Nigel Fountain was born in Southampton in 1944, and arrived in London via York University in 1966. A journalist, he has worked for many radical, alternative and mainstream publications including *Oz*, *Street Life*, *Socialist Worker*, *New Society*, the *Sunday Times* and the *Listener*. He is currently an editor on the London weekly magazine, *City Limits*. He lives in north London.

Pluto Crime

Edited by Ronald Segal

Murder in the Central Committee	Manuel Vázquez Montalban
October Heat	Gordon DeMarco
The China Option	Nancy Milton
Morbid Symptoms	Gillian Slovo
The Waste Remains	Judith Cook
Junk on the Hill	Jeremy Pikser
Dance Hall of the Dead	Tony Hillerman

'. . . Is there anything inherently illogical with the concept of socialist – or, at least, politically and socially aware – crime fiction? Pluto Press, publishers of serious left wing books, have inaugurated a crime list to prove that the two can mix . . . the first batch of pinko whodunits augurs well for the genre.' *The Times*

'. . . Sturdily resisting the temptation to call the series Red Herrings, the editors begin promisingly with four quite different types of thriller, varied in their setting and in the way politics enters into the action, but all taking an intelligent readership for granted . . .' *The Bookseller*

'Meanwhile, the proof of the four titles currently issued is in the reading: not half bad.' *Sunday Times*

Nigel Fountain

Days Like These

Pluto Press
London and Sydney

First published in 1985 by Pluto Press Limited,
The Works, 105a Torriano Avenue, London NW5 2RX
and Pluto Press Australia Limited, PO Box 199, Leichhardt,
New South Wales 2040, Australia

Phototypeset by AKM Associates (UK) Limited,
Ajmal House, Hayes Road, Southall, London
Printed in Great Britain by Richard Clay (The Chaucer Press) Limited,
Bungay, Suffolk

British Library Cataloguing in Publication Data
Fountain, Nigel
Days like these. — (Pluto crime)
I. Title
823′.914[F] PR6056.08/

ISBN 0-86104-797-4
ISBN 0-86104-796-6 Pbk

To J.A.S. for criticism, friendship, memory

October, 1908

1.

Lev was driving Abramovitch mad. Lev, the sole person he knew in London, in England. His day-time companion, the night-time provider of a flea-infested mattress in Alie Street.

Lev, Abramovitch had rapidly realised, was possessed by an anarchism drawn from books he had never finished, ideas he had never grasped, people he had never listened to and battles he had never fought. They had met in the Whitechapel Road the previous Monday. Abramovitch had been off the Hamburg boat for two days. He was soaked by the October rain, exhausted by walking the streets and bitter about his experience of the Jewish shelter. For a bed, Abramovitch had been willing once more to embrace the faith of his ancestors; for a meal, he had choked back his anger, as the Talmud was brandished once more over the lost, the demoralised, the unbelieving, the scoundrels, and the solitary Social Democrat himself.

On the second night there, the shelter had suddenly resounded with the screams of a white-faced youth, his cheeks vivid with acne. He was remembering everything, in a loud voice. The day had begun, in grey light from the tiny window, with the monologue of the youth coming out of his nightmares into the real world that had created them, cossacks, drums, flames, death: a pogrom.

The rabbi had offered another word.

'Tranquillity?' Abramovitch had shouted at the old man that Monday morning. 'Is that all you have to say? A chance to slave in the sweat shops? And wait for the wind to be stilled by the ghetto walls?'

The argument had been brief, the door had slammed behind him, and he had been back on the streets, drifting.

Abramovitch disliked idleness. Childhood in the Ukraine had been work, and study. If his parents had drifted from the path of the Talmud, they had retained that Jewish respect for books, and Abramovitch had extended it to newspapers, pamphlets, and, at a succession of schools, the replacement for the Talmud, socialism . . .

They were in the Jubilee Street club, Lev and Abramovitch, between Whitechapel Road and Commercial Road; just the two of them, a man making tea, and a girl. There was a fly too, surviving the chill of October. Perhaps it had been awakened by the heat of the club, brooded the Russian, or maybe Lev's droning made it feel at home.

Abramovitch looked at the girl, reading at a table; small, dark, with thick black hair pulled back from her face and fastened in a compact bun on top of her head. A single corkscrew of hair had escaped and curled across the wide, receding forehead. Her pink tongue darted out briefly as she flipped the pages.

'. . .In this country we cannot talk of a peasant uprising, obviously. Can we talk of any uprising? This is a land of committees, Piotr . . .'

Abramovitch had developed a range of automatic expressions and movements that enabled his own thought processes to remain intact while Lev rambled on. Grimaces, an occasional nod of acquiescence, even a 'too true' escaped his lips, while his mind roamed the world and his possibilities. 'Quite so,' he said.

He had to have a job, and then he would move on. That much was certain.

Lev cut a curious figure. A large white hat, returned from some colony to uncertain life on his head, a wispy beard, a black cloak, and a long grey scarf were the key elements of a dress style that he presumably hoped would emphasise his uniqueness. He didn't need to, thought Abramovitch. A Russian peasant revolutionary adrift for ten years in a land where he had failed to pick up more than eight words of English, who combined unemployment with an uncreative artistic life, was unlikely to be confused with the dockers, or the costermongers, or even his fellow Russians. This is a passing phase, Abramovitch told himself, things will improve; what did one bohemian matter, whatever his sense of self-importance?

'You say you agree, but where do you stand?'

My God, he's asking me a question, I have slipped up. I have to express an opinion.

'. . . Lot in what you say,' Abramovitch mumbled.

'Of course there is!' Lev resumed at a renewed pace. The failures of the 1905–6 Russian Revolution were dealt with at length, as were the problems of organisation amongst the peasantry. His words hung in the air, and Abramovitch made sure that that was where they stayed.

A job had been the reason why he had approached Lev: advice, contacts. It had not been a shrewd choice, but then he had almost crashed into him. He had heard of the Jubilee Street club from an old anarchist in Hamburg.

'Good man,' the anarchist had said, 'German, name of Rocker, Rudolph Rocker, he's done a fine job . . .'

Abramovitch had been unable to find the street, with his weak grasp of English, and on that Monday he would have tried anybody, to help him find a job, make contacts. That he had decided even before the episode with the Rabbi. On Sunday he had roamed the streets, watched the well-dressed on their way to St Paul's, been bored by the Thames and walked back past Aldgate to the park. There he had seen a ragged gathering. A white-haired old man was playing a harmonium, the crowd was singing a hymn. Abramovitch had even picked out the chorus. 'Tell me the old old story,' it was.

They were Jews, and the preacher was Christian. It was an uncertain alliance of hungry people in pursuit of bread, and a sermoniser in pursuit of converts. Ten yards away had stood a youth and a middle-aged women. 'Tell us the old old story,' she shouted, 'tell us the old old tale.'

They were well-dressed, curiously so for Aldgate. She wore a hat with a long feather that collected the drizzle gently falling over the park; the youth, a neat suit and a bowler. He might have been her son. He had fair hair, long and straight, with a scar on his cheek.

Her face was contorted with hate.

The youth searched in the mud, found a stone and threw it. It glanced off a little fellow in the crowd with an over-large black hat that concealed his ears. He was about thirty, but ageing rapidly. He edged deeper into the throng, averting his eyes from the hecklers and from Abramovitch.

'A living faith,' declaimed the preacher. He repeated the phrase, turning his eyes to the stone thrower. The youth turned away, and his gaze fell on Abramovitch. The Russian could understand the word – Yid – and the tone was familiar enough. He strode over and stared at the couple. They were a poor parody of the Black Hundreds, yet they were tainted with the same corruption that had crept across the streets of Moscow and Odessa and Kiev, the evil tide that had followed the ebbing of the revolution. He remembered the strength of that movement, *his* movement as it had swept across his land, and then the gangrene.

Katya was dead, killed on the streets of St Petersburg. She had ducked the cossack's sabre, but the horse's hoof had struck her and shattered her skull. The children died on the road to Siberia, under the knout. He remembered the moment of freedom and the time of death at the hands of the Hundredsmen as he thrust the stone thrower into the mud. England faded away for that second.

He looked up; a policeman was approaching. The youth grabbed at his leg, but he pulled himself clear and ran. There were cries behind him, but he was not followed into the alleys.

His mind returned to the present, and to the club. The girl was flipping over another page. Perhaps she would help. She did not have that aura of futility that hung over Lev. Her reading had a purpose, she was not passing the time. He walked across, she glanced up. Irritation crossed her face, swiftly.

'Yes?'

Abramovitch coughed. She spoke in English, but he guessed that she spoke Russian.

'I regret disturbing your reading, but I need assistance, advice, I need a job.'

She looked over at Lev. 'Idlers stay idlers.'

'I am not an idler. I have just arrived, through the underground, from Russia. I need money and a job.'

Her expression softened slightly.

'I have only been here a few days. I have met two people – two comrades – Lev over there, and you. You, I assume, are a comrade.'

'Assume what you will. I do not know you. You come in here, with a comrade as you call him. I call him an idler. I do not trust idlers; they drift to strange places.'

Abramovitch pulled up a chair and sat down. 'I have not come to you for your secrets. I asked you a question. I need a job.'

'I have no job.' She rested her book on the table, and cupped her chin in her hands. She had clear grey eyes. 'Who are you?'

'Piotr Abramovitch, member of the Social Democrat Party, from the Ukraine, working in St Petersburg from 1903 to 1906. I worked with the soviet during 1905 and early 1906. I was arrested in September that year and exiled in February 1907 to Siberia . . .'

'Where?'

'Samarovo, Tobolsk. I escaped in August and made my way back. They nearly caught me in St Petersburg, so I came out. I headed for Helsingfors, came through the bridge at Tornio-Haparanda.'

'They've closed the route. No one gets out that way.'

'I got out. It was still possible.'

'You may be one of *them*.'

'I am not Okhrana.'

She smiled. 'You probably aren't. The Tsar's intelligence men are smarter. They don't need to ask little part-time functionaries like me for sweat-shop jobs. Anyway, why are you asking me? Where is your mighty organisation?'

'I am out of touch. I went to Stockholm from Finland. I argued with them there, about stupid things, tactics, what I should do. They wanted me back in St Petersburg. I told them to go to hell.'

'And?'

'I went on to Hamburg. I had no money, my contacts were drying up. People are scared. I met this anarchist there, and he lent me some money. I came on to London; he told me to try this place, said that I might make some contacts.'

'What is it you want to do?'

'I want a job, then I am going on to New York. I have a friend there.'

'Where?'

He laughed. 'In the name of God! All these questions! Do you know everywhere? Delancey Street, in what they call the Lower East Side. I have never been there, as you will understand. And if I have to be interrogated like this, I probably never will.'

'His name?' She was unmoved by his complaint.

'Deborin.'

'A Social Democrat?'

'He was, probably still is.'

'How do you know where he is?'

'He sent a letter to Stockholm. We arranged it before.'

'Why should I help you?'

He shrugged his shoulders. 'God knows, my dear.'

'I am not your dear.'

'I'm sorry . . . comrade. Whatever we argue about now we will be together in the end, when the day comes, so we must help each other down our own roads.'

'You are an optimistic Social Democrat.' Her eyes narrowed. 'And I am an anarchist. We'll probably fall on each other like wolves the day after the great beast is slain.' Then she smiled. 'You know Houndsditch?'

'No.'

'There is a man who lives there, it is not very far. He is quite an old man, and most people in Russia and in the movement think that he's dead. Back in the eighties he was a fighter of the People's Will, formidable. They caught him one day and he was sent to Siberia, like you. And like you he escaped. But most people think he died out there amongst the Ostyaks in the wastes. He came here and opened a little bookshop, and he has been here ever since, in a place called Frying Pan Alley. He would know where you could get a job, perhaps with someone sympathetic. Not well paid, mind you, not good, but better than some, and you may find he can help you on your way. He can be bad tempered and has no love for you Social Democrats.'

She had heavy dark eyebrows, he noted, that accentuated the pallor of her face. Her eyes were deep and thoughtful. More of her hair was escaping and falling across her forehead, forming itself into a dark fringe.

'What are you thinking?' she asked.

'I was just looking at you.'

She pursed her lips. 'Well, don't. I think that is all you need to know.'

'What about the Okhrana?'

'What about them?'

'Are they here?'

She scratched her nose, and looked around the room.

'I think they are, some strange things happen. But maybe it is because we are away, inactive, we dream up ghosts of secret policemen, Tsarist spies, to keep ourselves believing that we matter, that we still exist.'

'I had a strange experience on Sunday.' He told her of the meeting, and the woman and the youth.

'So? An unpleasant English couple, two recruits for some little Black Hundred band, but they are in the wrong country. Down here they have their own gang of anti-semites, but they are small, weak, they mean little.'

'I saw him again today, the youth. When I was coming over here with Lev.' Abramovitch paused, feeling a twinge of guilt. He looked at his patron, who was slumped across the table, his beard soaking up spilt tea. 'I was coming by some Turkish baths in Aldgate and I saw him in the entrance. I didn't want to get involved again, no more squalid scuffles. We walked by, and then I looked back.'

She was not interested. She wanted to return to her book. 'And?'

'He was with a man, he didn't look English.'

'This is east London. A place of immigrants, drifters, people like you and me.'

'My youth is English and hates foreigners, or Jews. This man looked like one of us, but not a Jew. He reminded me of someone . . . Have there been deaths here?'

'There are always deaths here. Drunken deaths, murdered women, children. One of our people vanished, we are not sure, that way lies insanity . . .' Her sentence died away. She picked up a pencil and began writing on a scrap of paper. 'His name is Loskonoff now,' she announced. 'Or at least that is what he calls himself.' She pushed the paper across the table. 'And this is his address, and I have written you an introduction, and a little map to get there.'

He stood up. 'Thank you, uh . . .'

'Masha.'

'Perhaps I will see you again.'

'Perhaps.' She smiled slightly.

'Please tell Lev I will see him tonight, probably. I won't disturb his rest.'

'Nothing disturbs his rest.'

He inclined his head. She had returned to the book before he was out of the door. It was raining again, but Abramovitch was happier, the air was cleaner, night was drawing in.

It took him forty minutes to find the shop in the obscure dark little street. A cluster of candles flickered in the window. There was only a little girl in the shop, playing with a doll. A heap of newspapers was slipping off the counter, books lined the walls, spilled on to the floor, or were stacked in untidy heaps. The child shouted in English, and a man emerged from the gloom.

They spoke in Russian. Yes, he knew Masha, yes he was Loskonoff. He read the note. 'There is a job, I expect,' he said contemptuously. 'Seeler will employ anybody, Seeler is a swine. He calls himself an anarchist, then he sets up this little place, just to employ himself, he told me. Now he has ten poor devils working for him all hours of the day and night. Says that a man has to eat. He eats all right, he eats them every day.'

Loskonoff had a long white moustache. Curious, thought Abramovitch. He looks like an old English soldier. The little girl was about eight or nine. Her long skirt rustled in the dust. She swung her doll in the candlelight.

Abramovitch delved deep into his pocket. 'Here,' he said to her. 'Have this.'

It was a tiny Russian doll, the last part of a collection; he had kept it from Siberia. She took it.

'My doll,' she said emphatically.

'What is this?' shouted Loskonoff. 'Private property at

your age? What are we coming to?' He returned his attention to Abramovitch. 'Why do you want work?'

Abramovitch told him, and where he was staying.

'You stay with that drifter? That scoundrel? He has five of my books. He hasn't dared show his face in here for months. Is he a friend of yours?'

'I . . . he showed me the club.'

Loskonoff lost interest in Lev. 'You can eat here, tell me what is happening. I have been out of touch these last few months. All I see is this ridiculous English rubbish.' He picked up a paper from the heap on the counter. 'Some clown brought this in, some English calling himself a socialist in a neat little suit looking like a banker. The *Clarion*!' He brandished it at Abramovitch. 'You know what it says?' He gestured at the headline. Abramovitch didn't.

Loskonoff translated into Russian. 'It says "The Harlot and the Lady – An Appeal to England". This cretin Blachford, he speaks out of his arse!'

'Who is Blachford?'

'A fool of an English little patriot wearing a pink suit.' Loskonoff scribbled on Masha's note and pushed it into Abramovitch's hand. 'You'd better go. It is only two blocks away, turn left out of the door. Tell Seeler I sent you, that will stir his guilt if nothing else. Then come back here, you can stay the night. You will need something to eat if you are to work for that man. But just tonight! I cannot fill my house with every traveller.' He laughed.

Abramovitch sidestepped the little girl and left. It was quite dark. Loskonoff pointed down the road.

He was on the corner when he heard the voice.

'Piotr!'

'Yes?' He stared into the gloom. A figure separated itself from the shadows. A blow glanced off the side of his head, it came from behind. He crashed into the gutter, but looked up. It looked like the man who had been in Aldgate . . . and before. His thoughts moved slowly. Perhaps it was the blow, inducing a sense of timelessness . . . Something glinted in the dark, a long blade. There was another person, the youth with the fair hair . . . He was not wearing a hat, but gloves, yes, he was wearing gloves, and was holding the knife.

'I remember you,' said the first man. 'I remember Piotr Abramovitch. I saw you in St Petersburg. Why, you were a big man then, you and your filth. I keep in touch, Piotr. Good to see you in London, such a long way from St Petersburg, You are going home.'

The youth swung the knife, Abramovitch ducked and felt it skim his face. He reached out; he cut his hand on the outstretched blade, he tried to grab the youth's hand, but he had no grip . . . no grip. The young man stepped back. The Russian booted Abramovitch back into the gutter as he attempted to stand. *How many are there?* he thought. He screamed but there was no sound, just a hissing noise. The two assailants were breathing in spasms, men about their work. *Hard work killing me in the rain.* Where was the little girl? Such a pretty doll. His jaw was broken, that was why he couldn't shout. *Or perhaps I am dead.*

The youth knelt and pushed the Russian on his back. He took the blade to the tip of Abramovitch's right ear and scythed across. The artery was severed, blood streamed in the gutter, in the slime. Abramovitch made no sound.

London, early 1980s

2.

It was a Tuesday. Ferret and I had passed Monday evening in the Compasses. He had lectured me on why once the oil ran out the country would replace it at the bottom of the North Sea; why Europe was finished, and Russia and America; why I should join the struggle, and why he was drunk.

They threw us out at quarter to twelve. The cops drink there, he explained, that's why it was open all hours. I felt terrible the following morning, or afternoon. I didn't get up until one o'clock, which is always demoralising.

No one can work until their head is clear, I told myself. I didn't need much persuading. I took a walk to clear my head, from Highbury to Chalk Farm.

I was writing a history of the 1930s, a picture history. I still am. I select the pictures and write the captions, and a co-operative of four spiky-hairs are going to publish it and we're going to share whatever proceeds there are. Just then I had about four picture postcards of Stanmore in 1932 and the collected works of George Orwell. It was an inauspicious start.

Crossing Tufnell Park Road I wandered into the side streets which thread through into Chalk Farm. Railway arches ensure that the area has problems keeping up with Camden class. I took several dead ends before locating a north-west passage towards the Roundhouse. It didn't matter, then; it was a desultory stroll, on a grey day down a long street of Victorian terrace houses.

Just ahead of me was a little square of ravaged grass and bent beercans; a pub whose Victorian credentials were belied by bogus brass lamps; and a shop I almost didn't see . . . a shop hovering around junk status.

Because there were books outside, I stopped. 'First Editions A Speciality', proclaimed a scrawled notice, yellowing but optimistic, in the window. The only ones outside were some dog-eared 'Man From Uncle' paperbacks, and an LP, *Tribute to the Sweet*.

I pushed open the door, and a bell jangled. I was in a short corridor, lined with half-empty bookshelves. A peeling image of John Travolta on a mirror leered at me from out of the gloom.

I made my way into the main shop. Books were stacked untidily on and off shelves. They were mostly hardback, *Reader's Digest* selections, *Sorrell and Son*, *When It Was Dark*. Amongst them were a brace of Left Book Clubs; Hannington's *The Problem of the Distressed Areas*, and a *Forward From Liberalism* for ten pence, or so it said on the flyleaf. They raised the shop's tone, slightly.

There was a desk with a lamp which augmented whatever light was making it through the window. A cat was curled up on the desk. It glanced at me, but didn't seem too interested. Radio Three played opera to no one but me. I don't like opera.

In one corner there was a pile of *Illustrated*s. There aren't too many of those around. A lot of people seem to be unloading their *Picture Post*s these days, but I don't care about how the blimps are wrecking the Home Guard any more. In one issue a family explained how commercial TV wasn't turning them on any more. It wouldn't last, they reckoned.

I had just finished an article announcing that Natalie Wood was not, after all, getting married, when I saw it. A heap of pictures, cuttings, calendars, newspapers, the scrapings of years. I started digging, slipping back to the dawn of my childhood. A 1950 cutting from the *News of the World* about Liverpudlian prostitution, then my time machine took me back to the war and the good stuff. Pre-war *Tribune*s, some *Action*s, and a lot of stills; Hunger Marchers sitting down in the Savoy foyer, photographs of Hyde Park demonstrations. They didn't seem to have been pulled out of their elastic band since the marchers had gone back to Eccles. There was a studio portrait of some debutante with a sweet smile and cute little swastika badge affixed to her fashionable little bosom, the launching of a battleship with the Queen Mother looking older than she has recently, Seagrave waving from a streamlined car. Most of the pictures had neatly pencilled captions. There were a couple of copies of *New Weekly*, and those are rare. Harold Nicolson explained how the old gang should be seen on their way, with Oswald Mosley providing the maps. There were some family snaps, a dead lion with a family group, a dead deer, and a couple of dead monkeys, all with the same family.

The father was dressed in 'Sanders of the River' kit, with a gun, a thin wife and a boy and girl aged between eight and ten squinting into a tropical sun. There was an African attempting to look enthusiastic about the white hunter's decimation of wild life in his homeland. In another series, the family were sailing down, or maybe up, a wide river, and father had sprouted a neat little beard. In another, he co-starred with a kangaroo, dead of course. He may have got around but he certainly slowed down the fauna. Then there were some shots of open-air meetings with boaters much in evidence.

A door in the recesses of the shop opened.

She was about twenty-eight, I guessed, short brown hair, quite tall, with a spot on her chin. She was probably worried about it, I thought; I would have been. She wore a long smock, mass-produced in some Asian Woolworth's. It was an intelligent but bored face and my presence did not transform her mood. 'Yes?' she said, stating some pedestrian reality more than asking a question.

'You've got a lot of pictures and cuttings here.'

'Yes. Have we?' The accent was transatlantic, just.

'Yes.' It was catching. I fingered the pile to provide the evidence. 'How much?'

'I don't have a clue. Mr Astin left them there. He must know. I don't have much to do with that side. I cover fine arts.' She gestured at a Buddha with a skin problem in the corner.

'How about two quid for the lot?'

She looked at me, looked at the heap and shrugged, plunging her hands into the pouch of the smock.

'Fine, two quid. Do you want a receipt?'

I did. Was I interested in the Buddha? No, I wasn't. I put the purchase in a large envelope she gave me and made off down the corridor through the door.

I looked back. She had pushed the cat off the desk and sat cross-legged reading a copy of *Cosmopolitan* and rubbing the spot on her chin. The Buddha's habits and skin problem seemed to be catching.

It was about four o'clock. I walked towards Camden Town. It was still light, but there was a slight mist hanging over the streets. I wondered who Astin was, and why the girl worked there and where the cuttings had come from. I was drifting. The residue of the drink was still paralysing any will I might have had. I decided to go to Regents Park and look at the ducks, if there were any. I like ducks, busy little creatures.

The events only had a meaning in retrospect. At the time they had a dream quality. First there was the man, about twenty-eight; long brown hair, jeans, a slight limp, a beard. London University turns them out in thousands; they've set up production lines at the Polys, too. He hurried past me down Regents Park Road.

Then there was the woman, about fifty; well but boringly dressed, with what looked like dyed blonde hair.

I have always liked the houses around that park, tall and white, with muffins for tea . . . I ambled down the road, a vacuous smile on my face. The woman looked at the man. She was walking towards me.

The smoke and the sound seem separate now, but they must have been together, a grey puff, a bang and a flicker of flame. The noise was like a car backfiring, then there was a rumble as masonry collapsed. The lower part of the façade on one of the tall white houses had crumpled.

The house was between the man and the woman. They both stopped. She looked at him and he looked at the house. There were no screams, no panic, a few more bricks fell, then silence. A brick had dented the bonnet of a parked Cortina. Cars began to stop in the street.

I was immediately tempted to hurry on. *Nothing to do with me*, squealed a noisy little midget in my psyche, *get away*. Social responsibility and curiosity intruded. Doors opened, within a minute a crowd had formed. A man realising some childhood fantasy began to direct the traffic. Everyone to their own, I thought.

Smoke drifted out of what by then resembled a dolls house, deserted by some giant north London child. The man with the beard glanced back at me, glanced at the woman, and then walked on.

The police may have been slow when I had my head kicked in outside the Moonglow Chinese Take-Away, but they weren't slow then. The first Panda was followed by a Range Rover, a fire engine and an ambulance.

The amateur traffic warden was brusquely retired after his moment of stardom. The fire engine completed the ruin of the Sanderson wallpaper, the police erected a neat little fence, and the ambulancemen looked around for someone to put on their stretchers. Nobody volunteered.

The top cop had hair thick with Brylcreem, parted dead centre, in a style he must have carried from the Korean war. 'OK, who saw it?' he shouted. His underlings had pushed us back across the road.

The woman wasted no time in getting in on the act.

'Name?'

'Avis. Mrs Maud Avis, A-V-I-S.' She gave a competent account. I was rather disappointed; it left me with little to say. I tried a few stylistic embellishments but the cop was unimpressed. Mrs Avis was anxious to stay with the action.

'There was another young man,' she said, looking at me. Indeed there was, I thought. Where had he gone? The crowd had grown by then, and he was nowhere to be seen. 'With a beard, he was almost outside the house, but he walked on up towards the Park. He looked like a student.' She said it in a tone that implied he had all but lit the fuse. 'Jeans, brown donkey jacket, brown hair.'

'How tall?'

'About six foot. He dragged his left foot, I think.'

He looked at me. I appeared to be doomed to a walk-on part. 'I think that is all quite accurate,' I said.

'Can you give me your name and address, sir?'

'John Raven, 80, Highbury Hill.'

'I see, sir.' Just what he saw I wasn't sure, but his tone was faintly ominous.

He was outlined against the house. They had turned arc

lights on, perhaps it was a television crew. A small guy with a beard and a camera slung on his shoulder was arguing with a sound man.

'Any proof of identity, sir?' I was disturbed; he hadn't asked Mrs Avis. 'Any phone number?'

I gave him my number and my NUJ card. He seemed satisfied. 'Thank you, Mr Raven. We'll be in touch tomorrow. or possibly tonight.'

There were plenty of others waiting to testify. I was dismissed from the audience.

The park had lost its appeal. Who needs ducks after that? I walked back to Camden Town and the tube, wondering if Ferret was conscious. I wanted to star in my own production of the afternoon.

Ferret wasn't on the phone. His real name is Jack Murray, but he is always known as Ferret; a friend of the old mole, the revolution, he said. I reckoned it was because of his pointed nose and scuttling manner. He is thirty-four, small and dark. He had left Glasgow six years ago to continue a disastrous liaison with a woman who had come down to seek her fortune, and, I suspect, to escape from Ferret. It took her two years to lose Ferret and three to find the pot of gold in every TV researcher's knapsack.

I'd met him at a party and we had got on. He took to me, I suspected, because he liked to have someone to flagellate politically. He was a walking anthology of the left, having tried Labour, the Communists, the Nats for two days, the Socialist Workers, a short-lived Maoist group, the International Marxists, and had finally settled down with a cosy little group of Trotskyists who were apparently based in Stockport and were attempting to Bolshevise that town. This had the double advantage of allowing him to spin romantic stories of the proletarian upsurge there, whilst ensuring that he and the mass base of the organisation were kept at a safe distance from each other. The group were called Workers for Revolutionary Change, or 'those creeps the Wircs'. It was an unwieldy title, but this was common in such groups and represented a satisfactory permutation of the key syntax of red vocabulary. Ferret was effectively the London branch.

He lived in Stoke Newington. It took me an hour to get there.

He blinked at me from behind his door.

'Christ, haven't you had enough?'

His room was in a house of reds of varying shades, who met to abuse one another on the stairway on their way to work, the duplicator and the pub. Ferret had made a marriage of convenience with that section of the radical lower middle classes questing timidly for the proletariat. Occasionally he would go and ham up his days in the Gorbals, particularly when drunk, but otherwise would happily sneak off to the National Film Theatre. He was a sharp man, and a good organiser when he could be bothered.

I followed him upstairs, past an ancient 'THE DAY AFTER YOU DON'T BOTHER TO VOTE WILL BE THE FIRST DAY OF A TORY GOVERNMENT' poster. It was held in place by a flightless dart.

He paused on the landing to cough. I was vaguely nauseated to see that he was swallowing the phlegm, but that was preferable to spraying me with it, I supposed.

'Christ, I feel terrible,' he observed. 'I woke up this morning with all the lights on, and the fire on, and me sitting in the armchair like a corpse in an old people's home.'

In his room a kettle was pumping steam on to a shirt draped over the gas stove. I sat on his sofa. It was decaying, and propped up by a volume of Aleisteir Crowley. He collapsed on the carpet. 'I've been corrupted,' he moaned. 'Fancy a drink?'

I didn't. I told him what had happened. He had heard about it on the news. A great listener to the radio, is Ferret. 'You told the cops who you were? You just went up to them and told them? You're criminal, Raven!'

'What d'you expect me to do? I'm not building a workers' soviet in Stockport. I don't have to pass my time on the other side of the street shuffling round in the privet hedges.'

'Do you know whose house that was?'

I didn't.

'Raphael Hales's. You know who that is?'

'Some Tory MP,' I mumbled.

'*Some* Tory MP? That bastard makes Margaret Thatcher look like Rosa Luxemburg. Hates blacks, hates reds, hates workers, probably thinks his granny is a bloody bolshevik.' He sat up and waved his finger at me. 'You know what they are saying, those bastards on the news?' He gave me no time to guess. 'They are saying that it "may have been a bomb". You know what that means? Suppose some well-meaning idiot planted a bomb in his letter box, that means that the cops will be all over the place tonight, banging on doors, hauling punters in, and what are you doing? I'll tell you what you are bloody doin'; you're bloody helping them!'

'It could have been anything. It could have been a gas explosion. What am I supposed to do?'

He stumbled to his feet and glared down at me. He walked to the window and drew a face in the condensation. The face scowled at me. Ferret scowled at me. 'What was it they said on the radio? "Eye witnesses" saw a bearded young man whom police are anxious to interview. Eye witnesses? You are the fuckin' eye witness, you blind sod!'

'Yeah, I was an eye witness . . . me and this woman. He was in front of me in Regents Park Road. He vanished after the explosion.'

He asked me what the man was like. He said the police don't like people with beards very much, apart from members of the Special Branch and sailors, and they didn't like them very much either. He wiped away the face he'd drawn and gazed out of the window. 'Hales was on the radio. He said it was another example of the challenge to Conservative law and order encouraged by the Benns and Heffers of this world. I'd like to strangle whoever it was who planted that bloody thing. We've got enough problems already.'

'You've just been telling me what a fool I was to talk to the cops, now you want to strangle the bomber.'

'Look, Raven, you may be politically illiterate but you must have learned some of the script parrot fashion. You know the line. Shelf three, book seven, Trotsky on Marxism or Terrorism.' He waved at the bookshelf. ' "The emancipation of the working class is the act of the working class . . ." '

'*Communist Manifesto*.'

He clapped. 'Very good! Given ten years, you might get round to the *Future That Labour Offers You.*' He rested his behind on the window sill and scratched his crotch. 'I wonder if the bearded guy was connected; they've been picketing Hales's house recently.'

'Who has?'

'Some layabouts, squatters I think.'

'I love the way you reds stick together.'

He slid to the floor. 'No, they were all right. They just seem to think that if they occupy enough rat-infested holes, ICI will go bust and Thatcher will come out with a white flag. Well, they're wrong, but they had quite a good scheme. Hales had this place in south London and they squatted it. He was always going on about housing and parasites and he had this lovely little home and never went near it. So he sent some strong-arm boys in to send them on their way. They picketed it, and the Regents Park establishment, to show what a flaming hypocrite he was.' He paused. 'Got a cigarette?'

I threw him a Silk Cut. 'Bloody kids' stuff,' he muttered. 'Every squatter in London will have PC Plod on his doorstep tonight. What did the cops say to you?'

'That they'd be in touch. Tonight or tomorrow. I don't want to be in touch. I want to get out of touch. I'm getting a terrible thirst. Coming down the Compasses?'

'I haven't eaten. I can't exist on Guinness and scotch for the rest of my life.'

He buried his head in his hands and dragged on the cigarette. 'And I haven't been to work today. Terrible . . . First day I've missed in three months. The site is really going well, we've fixed it so the gaffers can't move a brick without us having the safety regulations on them.'

'You could have a pie in the Compasses.'

'Aye, shit and kidney.'

I lit a cigarette. 'Something else happened. Have a look at these.' I handed him the folder. He thumbed through and found the 1938 *Tribune*s and began an argument with Victor Gollancz about the way forward after the Spanish Civil War. I pointed out that Gollancz and Franco were now discussing the issue in another place and that neither he nor the Wircs would be able to do anything about it. He agreed, but said it was symptomatic.

'Where did you get this stuff?'

'A little shop near Camden Town, just before Hales's world collapsed around him.'

'Lots of shots of our colonial kith and kin,' he mused. 'The *New Weekly*, eh? Good stuff; what are you going to do with it?'

'It's for the book. You know, the one on the 1930s.'

'Oh aye. How someone with your political nous is capable of writing about the 1930s is as big a mystery to me as the demon bomber of Camden Town.'

'Great to have you aboard, Ferret. Drink?'

He stood up, rolled on a pullover, added a donkey jacket and draped a frayed red scarf about his ears.

I pointed at the cuttings. 'Can I leave the stuff here? I don't want to wind up losing it at closing time.'

'I don't want to wind up losing myself at closing time. Yeah, leave it there.'

It was seven thirty, dark and misty. The Compasses was brightly lit, but cold and dank. It immediately depressed me. I felt like a traveller from nowhere in a land that should have been my own. It was vile, full of failure, of the drunk, the ill-dressed, the chronically poor, failing, coughing, smoking, dying, dancing, acting. It was my paranoia, I consoled myself. People were lurching into arguments and body contact out of fear and loneliness. Country music celebrated their impotence, music of defeat masquerading as the music of defiance, rebellion; movin' on music for souls with nowhere to go.

It was warmer by closing time.

3.

The phone rang on. It was two minutes before I was capable of answering it. The voice was cordial enough. 'Mr Raven?'

'It is he.'

'What?'

Obtuseness, especially at nine in the morning, is unwise

'Yes, this is John Raven.'

'I wonder if I could come round. This is Detective Sergeant Garret over at Kentish Town. It's about yesterday's explosion.'

For no reason at all, apart from a mild dislike of having my territory invaded, coupled with the poster on my wall, a gift from Ferret, I decided to go to the cops. The poster depicted two building workers being assisted off a picket by a group of enthusiastic policemen.

'That's all right. I've got to be over that way this morning, I'll come and see you.'

'Fine. What time will you be over? We're in Holmes Road.'

'About eleven?'

'Fine. I'll see you then.'

He hung up. I was immediately annoyed with myself. Half the day would be wasted because of my mild paranoia and Ferret's politics. I stumbled across the room.

It isn't much of a place. It is on the second floor of one of those late Victorian mansions that flourish in north Islington. It can be used for optical illusion experiments. Stand Sylvester Stallone in one corner and he looks, with the aid of the sloping floor, like a fairground midget. It is cheap because I have been there for ten years. When Kathy lived there, it had elements of civilisation. But since her departure for Italy, standards have declined.

I picked up the paper downstairs, made a cup of tea and a slice of toast. The marmalade had run out.

The *Guardian* had it on the front page, so God knows what the *Sun* had done with it. 'MP's HOME BOMBED', it said.

'Police are investigating the explosion which severely damaged the home of Tory MP Raphael Hales in Camden

Town, north London, early yesterday evening. No one was injured in the blast. The house was empty at the time. "We are treating this as a criminal act," said a police spokesman. "The anti-terrorist and bomb squads have been called in."

'Mr Hales has emerged recently as a critic of some aspects of his government's policy. He has been attacked recently for his alleged links with far right organisations. His views on trade union reform and race are believed to have made him many enemies on the left.

' "I don't know who caused this explosion," he said in a press statement last night, "but if some group of left wing thugs think they can silence me with bombs they are sadly mistaken. Truth is more powerful than their violence. I am going to continue to crusade against the Communist challenge to this government and the nation." '

The rest of it was filler. I wasn't happy. I looked out of the window: more mist. They had the floodlights on at the Arsenal. I had a cigarette and walked to the bus stop.

Garret wasn't my idea of a cop. He sat behind his desk and twiddled with his beard. He would have looked more at home with Ferret's mob in Stockport, I thought. Or perhaps that was where he went in his off-duty hours, or in some of his on-duty hours.

'It's quite straightforward, Mr Raven, a bit *boring* really.' He laughed.

I laughed. I like to be good company.

'All we want is for you to go through what you saw, from the beginning. We'll draw up a statement and you can sign.'

Ferret floated into view, finger pointed accusingly in my direction. I vapourised him.

'I had just been to a shop in Camden Town and bought some material for a book I'm putting together. It was a pleasant afternoon and I decided to go for a walk.'

'Fine, fine. Just tell me what happened.' A stenographer behind me was taking notes. Garret listened until I had finished, then offered me a Silk Cut. Clearly he was the nice KGB man. I took the cigarette.

'Tell me more about the chappie you saw in front of you. Describe him.'

Ferret returned, and refused to be knocked off a second time. Oh Christ, I brooded, here comes this daft, harmless, bomb-planting squatter. Perhaps revolutionary justice will strangle him first . . .

I cleared my throat. 'Difficult to say, really.'

Garret looked at me, through me. He was wondering why it was difficult to say, but he said nothing. I decided to tuck in behind Mrs Avis. 'Dark brown hair, longish, jeans . . .'

'Anything else?'

'Nothing that springs to mind.'

'Bit of a limp?'

'Yeah,' my voice tailed off. 'Yes, maybe he had a limp.'

'What about his face?'

I was on safer ground here; after all, he had walked past me, I had caught sight of it, miserable-looking guy . . . but his back was to me, most of the time.

'I never saw his face.'

Garret leaned back in his chair, rested his feet on the desk, and looked every inch a man at peace with the world and his environment.

'What did he do when the bomb went off?'

'I don't know what he did. I never saw him again.'

'You mean he didn't stop? You stopped, didn't you? Mrs Avis stopped, people came out of their houses, got out of their cars, and he didn't stop?' Garret was moving into the speedy interrogator routine while maintaining his air of relaxation. Maybe he could combine both at the same time, I thought. Ply me with fags with one hand, beat me with a rubber hose with the other.

I was always a terrible bridge player; it used to infuriate Kathy. I thought that if I won the bidding, that was it. Then I would sit there with a collection of dud cards on the table while she swore at me. Yet it shouldn't have been difficult, it was merely a question of keeping Ferret out of my mind.

'I wasn't paying any attention to him. I was looking at the house, where the noise came from.'

'You saw Mrs Avis?'

'Yes.'

'So why didn't you see him?'

'I didn't say I saw her then. I saw her before, and of course I saw her afterwards. I noticed he wasn't around.' I decided it was time for a moving plea on the missing long-hair's behalf, coupled with a few words of statesmanlike reassurance. 'I think you're labouring the point,' I said. 'After all, Mrs Avis was there, and I was there, and we didn't blow the place up. So why should he have done? We were all just walking down the street.'

'You stayed. He didn't.'

More fool me, I thought. I shrugged. There didn't seem much else to say. 'Well, you've got the Bomb Squad on it.' I laughed. Christ knows why.

He smiled. 'Yes. Well it's inevitable, isn't it? They like to keep their hand in, them and the Anti-Terrorist lot.' He swung his feet off the table and leaned forward confidentially. 'To tell the truth, Mr Raven, I'm just handling the routine part of the operation at this end, shoving bumf to and fro.'

'I never realised that Hales lived there.' *I'm innocent you understand? Nothing to do with me, just off to see the ducks.*

'No.'

'It said in the paper that he had a lot of enemies.'

It was his turn to shrug. 'So have a lot of people. If you shoot your mouth off like Hales, then you attract attention.'

'You don't like Hales?'

It was an unwise question. He was trying to inch me out of my shell, and I wasn't sure that I had one. 'I don't have any views about Hales, Mr Raven,' he said slowly. 'Do you?'

'No.'

'I'm a police officer. I don't care if it is Hales who is bombed, or Dennis Skinner. I would sooner that no one was bombed.'

'You are sure that it was a bombing?'

'You can't be sure of anything in this life, can you?' He smiled again. It was a pretty shallow little effort, but mine had been unimpressive. 'All I can say is that if anyone did it, it's our duty to make sure that whoever that was gets done.'

'Yeah, right,' I muttered feebly.

The stenographer stirred. She was clearly not interested in our philosophical views on public life. 'Is that all right,

Molly?' he asked her. It was. The statement was placed in front of me. It was all the innocuous stuff. Mystery man hardly got a mention. I signed.

I was out of the station within two minutes. On the other side of the road a man was standing. Just in front of a little French-Arab restaurant I used to go to with Kathy. I went off it after she walked out. The morning had done nothing to renew my interest. The man walked over. He was wearing a black leather jacket, and he looked like a fourth-division manager who had unexpectedly made it to the semi-final of the FA cup. 'Sorry to bother you.' He smiled brightly. 'I'm from the *Mail*. Have you been in there about the bombing?'

It was getting worse. Another two were approaching. I hesitated and thrashed around. 'Official Secrets Act,' I muttered, and scuttled off down the road.

I retraced my steps of the day before, through the back streets, past the kebab houses, towards Chalk Farm. I decided to ring Winston Pix, a sporadic kind of picture agency which was an occasional source of income. I sat there and filed old prints, and an old Italian called Spizzichino shouted at me.

But I found myself back outside the junk shop. I heard a banging on the window. The girl mouthed at me through the glass. I remembered the folder. What had I done with it? It was at Ferret's. I breathed easier and went in.

'Thank God for that,' she said. On Radio Three someone was recalling a big night out with Evelyn Waugh.

' "His first wife had just left him and he was bitterly unhappy, and drunk," ' boomed a fruity voice out of the radio.

'Astin's frantic,' she said. 'He never told me.' She gestured to the back of the shop. 'He's out there now; I shouldn't have sold you that stuff. He was just sorting through it. He never told me.'

'He never told me either. The stuff was out there and I bought it.'

She put her hands on her forehead. The spot had gone down. She smiled the insincere smile of someone about to borrow a quid.

'More than your job's worth,' I said.

'What?'

'If you don't get the pictures back.'

'What? Oh yes. That's right.'

She stood up. 'Jesus. I wonder why I do this job. Still it's peaceful, forty pounds a week and plenty of time for reading.'

'Nothing like learning,' I said. We hesitated. There was a crash from the back of the shop. A Victorian glass case of flowers, with a very un-game like bird nestling amongst them, shuddered. Mr Astin came in.

Astin resembled a bogus RAF officer straight out of Terence Rattigan, thirty years after expulsion from the golf club for cheque bouncing, alive and ill in Thatcherland. His upper lip featured a dead or dormant wedge of nicotined fur that colour-co-ordinated with his woolly cardigan but clashed with his crumpled black trousers. His shirt wasn't too clean; it wasn't too anything.

'This is the gentleman, Mr Astin,' she said.

He looked around, pausing to scrutinise the bird. It had stopped shaking. If it wasn't worried, then I wasn't worried. 'What gentleman?'

'The gentleman who bought the pictures.'

'Bought the pictures? Stole the pictures!'

'I didn't steal them. I bought them yesterday afternoon from your assistant.' I attempted a magisterial tone, aloof, above the squabbles of petty tradesmen.

'They weren't for sale.' His hands opened and clenched, he spat the words out, and glared at me, or rather over my left shoulder, having trouble with his range finding. 'They weren't for sale, I don't hand out my personal property to anyone who just happens to pass by.'

'You weren't here. The stuff was on display and I bought it, two pounds for the lot.'

'Look here,' he focused on me at last and looked as nasty as he could. In his day that was probably pretty nasty, and it was still impressive. 'I want those pictures back and you are going to give them back. Right now. You can have your squalid little two pounds back and then you can get out and not come back.'

Kathy always said that I'm great at Custer's Last Stand scenes. Arguing about the bill when I've already paid the money, or complaining about the sound track when the cinema is burning down. I decided that this was going to be different.

'Since you failed to inform your assistant that you display your personal property in what I took to be your shop – ' I waved my arm around the shredded wild life and *Readers Digest* selections – 'it is hardly surprising that I should be tempted to buy it. When I came in here I had no idea that you were worried about the pictures. Had you asked me politely I would probably have given them back. Since you insist on ranting at me, you can sod off.'

The girl sat down and groaned silently. I had hopes that she would be impressed by my eloquence. She looked up, and my hopes were dashed as she spoke. I thought I was beginning to locate her around Brooklyn. 'Jesus, don't be such an asshole.'

' "It was around then that *Vile Bodies* was published," ' added the radio.

Astin blocked the door, apparently intent on preventing my departure. He was angry and nervous, but not about me. 'Give me the pictures.'

'I haven't got the pictures. I don't carry my possessions around in an ox-cart.'

A string quartet struck up. She turned the radio off. 'If Mr Astin wants the pictures back,' I told her, 'he can write me a letter of apology, enclose a two pound postal order, cheques not accepted, and hope for the best. Send the letter to 80 Highbury Hill. The name is John Raven,' I said loftily, pushing past him, and opened the door.

He said nothing, just stood and watched me leave. His anger had evaporated. He was tired and worried and even older than the seventy years I had originally awarded him.

I decided to give Chalk Farm a miss for a while. If it wasn't bombs it was senior citizens. I was depressed. The week had hardly started, and I was broke and doing little apart from chat shows with the Force. I gave Spizzichino at Winston Pix the ring I had been promising myself. Winston did a good line in chocolate biscuits.

I stayed there all afternoon and most of the evening. He had been around, had Spizzichino. I spent about twenty minutes filing and five hours pumping him about his life. He had a shabby little office above a tailors' in Covent Garden. Regularly every twenty minutes one of the two old tailors would enter, pad silently to the cupboard that passed as the lavatory and pad out again. At the door they inclined their heads, with identical movements. It must have been the years spent together over the cloth. I left at nine; it was raining. I hated the city that night, it was full of wasted midgets who had fallen to earth years before, in dark shades and pink fluorescent socks, and had failed to book a return trip. London grew steadily more unpleasant, more loathsome on wet evenings with the bus fare and half a pint's worth of money in my pocket. A middle-class couple were walking towards the Talk of the Town, she in a long evening dress and he in a dinner jacket, tribal uniform for the big night out. The midgets didn't like them too much. He was unhappy, probably a mile away from his gleaming Rover 3500. What a crummy place for a big night out, tat everywhere. I climbed on a nineteen bus.

The floodlights were still on at the Arsenal; perhaps they had lost the ball. They weren't on at 80 Highbury Hill. I let myself in and climbed the stairs. My door was open, I flicked the light switch. The table and cooker were still in the same places but the rest of the flat had been redesigned. My desk was open, the so-called sofa was bleeding horsehair, a chair – the chair – was toppled over. In the bathroom the shaving cupboard was off the wall and the contents deposited in the sink. I hadn't bothered to make my bed that morning, a wise move since the interior decorators clearly preferred it without the mattress. Ferret's victimised building workers were all screwed up in the corner. Someone who had failed to find the bog had used the carpet. That was sad. The carpet was the best thing in the room; Kathy had given it me to usher in a Habitat phase in my life. My books littered the floor, and there was little left of my small record collection to take to the desert island that I wished, devoutly, that I was on.

4.

I rearranged the room according to my own untaxing standards of decorum. It still lacked a certain something. Then I went to bed. The following day was grey; I idled through the morning, eating toast, reading the paper.

I decided to make a phone call, and Astin was in the telephone book. I rang the number. She was in no hurry, but answered in the end. She wasn't overenthusiastic to hear from me. 'Has Mr Astin got any rough friends?'

'What?' She was mildly exasperated. 'I'm trying to run a shop, you know. I don't spent much time in his company outside working hours. If you want to play games with Mr Astin, could you leave me out of it?'

'I wish I could leave me out of it. I gave you my address yesterday.'

'You gave *him* your address.'

'Someone turned my place over last night.'

'I'm very sorry.' She didn't sound very sorry.

'Well I just wondered . . .'

'Wondered what?' Anger intruded.

'I wondered if you knew anything about it.'

'God, you've caught me at last. I go round every night with a brick in one hand and a sledgehammer in the other. I was getting bored with Camden Town so I thought I would give your place a try.'

Whatever my views of her, some co-existence was necessary. 'I wasn't implying that. I just thought that Astin might have sent someone round. I'm sorry I got you into trouble, if I did; it wasn't my fault, or your fault. I'm even sorrier that someone kicked my room around.'

She sighed. 'Yeah, well I'm sorry, too. Did they take the pictures?'

'They couldn't. I didn't leave them there. So if that's what they wanted they were disappointed. Are you doing anything this lunchtime?'

There was a pause. 'It depends.'

'I just wondered if you would like to have a drink.' I wasn't sure what I might get out of it, but it was worth a try, she might know something, and it passed the time. I didn't have much on.

'I'm supposed to be running a shop. Astin isn't here, you know, or you could ask him.'

'I don't think you get all that much trade. Why don't you close down for an hour, take a walk down to the Spread Eagle in Parkway, and I'll see you there in an hour?'

The Spread Eagle is a large white pub hovering between Irish Camden Town and television employees' Camden Town. It looks like a golf club hi-jacked from suburbia.

We arrived together. 'I still don't know your name,' I said.

'Moira,' she said. 'Moira Marchant.'

'Do you want a drink?' She had a whisky and lemonade; revolting, I thought. She was wearing a long, blue, shroud-like smock and blue jeans. I said I was sorry about the day before. She offered me a cigarette, which I accepted, lit one herself and blew out between compressed lips. 'I went there for a quiet life. It isn't quiet anymore.'

'Do you think that Astin did the break-in at my place?'

She took another pull on her cigarette. 'You didn't put any ice in.'

'No. Do you want ice?'

'I always have ice.'

'I'll get you some.'

'Forget it.'

She had a wonderful way of putting one at ease. She returned to my question. 'He's an old man. An old, tired, jaded, bitter man. He doesn't go round breaking into people's houses, but he might know who did; he might even have put someone up to it.'

She swirled the drink in the glass, waiting for a clink that never came. I waited for her to come out with some revelations. 'I've worked for him for six months. He's become more ratty the longer I've been there. He was always a bit funny, but we got along, mainly because he spent most of his time out of the shop. When he was around, his wife used to ring up and harangue him, or me, so perhaps that's why.'

'Where does he live?'

'Tulse Hill.' She laughed. 'One day he came back – he had been drinking, not that that's rare – full of old world bonhomie, he invited me to dinner to meet the "little woman". I managed to get out of it. Anyway you aren't interested in that. The last week or so he has been very agitated. Last Saturday this guy came in to see him. They went into the back room. I heard them shouting. This other man was saying something about "obligation" and Astin's "duty". I wasn't really listening, but it was impossible not to pick up some of it.'

'What did he look like?'

'Early forties, fair hair, well-dressed, dark blue suit; he looked like a businessman.' She paused, puckering her forehead in concentration. 'He was a businessman. He left a card which Astin stuck in his mirror.' She ran her finger around the rim of the now empty glass. 'Michael Fuller, Wakely Investments,' she recited.

'It was about lunchtime when he left. Astin came out looking even greyer than usual, said he wasn't well and went off. I was pretty sure he wouldn't come back so I closed early. He didn't show up again until the day you came in, just after you left. He started messing around in his office. Then he came out and started turning over the shop. I tried not to pay any attention. It's his shop, if he wants to turn it over, fair enough. He was quite frantic really.

'By the time he was more or less shoving me over in his anxiety, I got round to asking him what he was looking for. He told me he was looking for a pile of cuttings and photos. So I said it was probably the lot I had just sold to you. He was livid, said I had no right, what did I think I was doing? I told him I thought I was running a shop, which entailed selling the stock occasionally. He stomped round the place; I thought he was going to bust a gut or something. Then he asked me who I had sold them to, and I said I didn't know who you were and that I didn't make a habit of delving into our few clients' biographies.

'I thought he was going to fire me there and then, but he just went into the back room again. He didn't come out again, I said goodnight when I picked up my coat and shut up shop. He didn't say a word. Then yesterday he was in early, and Fuller came back. They talked for a while, quietly this time, then Fuller left.' She paused, and looked at her glass.

'Do you want another?'

I did. She returned with a half, and a whisky and lemonade, with ice. I asked her what she thought of Fuller.

'I didn't think anything of him really. A bit of a smoothie. He ignored me. After he went, Astin spent about half an hour in the backroom on the phone – unless he was talking to himself – that sounded quite lively, too. Then he came in and told me I would have to run the place on my own for a couple of days, he was going off to Wales. Then just when I thought he was getting ready to go, you showed up for the ding-dong. After you left he was back on the phone, but talking quietly. He looked a bit odd when he came out, then he left. Maybe he was ringing up some local burglars to have you turned over.' She sipped at her drink. 'Maybe he wasn't. I didn't think of it at the time but it's possible.'

'Why?'

She looked at me in a resigned, bored way. 'It is possible because you had something that apparently he wanted, you had a row, and then your place was turned over. I don't have any other evidence, but this is known as deduction. I can't imagine him doing it because he's too old, but perhaps it tied in with Fuller. In fact I think it must have done; I can't imagine Astin finding any robbers off his own bat.'

'Why do you see Fuller as a potential robber?'

'Jesus, I really have to do all the work, don't I? I don't see him as a robber, or wouldn't have done. I'm just fitting what you told me to what I know. It was probably someone else who turned your place over. Someone who had nothing to do with it. Suit yourself. But he did write your address down. So make what you want of that.'

Moira Marchant was losing interest. My interest remained. It was my flat. I decided to pursue the theory anyway. 'What do you know about Astin?'

'Not much. I think he's a fairly embittered and miserable guy. He asked me once what I did when I wasn't sitting in the shop, and when I said anthropology he laughed. Said that he had seen all the blacks he wanted to. I said that anthropology wasn't about blacks. He said he'd been all round the Empire and he knew what was what. I dropped the subject.'

'He was in a bad temper yesterday.'

'You catch on fast.'

'Yeah, I'm really greased lightning.' I was becoming rather tired of Ms Marchant. 'Let me rephrase it. I thought he was possibly . . . scared. Do you think he could have been scared?'

'Yes, it's possible. Fuller's visits certainly didn't cheer him, not that anything cheered old Selly.'

'Selly?'

'That's what his Tulse Hill bride called him. Selwyn Albert Astin. Why didn't you tell the police?'

'I wanted to talk to you or him first and I'm getting fed up with the amount of time I seem to be spending with the police.'

'Why?'

I told her. She was amused. We began to show disturbing signs of getting on. 'You should tell Astin. I'm sure his opinion of you would go up if he knew you were defending Hales.'

I asked her if Astin was right wing. She shrugged. 'I don't think he is a member of the Socialist Workers Party. He had a lot of political stuff around the shop and a lot of that was pre-war, fascist or fascistic. I borrowed some of it.'

'Why?'

'Because a friend of mine was – is – doing a thesis on Mosley and asked if he could borrow the books. Astin grumbled about it but said the stuff wasn't much good to him anymore. Mind you, he said I had to bring it back, so he didn't want to sell that either. Beats me just what he did want to sell, other than ninth-hand Barbara Cartland and propelling pencils.'

'I'd like to see the books. I could plagiarise your friend's thesis for the book I'm doing.'

'Well I don't want to see *him*, he isn't a friend now, and if you can get anything out of him you'll be doing better than I ever managed.'

The conversation died. We gazed at the rows of drinkers, backs shaking in mildly alcoholic laughter. The makings of four o'clock hangovers being prepared. I wanted to know more about Astin, and his shop, and why he had been so anxious to get the folder back.

'I'm going to have to go,' she said. She pushed her brown hair behind her ears.

'I have a proposition to put to you.'

She looked faintly resigned; joke, sexual come-on, favour, would all be the subject of equal indifference to Ms Marchant. 'Oh yes, what?'

'Could I look through Astin's files?'

She stared at me as if the proposition had been indecent rather than illegal. 'Why?'

'I would just like to see if there was anything . . .'

She raised her head and smiled, It was not a friendly smile, but not hostile either. 'Plan of your house, eh? Where you buried the treasure? A real adventure, huh?'

'Well, could I?' I decided to ignore the witticisms.

'I don't really care,' she said wearily.' All you'll find is a lot of invoices and some dead flies.'

No potential customers crowded the entrance. She unlocked the door and we went in. She led me to the back office. 'If you're going to dig around you'd better keep the door closed. Leave everything as it is. God knows what will happen if he comes back. I don't want to get involved.' She shrugged, 'I don't know why I am letting you do this.'

'Well, thanks anyway.'

'Yeah.' She gestured around, and pointed out the business files, 'I don't think those are classified. I haven't really looked at the rest. The bluebottles are guests. A great one with the fly spray is Mr Astin. Not a great one for clearing up.'

She closed the door as she went into the shop. There was no further sound, no customers. I sifted for half an hour and found nothing of any interest. Even the bluebottles were cadavers from the previous summer. Then I sorted through the wastepaper bins. Hundreds of dog-ends, old *Daily Telegraphs*, a pair of blue socks, some blotting paper, and a screwed up note. I unscrewed it.

It was on headed notepaper, 'Sirius, Rhydd-ddu, Gwynedd' it ran, and below there were a few ill-scrawled words, 'Dear Selwyn. Expect Bangor 5.30. You will be picked up from there. Regards.' The signature was illegible. I lit a cigarette, squatted amongst the debris and re-read it, looking for further enlightenment. So that was where Mr Astin was, a late autumn holiday in some corner of Wales. Lucky old Selwyn.

The door opened. 'Well?' she asked.

'He doesn't lead a very interesting life, does he? Still, I think I know where he's gone. Somewhere in Wales called Rhydd-ddu.'

'What kind of name is that?'

'Welsh isn't it? What you would expect in Wales. We've got odd names; you've got odd names as well, what about Medicine Hat?'

'What about Medicine Hat? That's in Canada, I'm not a Canadian.'

'OK, Hackensack, Hoboken. You've come a long way from St Louis.'

'I haven't been anywhere near St Louis. I come from Staten Island.'

'Great, lovely place New York. Turn Manhattan into an isle of joy?'

'Staten Island, I said. Staten Island is at the end of a ferry. Staten Island is shit, which is one reason I'm here. And this place is shit, too. So where's this Rhydd-ddu place?'

'North Wales, I think, near Caernarfon. I had a Welsh relative, you know.'

'That's nice to know. What are you going to do now?'

'I haven't a clue. Go home and think about it. What are you going to do?' It wasn't really an attempt to build our relationship, more idle chat.

'I am going to sit here, then go home, and wait until Astin shows. Then he will give me a pay-cheque. Then I'll go home again. I lead an exciting life in your wonderful country.' She stroked a wooden elephant on the mantlepiece. 'What was in that stuff you bought?'

'Not much. I left it at this friend of mine's place, just a

collection of cuttings. Come and have a look at them.'

'I've got a lot on,' she lied. 'Well, I suppose you'll be going.'

I was disappointed, although I had no reason to be so. 'Yes, I suppose I will. Well, see you. Thanks.'

'You might, if you stand outside the window. I'm usually here.' She led me to the door and closed it behind me. I went home.

5.

'Mr Raven? We've met before, I believe.'

'Have we? When did we do that, then?'

'Yesterday. Remember?'

I remember. He was a young policeman who had hovered in the background when Garret had ushered me into his office. His nose was pink-tinged, and his eyes red. He was like a curious bird, a secretary bird I had once seen at the Zoo. His sideboards were as long as regulations permitted and police concepts of fashion demanded, and he wore the standard dark suit of a plain clothesman. Funny how they model themselves on villains: he would have been equally at home nailing a bookie's knees to the floor or arresting the perpetrator.

'I've called about Tuesday. I expect you are getting a bit fed up with all the fuss eh?' He laughed self-consciously.

I gave my best world-weary smile. It was half past nine in the morning. 'All my days seem to start with your lot now.' But they end differently, I brooded.

'Well, you know how it is.' He gazed over my shoulder. He didn't like doorsteps.

'I didn't, but I'm picking up fast.' It was a sunny day.

'Typical anti-cylonic weather, cold, clear and crisp,' boomed my geography master from his residence in Form Five/d down Memory Lane. In the street a pale blue Vauxhall Cavalier was trying hard to pretend it wasn't a police car.

'I'm PC Purkiss. Can I come in?'

We went upstairs. The smell of rancid bacon followed us up. Pedro in the basement was obviously still on hard times. One day his band was going places, he kept telling me, 'I'll play with Springsteen, man, you wait'. Meanwhile the sound of his saxophone continued to come from the pit, long soaring solos backed by the roar of the tumble dryer. One day it would come from a thousand juke boxes, but that day was still far off. I pushed open my door. I was relieved that I had not reinstated the building workers. The flat looked derelict but respectable, like a Labour Party branch.

He accepted a coffee and looked at books, lingering over a volume of Victorian country photographs. I went off to shave. By the time I returned he was into a book of pictures of the Army in India. Men with moustaches on sunny days sitting under the banyan tree.

'Those were the days, we knew where we were then,' he was gazing at a picture of the 22nd Madras Native Infantry, dated 1861. 'Now they're all over here,' he laughed. I didn't. 'You've got a lot of these old pictures?'

'It's to do with my job. I'm a sort of journalist, a researcher.' This bout of nostalgia could go on too long, I decided. 'What do you want?'

'Journalist, eh?' He chewed over the information, looked at me, took a peck at his coffee. I thought that he should have perched on the rim. 'We're holding an identification parade and we would like you to come along.'

'It's a bit sudden. One minute I'm in bed, then I have to trot off to an ID. Who am I supposed to identify?' It was too early in the morning. For two pins and a guarantee of no prosecution, I would have sunk my teeth in the lower part of his leg. He was aware of that, and would doubtless have been happy to reply in kind, but he didn't. He laughed, the only-doing-my-job speciality chortle.

'I'm sorry about the timing. We tried to get hold of you yesterday, but you weren't in.' He adopted a confidential, between-you-and-me technique. 'The fact is we're to-ing and fro-ing with the anti-terrorist people. They want to get the thing sewn up fast and we're trying to fix the identity of the bloke you saw in the road.'

The alarm bell clanged, and it was Ferret once more on the end of the rope. 'All I said was he was walking down the road. He didn't have a plunger concealed about his person that I could see. He wasn't carrying a little plum pudding with a fuse hissing at one end. He wasn't doing any more than me.'

'No, and we are not *necessarily* saying he did. But between you and me there are some things we're not too happy about.' He wasn't the only one. Pedro had stopped playing. It was suddenly quiet.

'One of them is that he did walk on. Another is that – I've got nothing against anyone's political views, I want to make that clear – is that he might be a . . . a bit of an extremist. We do know that they have bothered Mr Hales before.'

'Hales bothered a lot of people before. I'm not very happy about it.' I was bloody miserable about it. Ferret had abandoned the bell-rope and was now waving his Scottish digit accusingly, Glaswegian invective raining down.

Purkiss was losing his synthetic warmth, like a phony coal fire with the radiant switched off. 'You're not very happy about it. We're not very happy about it.'

'Yeah, you too are only doing your job.' I shrugged. 'Forget it, I was thinking of someone else. When is it?'

'Midday.'

'So this bloke has agreed to the parade, whoever he is?'

Purkiss sighed. 'We wouldn't be holding it otherwise, would we?'

Quite, but why? Assuming they had located the right man, why was he denying he was in the road? Because he had panicked? Because he planted a bomb and he was coming clean? He wouldn't need to be on parade if he had. Because he was gambling that I looked the kind of person who would back him up and say he wasn't there? The last possibility looked the most likely and didn't cheer me at all.

Purkiss drained his cup. He said he would drive me over.

'Who else is doing the parade?'

'I don't really want to go into that.'

'Mrs Avis?'

He looked at me as if I had uncovered a state secret. 'Yes', he replied after a pause, 'Mrs Avis'.

'Do you know anything about her?'

'She's just a housewife, I think. We don't do detailed investigations into our witnesses, but she's been very helpful.' There was a faint implication that this was more than could be said for some people. He looked round the room. 'I live round here, just up the Holloway Road. Quite a nice little place you've got here.'

I couldn't imagine why he might think that. My fears grew. What did he know about last night? I decided against finding out. 'Yes,' I said, 'it could do with a bit of tidying up.'

He stood up, 'Well, it's difficult if you live on your own; you do live on your own?'

'Mostly.'

He laughed knowingly. 'Well, shall we go?'

We went, driving across sunny north London, agreeing that it was a nice day. 'What has happened to Hales's house now?' I asked.

'What d'you think? He's got the builders in.'

'You've uh . . . completed your investigations?'

'We've been through the place.'

'Find anything?'

He glanced at me. 'Well, I don't really want to go into that, Mr Raven. You know how it is.'

I knew how it was.

'Still,' he said, 'we've got a bit of time, fancy taking a look?'

I did. Why does he want me to take a look? I thought. Resolve stiffened by the horrific scene of the crime? We drove round the back of Camden High Street, across Parkway and into Regents Park Road. I just couldn't keep away . . .

The sightseers and the police had gone. A plastic sheet hung over the shattered façade. A builder in National Health rimless specs was sawing a plank in the front garden, or what was left of it. He looked like a potential recruit for Ferret from the way he eyed the Cavalier, and us as we got out.

'Everything all right?' asked Purkiss.

'The sun is shining, I'm being paid, everything's fine,' observed the builder. 'Who are you?'

'I'm PC Purkiss from Holmes Road. This gentleman saw the explosion.'

The man was about thirty-five, lank brown hair drooped across a wide, intelligent face. He sat on the garden wall and started rolling a cigarette. 'Oh yes?' He looked at me. 'Key witness in the bombing outrage, eh?'

'Too right,' I observed gloomily. 'Is it much of a job?'

'Not really, should keep us busy. Mind you, whoever did it knew what they were about.'

'How's that?'

He gestured at the debris. 'I reckon they buried the stuff there, in two separate holes, and it peeled the front off. Neat bit of work, high class. What beats me is how anyone could do it in broad daylight. You would have thought someone would have seen it.'

'Well, I didn't. Anyway you don't expect people coming round and blowing the neighbourhood sky-high.'

He stuck the cigarette to his upper lip and continued talking. A neat trick. 'Don't know what to expect these days do you? Anyway, one man's explosion, another man's work for a month. I better get on.'

'So had we,' said Purkiss. We drove on to the police station. I felt like I had felt on my way to sit final exams, and I knew why; maybe I was. The policeman said nothing, just took an occasional short stare.

It was a busy day at the Kentish Town nick. An old man had got blind drunk, quite an achievement before lunch, and was angered at being disturbed in his cups. He wore a check suit and looked like a bookie's runner, with grey hair which lay greasy flat across pink scalp.

'No right,' he mumbled to the desk sergeant. 'No right at all. What does Bermuda matter to me? Why should I be expected to pay?'

'You tell me,' said the sergeant.

The drunk saw me. '*You* tell him. It's a bloody disgrace.'

'Difficult,' I said.

The drunk digested my observation and stared at the floor. Slowly he sank to the floor, a child observing the ways of ants. He glanced up at me and smiled. Then he threw up. The vomit dribbled across the foyer.

'Oh for Christ's sake,' shouted Purkiss. 'We've got an ID in ten minutes. Do you have to turn this place into a doss house? What do you think Herne will say?'

The Sergeant leaned across the desk. 'We've got enthusiastic policemen on this force as you will doubtless have noticed, Purkiss. Randolph has only been here three days and he has spent them collecting specimens outside the Old Mother Redcap.'

'Well, it isn't right.'

'No, it isn't, Purkiss. Not right at all,' He shouted into the void. A woman appeared with a mop and bucket, familiarity with the scene did not prevent her look of disgust, but it was tinged with resignation. The drunk was frog-marched out.

Purkiss took me to the office where Garret had interviewed me and left. I lit a cigarette and read the *Horse and Hound.* There was a wide range of interests in the police. A few shouts about Bermuda drifted down the corridor.

The door opened and Garret entered. 'Sorry to keep you, Mr Raven. Thanks for coming. This is Detective Superintendent Mellowes.'

I knew Mellowes. He had been the man who had spoken to me after the explosion. He smiled a big insincere smile and proffered his paw. It was extremely large. I always thought *I* had big hands. 'Good to see you, Mr Raven. It won't take long. All you have to do is walk down the line, take your time, and then let me know if you recognise anybody. Then you can go.' He recited it in a sing-song style born of constant repetition.

Garret bustled around the office and settled by a filing cabinet. He was less relaxed with Mellowes around, less one of the lads. I caught a glimpse of what I thought was my statement. 'Is Mrs Avis here?'

He raised his eyebrows. 'Mrs Avis?'

'The lady I was with in Regents Park Road.'

'Oh yes, Mrs *Avis*.' His forgetfulness routine was unconvincing. 'Yes she's just done it.'

'Any luck?'

They glanced at one another, 'Depends what you mean by *luck*, Mr Raven,' said Mellowes. 'Anyway, we can't talk about it just now. Could you come along?'

I followed them out of the room down the corridor and into a courtyard. I remembered movies of prisoners marching round quadrangles, but I wasn't inside. I could leave when I wanted, I was a free man.

There were ten people lined up. A couple of clear outsiders, representing the fat community and the long thin community, both with long brown hair. Only one of the ten had been in Regents Park Road and he was third from the end. I felt sick. Why had I got involved? Why had *he* got involved? I strolled down the line, slowly, and then once more. The fat man coughed, and I used it as an excuse to pause in front of him. He looked affronted, but scared. It was the first time I had really looked at the face of my unwilling . . . accomplice? I was getting in too deep. His beard was neatly trimmed, perhaps he had cut it especially for the parade, his brown hair was neatly parted on the right side of his head. He was wearing the jeans from Tuesday, but with a white shirt and a large, out-of-date kipper tie. He looked straight ahead, but he knew.

I could still tell Mellowes, I thought. I fantasised about consigning all fifteen to Life in Botany Bay. Mellowes stood at the end looking confident, calm in a dark grey suit. Not a greasy hair was out of place, he was in charge.

I walked back, and out of the courtyard, with Mellowes leading the way. 'Well, sir?'

I stole a last glance at the line, which had broken up, with nervous laughter ringing round the courtyard. My man didn't look like a bomber; he looked resentful, and a bit dumb. *See how popular you can make yourself, Raven.* I felt Ferret's antennae settling on to my brain. Mellowes was looking at me, a mixture of curiosity and contempt spreading across his face.

'No, I'm afraid I can't help you, Superintendent. I can't

pick anyone out from that lot. Are you sure you've got the right one?'

Curiosity lost a battle with incredulity but contempt took a major billing. 'We thought we had,' he spat at me, 'in fact we still do. Still . . . Thank you very much, *Mister* Raven. If you would care to come back through.' I followed him down the corridor, the disgraced small boy who had cocked up the speech-day. We went back into Garret's office.

'Well, that's about all there is for the time being.' Garret didn't bother to try a smile. 'We may be in touch again. It's a pity you couldn't help us.' The implication that I might have cause for regret was plain enough.

'Yes, I'm sorry,' which was was true enough. Christ, I did feel sorry, but not for them, and not for the third from the end. 'Did you get a different response from Mrs Avis?'

'Yes we did. She picked somebody out.'

'Who was that?'

Mellows had been thumbing through the statements on the desk. He fingered mine. 'You know bloody well who it was,' and looked directly at me. 'The same one that you picked out, the third one from the end.'

'I didn't pick anyone out.' He put the statement down, as if fearing contagion. 'No, you didn't, and I would be simply fascinated to know why.'

I got angry, a mixture of guilt, fear, and, I console myself now, bloody-mindedness. 'I didn't pick anyone out because I didn't recognise anybody, that's why. I've been as helpful as I could. I didn't need to come on your parade and now I'm being treated as if I've just blown up the Bank of England.'

'Well, we're truly sorry to have disturbed your beauty sleep, Mr Raven.' I wasn't wondering if Garret was the nice KGB man anymore; compared with Mellowes, he had to be. Perspiration was breaking out on his forehead; droplets oozed out from the brylcreem. 'I don't know where your loyalties are, Raven, but by Christ I'd watch out from now on, because we will.'

'Thanks very much. I don't know who the bloke . . .'

'You knew all right, I could see you weighing up your shabby little options . . .'

'I didn't know, and I don't know. Who is he?'

Mellowes moved away from the desk and came in for the eyeball to eyeball. 'He's the kind of long-haired red who does bugger all except get our lads out on Sundays while he and his mates prance around the streets of London shouting slogans about liberating some other bunch of long-haired layabouts. Before long he's going to be doing a long stretch and be a burden on the prison service instead of us. And I'll be very pleased when that happens.'

'I didn't know you ran the judiciary as well.'

'Very witty.'

'What's his name?'

It was Garret's turn to get in on the action. 'His name is Martin Gold. And I wouldn't be at all surprised if that came as no surprise to you at all.'

'Well you'd be wrong. And what has he done? He was walking down the road. So bloody what? I was doing the same and you haven't pulled me in.'

They looked at one another. Clearly the idea had crossed at least two minds. 'Gold has pestered Hales for months, picketed his house, tried to bust up a meeting, we nearly got him for throwing a brick at him.'

Perhaps the Almighty knows what came over me. 'What was wrong? Didn't you plant it on him in time?'

I swung gently off the ground as Mellowes grabbed my lapels. I could feel the seams going. It had never been a particularly well made jacket. 'Get lost, Raven.' He lowered me slowly to the ground.

'A pleasure.' It was. I bumped into Purkiss on the way out. He smiled – the word had yet to get round the station. He didn't offer me a lift home, but then I didn't go home. I decided to follow up the other consuming interest of the week, Michael Fuller of Wakely Investments. I got a tube to Old Street, several tubes, and kept a regular watch behind me, I saw no-one.

Old Street is a sterile place, a roundabout with a few shops clinging to the edge of the speedway, and concrete lumps, devoid of any human logic, stuck in the middle. 'It was probably pleasant before they built this lot,' I had once said to Kathy.

She had laughed. 'Never. Read the *Home Front* by Sylvia Pankhurst. Old Street, Hoxton, it was always a wasteland.'

It didn't stop them gutting the wasteland. Now the locals can either contemplate the area from the lofty horror of the highrises or, if younger, ride their Suzukis round and round the one-way system.

Just down from the roundabout, and over the road from where William Blake lies six foot under, swearing at the shambles he failed to stop a hundred and fifty years ago, is Companies House. In it are files on all British companies; very useful, Ferret is always telling me.

'The gaffer said he couldn't pay a penny over two quid. Lying bastard, tiny little company he said he was. Well young Terry went down there . . .'

'Young Terry who junked his PhD to join you on the sites and really get his hands buried in the proletarian muck . . .'

'Don't you knock Terry,' Ferret had shouted, 'he came from a good Nottinghamshire mining family, none of your stuck-up Southern petit-bourgeois, he uses his knowledge in our struggle. Anyway Terry went down there and found that bastard, that lying bastard was part of Ortram.'

'Who?'

'Ortram Construction. God you're bloody ignorant. Huge company, built half of Saudi Arabia, what there is of it. Once we found that out, the place was sewn up in half a day. Useful place, Companies House.'

And it is a setting for Kafka fantasies; solicitors' clerks digging through mounds of balance sheets, people's Maseratis and nice houses in Pinner neatly reduced to rows of incriminating figures, five-year fraud sentences lined up in black and white, if you can pluck them from the ranks of figures.

I waited for the file to arrive. The man next to me was reading the *Daily Telegraph*. Mrs Thatcher smiled at me from the front page, but I wasn't convinced. He was reading the sports pages and wheezing. He clearly passed a lot of time in that sweaty environment. He leaned across. 'It's all go, isn't it?'

'Tedious with it.' I like to be part of a club. The file arrived telling a familiar tale. Wakely was a property firm, and Fuller the managing director. It had started up in 1961. It seemed to have had a low turnover until the early 1970s when money began to come into it. Some chap called Appleton had joined the board around that time; an American, I noticed. There were no returns since 1977, which was illegal, but not unusual. Why would a successful property shark like Fuller be worrying about an old never-was like Astin, or more alarmingly with a nothing in particular like me? Fuller got around; he was listed as a director of three other companies which I didn't bother to follow up. The *Telegraph* reader's respiratory problems were beginning to depress me.

He had slumped across the chair. The effort of reading was clearly too much for him. His mouth gaped, and he began to snore. I left.

I was fed up, depressed by the cops, tired of being broke, bored with futile investigations. I decided to go to the pictures; there is nothing like the peace and quiet of the Academy on a Friday afternoon. I caught a bus to Oxford Street. I had twenty minutes before the film began. I toyed with the idea of visiting the Old Kentucky Pancake style steak hamburger and pizza bar but thought better of it. I decided to make a phone call, having taken Fuller's address from the file. It was in St John's Wood, so it should have been easy to find. But there were no Fullers in Acacia Road. He must have moved. I tried the office.

'Wakely Investments,' said a bright, cool voice down the phone. I pictured a neat blonde with streaked hair and shades and a boyfriend with a Datsun sports car. She would be wearing a dark red pencil skirt.

'Wakely Investments,' she repeated, 'Yes?' She was probably a middle-aged lady. But then I like middle-aged ladies, I've been waiting for a Mrs Robinson ever since I was ten.

'I'm sorry,' *Why am I always apologising?*, I thought, 'I wonder if I could speak to Mr Fuller?' What did I have to say to Mr Fuller? *Smashed any good property up lately*?

'Not here I'm afraid. Can anyone else help, can I take a message?'

'Aaah . . . no. Could you tell me where I could get hold of him?'

'I'm afraid I can't. He's not in town at the moment, he's gone away for a few days. Could you tell me who it is calling?'

I didn't like that at all. 'Just a friend, it isn't important, my name's Peter Butcher.'

'B-U-T-C-H-E-R? Is that right?'

She could spell it how she liked, I'm not mean. I invented it, she could embroider it. I said that was right. 'I tried to find his number in Acacia Road but it didn't seem to be there.'

'Acacia Road?' She sounded mystified. 'I don't think he has a place there. Anyway I believe he is in Wales but I can't tell you where.'

That sounded interesting.

She couldn't or she wouldn't?

'Wales?'

'Yes, Wales.' She was tired of our lively banter. Perhaps I should invite her for a drive in my Lamborghini, I thought. I decided against it.

'Thank you very much. I'll ring back next week. Thanks.'

'You're welcome.' From the sound of it I wasn't and she could do without the follow-up call.

I hung up and walked down Oxford Street. What was so interesting about Wales? I went in to the Academy. It was a good movie.

6.

It was the weekend, and nothing was happening. If there is a heaven, a hell and limbo, then I suspect that north London on a grey, damp weekend will be limbo. I shopped, cleared up the flat, went out to eat with a couple of friends. I was lying in bed on Sunday morning when the phone rang.

'John.'

'Ferret.'

'Fancy a drink?'

In theory I always fancy a drink on Sunday morning. It is a part of a vision that I have of another me, cavalry twilled, with a Ford Capri, a wife and a good golf handicap, whatever that might be, having a drink at lunchtime before roast lamb and mint sauce. Usually I am too hungover on Sundays to do anything, but that day I was suffering no after-effects. It was a chance to live out my fantasy, although Ferret was unlikely to have spent the morning on the links.

'Yeah, all right, where?'

'I'm selling the paper on the estates in Dalston. Fancy coming to the Norfolk about one?'

'What time is it?'

'You're really in touch, aren't you? It's half past ten.'

I arrived just before one. The Norfolk is a long thin L-shaped bar with a juke box. Once it had been crammed with locals listening to other locals impersonating Andy Williams to piano accompaniment. Recently it had been increasingly occupied by Ferret's friends, or, to judge by the tenor of their conversations, his enemies. The reds came from miles around to abuse one another.

Ferret hadn't arrived. I got a drink. The juke box was off; a sign that genuine, live, pub entertainment was making an unwelcome come-back. I preferred the juke box. A short plump man strolled to the stage and welcomed everybody to the pub. The reds and locals shuffled uneasily. The man seemed to imagine that he had made the Palladium at last and launched into a selection of Abba's hits in the style of late period Sinatra. It was an uneasy marriage.

I read somebody's *News of the World*. Hales was doing well. He had his own centre page denunciation of his bombers complete with general attacks on marginal sections of the community.

Ferret came over with his papers stuffed under his arm. The publication was *Workers Speak*, the newspaper of the Workers for Revolutionary Change. On Sundays he took time off from flogging it on his site and at factories and took it down the housing estates. He asked me if I wanted a drink, I accepted, he got them and sat down.

'Bad morning.' He lit a cigarette and stretched himself out

on the red plastic. 'Half the buggers were out. One bloke who's bought it for the last month wouldn't buy it because his wife didn't like it. A woman who had her old man in wouldn't buy it because her old man didn't want it and *she's* been buying it for three weeks. And another bloke who I thought we might recruit wouldn't buy it at all! And that's after two months.' He shrugged. 'And some fascist tried to help me over the balcony.'

'It's dedication that counts, Ferret.'

He missed or ignored my attempt at irony. 'What do you know about dedication? Why don't you come out one morning?'

'Because it's cold. Because I don't agree with you. Because I wouldn't know what to say. Because I don't want to join, so how can I try and trap some other poor sod in your web?'

'You don't want to join because you are idle. You don't really disagree. You just want to sit round and moan and not do anything. We've got the most right-wing government north of Johannesburg and west of Moscow and you are doing bugger all.'

'I'm not moaning, you are. I'm just sitting here drinking my drink and harming neither man, woman, tenant nor beast.'

He drained his glass. 'Well you can do a beast some good. Mine's a pint of Special.'

I went to the bar. When I came back he was reading Hales's article. 'What a bastard this guy is,' he tapped the paper as if prodding the MP's lapel. 'God, he should know what scroungers are.'

I put my glass down, the beer slopped on the table. He asked me if I had heard any more from the police.

I smiled a confident smile. 'You don't read the papers. They had an identity parade on Friday morning. They invited me.'

He slammed down his glass, the reservoir on the table was expanding. 'You declined the invitation, of course?'

'Now why should I do that?'

He articulated the words slowly, precisely. 'Whoever did it should not have done it. Not because it was criminal, but because it was criminally stupid. Whoever did it had the right idea. You should not have let the cops loose on him or her.'

It was developing into another of my 'last stand' routines. I commenced with a broad humanist perspective of the evils of violence from whatever quarter. 'What bloody difference does it make who he was trying to blow up? He could have killed somebody, *anybody*. Some poor sod walking down the street – specifically me – it's always some harmless so-and-so who gets blown up. It isn't a question of tactics, it happens to be wrong to go round blowing people up.'

'Go tell that to the Israeli air force. There is a difference between the violence of the oppressed and the . . .'

'Violence of the oppressor. You can stuff that Kung-fu wisdom.'

'Look pal, did you go on that ID?'

'I did.'

'You crud.' He hunched up like a Granny with overdose of umbrage.

'You haven't let me explain. I went on the parade, but I didn't identify anybody.'

'Why's that then? Did they turn out the Dagenham Girl Pipers?'

'They wanted to identify the bloke who was walking down the road, the one who kept on walking. He was on the line, but I didn't pick him out. Now think about it. I didn't have to go on the parade, but nor did he. He must have calculated that he had to, if he was to have any chance to clear himself, and must have gambled that I either wouldn't or couldn't identify him, which would strengthen his position.'

'Well, God help him if he has to rely on you to do the Clint Eastwood number.'

'Thanks very much. What would the cops have thought if I hadn't shown? Come to think of it, I don't know why I didn't pick him out, apart from the thought of people like you shouting abuse at me.'

Ferret's foreign impersonations were excruciating. 'You putta da finger onna him. We putta da finger on you. So they didn't get him?'

'Of course, they bloody got him. Christ, you should read the papers.' I pointed out his pile of *Workers Speaks*. 'If you rely on that thing for up-to-date news, then you're going to be in trouble. The number of times that comes out, it's a wonder they've managed to get the Russian Revolution in the stop press.'

'You want to contribute to our new printshop fund?'

'Knock it off. His name is Martin Gold, and they are still holding him. They knew who he was, and the woman – Mrs Avis – picked him out. They knew I knew who it was, too. They weren't too keen on me after the parade.'

He laughed. 'Oh . . . Nasty cops rude to you, eh? You're a classic liberal, Raven. You get the worst of all possible worlds. You compromise your principles by talking to them after the big bang, compromise yourself by going on the parade and not picking anyone out. No wonder you pass your life in bed, you compromise yourself by putting your foot on the carpet. You have an unerring aim for the sea of custard. You know that?'

I was furious. He wasn't inaccurate, quite the reverse, and I was sickened by the taste of custard. The drinkers hemmed us in like some impenetrable forest. 'I'm just about fed up with this fucking routine! I've spent my entire time these last five days being shouted at, abused, prodded, and I've had my flat turned over.'

'What do you mean, had your flat turned over?' He gazed at me from above the rim of his almost empty glass.

I told him.

'So you reckon they wanted the pictures?'

'What else?'

'It doesn't sound like the bombers. Martin Gold . . .' He shook his head, 'I've never heard of him.'

'Ever heard of Fuller? Or Astin?'

He hadn't. Over by the bar an arm waved a greeting at Ferret, like a fern growing in the heights of a rain forest, a muddy dark blue fern, the remnants of a naval greatcoat. Inside it was a tall lumpy man with a drooping moustache and short black hair. He looked in his late twenties, and as resentful about that as about every other aspect of his life.

Under his arm I glimpsed a thick padding of *Workers Speaks*. Ferret waved back, looking faintly sheepish. 'That's Odgers,' he muttered.

'Want a drink, Ferret?' Odgers shouted loudly enough to make most of the bar feel a sense of exclusion from his largesse. They weren't happy about it.

'Yeah,' said Ferret, trying to whisper a shout. 'A pint of Special.'

'Nice chap, your mate.' I gazed at the remains of my pint. 'Nice of him to offer everyone a drink like that.'

Ferret, and it was unusual for him, looked embarassed. He leaned over; 'His name is Odgers, Cal Odgers. He is a very good . . . a very good *comrade*. Been in the group about eighteen months, sound as a rock.'

'And heavy with it.'

Ferret blinked. 'If you mean *serious*, yes he's serious. He doesn't piss around all the time like some people, if that's what you mean.' He attempted self-righteousness to dilute his unease. 'He's got a job at that toy factory down the road. He's running for AUEW shop steward.'

I rolled the dregs round my glass. 'Well some old Labour bloke told me that whenever he heard the word "Comrade" he watched out for his watch-chain. Where did he do his degree in Oriental Philosophy?'

'Oxford Poly, it wasn't Oriental Philosophy, and he walked out.' Ferret still wasn't happy with his associate. 'Anyway he's a good lad.'

Odgers sat down. Ferret made the formal introductions. Odgers assessed me with mechanical movements of his eyebrows before going to Ferret for the key moral judgement. 'Member of the group?'

Ferret handled the translation. 'No, he's just a mate of mine, is John. Coming our way I think.' He emitted a cross between a sneeze and a laugh. It was unconvincing as either.

Once I was thus categorised, Odgers dismissed me from the conversation. 'I sold eight. Some good people on that estate, Ferret, think we might make some progress. There was one old fellow who was in the RCP way back, wonderful old man.'

'RCP?' I asked.

'Revolutionary Communist Party,' replied Ferret tersely. 'Original British section of the Fourth International, broke up in the late 1940s.' Having dispensed his slice of Trotskyist history, he returned to Odgers. 'Eight papers, eh?'

'Yes. This old boy had the Communist Party all summed up. He was in it for a bit in the early 1950s. Said he left in 1955 because he didn't like Malenkov.'

Ferret permitted himself a hint of exasperation. 'I didn't know Malenkov was around long enough to piss anyone off apart from his wife and the punters at the power station they landed him with. What was wrong with him just settling for hating Stalin?'

Odgers shifted uneasily. 'Well, he was a bit odd about it, really. Said that Stalin and Trotsky should have got together when Hitler invaded Russia.'

'Joe buried the ice-pick in Trotsky's toupee in 1940,' observed Ferret acidly. 'It would have been a grave digger's job.'

'Yeah, well I said that – almost.' He laughed self-consciously. 'Actually he was a bit odd about Trotsky. He was a bit odd about Mao, too. Said he wrote him a letter but he never wrote back.'

'Did he try ringing him up?' I asked.

Neither of them found this amusing. They glared at me. 'What do you mean,' said Odgers, 'ring the Chinese embassy?'

'Forget it, Cal. John's being witty.'

'Yeah.' Odgers was losing out on the broader political questions. 'Anyway he works at the Town Hall, got a desk job now. He is in NALGO, used to be in the G and M. I think he might join, he said he had the SWP around but he told them to piss off.'

'Right,' said Ferret approvingly. 'We could use someone down there, what with those Labour Left posers.'

My glass stayed empty. 'Want a drink?' I asked Ferret. He did. My eyes were harpooned by Odgers.

'Sorry I didn't get you one,' he lied. 'Pint of Special, I'll give you the money.'

I told him to forget about the money, which effortlessly he did. The Sinatra substitute had relinquished the stage, I noticed, as I elbowed my way to the bar. An old man, a dehydrated Al Jolson, gripped the microphone.

'When no-one else can understand me –'

A group of cheerful drunks in the corner joined in, 'Aah ah, aah ah,' they chorused.

'You give me strength to carry on –'

The drunks reprised.

'I guess I'll never know, the reason why, you love me the way that you do –'

'Beats me why they ever bought Nicholas in the first place,' observed a regular to the barman.

'It's the wonder, the WONDER of you.' It was weird, a shrivelled Jolson rendering a cheeseburgered Elvis.

Back at the table Odgers was warming to his theme. 'I reckon if he is any good, *any good at all*, we can really start to make an *intervention.* Get in there, split off some of the Labour left, begin to make real progress.'

Ferret was bored. 'Right pal.'

'Bloody right I'm right. You coming to the meeting on Tuesday?'

Ferret would be at the meeting on Tuesday. The barman abandoned bonhomie and switched to abuse: it was five to two. 'Got some stew at home,' said Ferret. 'Care to come back?'

Odgers made up my mind for me. 'Love to, Ferret, but I've got to go and see the fucking wife. She's kicking up about not getting her money this week. Silly cow.'

'How's Terry?' asked Ferret.

Odgers shrugged. 'He was all right, but you know Teresa, she's been playing up. She's set me against him, but that kid, you know – when he's been with me an hour – we get on fine. Anyway I've got to go. See you Ferret,' he flicked his eyes to me. 'See you'.

'Yeah,' we muttered, and retired to Stoke Newington. There was a smell of burning turnips as Ferret opened the door.

'Ah, turnips flambés.'

'As a matter of fact,' said Ferret with dignity, 'it is rabbit stew For Whom The Bell Tolls. The bit where that punter is up the mountain with the fascists all around, drinking red wine out of a goat skin and eating rabbit and slipping into the bear skin with that girl. The wine's left over from last night, and I got a carry-out! He brandished a large can of beer and a quarter of Scotch.

Avoiding the turnips, I found that it wasn't too bad. I settled back with an apple yoghurt in one hand and a Scotch in the other. I gazed out of his murky window. Pale sunlight filtered through. 'Where's the envelope?'

He walked to the bookshelf, picked up a packet of cigarettes, tossed me one and sifted through a pile of *Socialist Workers*. He found the envelope, sat on the carpet and thumbed through. He was wearing odd coloured socks, one red, one green.

'That's a sign of madness, Ferret!'

'What?'

'Your socks.'

'Oh aye. You should talk to the kids down the road. I was on my way to the launderette yesterday – that's why I've got odd socks – they were the only clean ones, and they shouted at me. "Mister, you've got odd socks." So I said, "you're right there," all cheerful like. It was amazing. One little psychopath said to his mate, "He's mad! Throw something at him!" So there they all were throwing stones, really charming.'

'That was yesterday, Ferret. Why have you got odd socks today?'

'Drink, my boy, drink and lethargy.'

'They were right.'

He pulled out the contents of the envelope. 'It seems awful mean to turn your place over for a few tatty old *Tribunes* and a couple of dead kangaroos.'

I looked at the pictures. Nothing was revealed, so we delved back into what appeared to be the early 1920s. Before the big game photographs was one of the couple standing on some foreign quayside. The sun was shining in their eyes, they squinted at us, we looked at them.

'The saga of our colonial forebears,' observed Ferret. 'But why is it all mixed up with *Action* and *Tribune*?'

'Because Astin was searching through piles of junk and mixed up separate lots?'

'Could be. Or maybe they were a political family.' He laughed, 'Of course people like this were above politics, or below.' He sifted back to the bottom of the pile and pulled out a curling sepia picture of a dog with a lopsided ear. It was attempting to look fierce. Ferret sipped his Scotch. 'Strange how animals make things seem contemporary, an emissary from the present into the past. You see those pictures of Dutch peasants snowballing each other and there is some daft animal running around with them, with those long dead people.'

'Well, that dog has gone to the great kennel in the sky.' I pulled out another picture, a family group with a stern patriarch, a rigid but withered wife, and a son about ten years old wearing that familiar Edwardian item, a sailor suit. I pointed at a young woman on the periphery of the group, 'Daughter, son and parents.'

Ferret scrutinised the young woman. 'Na, she's not dressed right, looks more like the governess.'

'I never knew you had a nanny, Ferret, didn't think it was the Glasgow style.'

'Fuck you! I'm interested in social history, it is *our* history, even if these cadgers were ripping off my grandparents.' He spoke with slightly pompous dignity. The next picture was in a frame.

'Nice bit of work this, John, this is silver. Perhaps they turned you over for the cost of it, nice bit of work.'

He looked closely at it. Again it was the patriarch, with his wife and child and must have been taken about the same time. The scene was a public meeting. The patriarch addressing the meeting from a table draped in a union jack. It was in the open air, and the man's hand was frozen in gesticulation, emphasising a point made seventy years ago, or more. Ferret slopped some more Scotch into his glass and passed the bottle to me. 'Well, what are you going to do with this lot?'

'Leave them here. I'm not taking them back to Highbury to get nicked.'

'Then what?'

'When Astin and Fuller get back from their holiday in Wales, I'll have a word with them. There's not much else I can do, is there?'

'I suppose not.' Ferret crawled unsteadily to his feet, struggled to his desk and turned on the radio. A vicar was explaining a minor theological point to an earnest youth.

The afternoon drifted away. Sunday evening loomed, the worst evening of the week. At half past three, I told Ferret I was leaving, and by half past six was on my way. I walked down Kingsland Road to Dalston Junction.

'After the revolution, Kingsland Road and Holloway Road will be turned into game reserves,' Kathy had suggested once. 'They are the most god-forsaken streets in the entire world.' Especially on Sunday evenings in late November. They had probably helped her on her way to Italy.

I took a bus to Highbury Corner and walked across Highbury Fields, past the tall Georgian houses to Highbury Hill. The three men were coming down the steps. I saw them just before they saw me.

Two of them could not have been much over twenty. The third was in early middle age, with sparse sandy hair and an expression of querulous outrage that had probably frozen on his face when he had been caught nicking scrap iron during his early youth. It was not softened by my arrival. He was wearing a red anorak of the kind doled out by petrol companies. It was past its prime. His companions were at an earlier stage along the same road. One, a neo-skin head, gaped. The other, a Ted, had a lot of work to do on his quiff. Still, it was good to see some intermingling of usually conflicting cultural groupings. I tried to pass them on the steps.

Anorak swung his shoulder, his hands buried in his pockets to block my progress. 'Your name Raven?' His parody of middle period Cagney was so laboured I almost laughed, but didn't. The familiar feeling came over me.

Why aren't I still on my Sunday walk? I thought. *Why aren't I skindiving*?

'Why do you ask?'

'Don't get funny,' said Quiff. 'DON'T GET FUNNY.'

He prodded me at that point below the throat where the rib cage meets. I wasn't getting funny, nothing could have been further from my mind than random jest.

'Do you spend all your Sundays prodding people?' I was sweating and my voice was curling at the edges. I had a vision of a vibrating British Rail cheese sandwich.

'I prod who I like.' Perhaps he did. I didn't want to find out.

'Look, chief,' said Anorak with the tone of sweet reason General McArthur must have used when accepting Japan's unconditional surrender, 'your name is Raven.'

This was true, I wasn't happy about it. 'No it isn't.'

They wavered. 'Don't get funny,' repeated Quiff. I hoped he sounded marginally less convinced.

'Then who the fuck are you?' Anorak was disappointed.

'My name is Peter Butcher.'

'Who the fuck is Peter Butcher?' The third guy had managed to open and shut his month.

'What does Peter Butcher want?' asked Anorak.

I summoned my dramatic powers. 'Look, I don't know what you want. I've come to see Raven because he owes me a tenner and what I get is you three muscling me up.' It was a good performance. I reached for a cigarette, and Quiff helped himself. This was a good sign, and it got better.

'He isn't in.' Anorak looked at the house. 'No one's in. He owes us something too, which is why we're here. You sure you aren't Raven? Not getting absent-minded or anything?'

The time had arrived for a counter attack, a little righteous indignation. 'No, I'm not getting bloody absent-minded and I'm not Raven. Kick his head in if you want to and get my ten quid off him too. If he isn't in then I'm off.'

'All right, all right, I believe you.' Anorak looked at his companions, who looked approvingly at me. Someone else who had joined the club of people being ripped off by John Raven. I began to think he was a bit of a slob myself. 'Do you know when he'll be back?'

I shrugged. 'I thought he would be in now.'

'So did we. You haven't seen him recently?'

'Not in three months.'

'Yeah? Well, if you do, tell him we'd *really* like to see him about some pictures.' Anorak gestured expressively. 'And if we see him, we'll pass on the message about the tenner. No hard feelings, eh?'

The episode was shading into farce. We had all formed a common bond against this defaulting debtor and art thief. 'No, no,' I said. 'He's a ponce anyway. What's all this about pictures?'

Anorak became, as much as it was within his nature, bashful. 'Oh, nothing, just some pictures he nicked off an old mate of ours, that's all.' He glanced at his companions. 'Well, sorry about that lads, thanks for coming along, sorry it didn't uh . . . didn't quite work out. I got to go off now.'

And he did. Surprising his associates almost as much as me, he strode off towards the tube station.

The three of us stared at one another, partygoers after the host has announced an early night, huddled around a lamp-post in Highbury Hill.

'Here, uh . . .' Quiff was a trifle embarrassed.

'Yes?'

'You couldn't lend us a quid, could you? We haven't got the fare.'

I let out a genuine, strangled laugh. 'You must be joking. I've got fifty pence to see me till tomorrow.' It was true.

He was crestfallen. 'Oh yeah, well, no bother. See you around.'

They remained at the corner as I walked back towards Highbury Fields. They lose their appeal by seven on a November evening. I sat on a bench and scrutinised the remaining leaves on an oak tree. I made it home by seven thirty. There was still no-one in. I locked my door, pulled the curtains and brooded. Depression, a combination of fear and hangover swept over me. I went to bed early and watched a snow storm on my flickering, dying televison.

About ten, the phone rang. Her voice was odd. I asked her how she had found my number, paranoia came easy. She had looked in the book.

'I didn't expect you to ring.'
'Nor did I,' said Moira Marchant.
'Job going all right?'
'It's *going* all right. I've just had a call from Astin's wife.'
'Sociable old soul. Still, Sunday can be a lonely day.'
'She was upset. He's dead.'
The sweat returned in the cold room with the flickering televison. 'Astin?'
'Who else? Apparently he was involved in an accident, fell off a cliff. I couldn't get much out of her.'

7.

I saw her the following evening at the Spread Eagle. She arrived about nine. I had been there an hour, drunk two pints and found nothing in the paper about Hales or dead booksellers. Spizzichino had paid me thirty pounds, so there were grounds for faint celebrations.

She was wearing a blue dress which made her look as if she had come from a cocktail party. 'You look as if you've just come from a cocktail party,' I said.

'Laundromat,' she said shortly. 'Nothing else left.'

'The only time anyone wears anything interesting now is when they go to the launderette. They should install bars.'

'What?' One had to be precise with Moira Marchant; obscure witticisms crumbled before her. I bought her a gin and tonic: the dress was something to live up to.

The pub was filling up, but there was still some room in the corner. She stretched out.

'So what did Mrs Astin say?'

'What I told you last night. I think she was drunk.' She paused and half smiled. 'Mind you, I often think she's drunk when she rings up. She told me I didn't need to come in today because the "whole thing was finished". He fell off a cliff and died on the way to hospital.'

'Just fell. Not pushed or shoved, just fell.'

She looked at me. 'It's all your idea about plots, you

know. She sounded a bit resigned, almost as if she had been expecting it and there was nothing she could do apart from be bitter. And from the way she spoke, that is *pretty* bitter. She said she would see about paying me off because the shop was going to close.'

'And that was it?'

'I told her how sorry I was, came out with some guff about how much I had liked working with her husband. Funny what lies you can tell . . .' She shrugged. 'Well I didn't want the poor old guy dead.' She took a tentative nibble at her thumb. 'She laughed and said "oh yes", obviously didn't believe a word of it.'

Moira Marchant had ripped the flesh of her thumb, a pinhead of blood had appeared. She swore and asked me if I wanted another drink. I had a half. I was getting drunk, not happy drunk or paranoid drunk, but faint meaningless warm drunk. I watched her as she returned with the drinks, noted the outline of her legs, her figure. My mind slipped away from Astin and Hales. As she put the drinks down, she smiled. I was surprised; it was warm, the sun emerging from the clouds on an uncertain August day. Usually when she smiled it was out of habit rather than feeling, a signal dutifully raised by an indifferent railwayman. It vanished as quickly as it had come. I noticed she was wearing perfume. I asked her if she had heard from Fuller.

'No. Should I have done?'

'Well he was Astin's host, wasn't he? Even if you didn't officially know. I just wondered. I did try and contact him, I was playing games I suppose, I didn't have anything particular to say. He's making tracks to Astin, and maybe me.'

'How do you mean?'

'I looked up Wakely Investments, Fuller is a prosperous gentleman. Then I rang them up. The woman at the other end said he had gone off to Wales.'

'Well, score five points.'

'Thanks. She said he wouldn't be back for a few days. That was on Friday. Then on Sunday I met three charming people who said they intended to kick John Raven's head in.'

'You,' she observed, 'are John Raven.'

'Not last night I wasn't.' I told her what had happened. 'I can't wait for them to come back again.' I concluded.

She lit a cigarette. 'Why don't you go back to the police?'

'I can hardly keep away from them, but it's becoming a rather stormy relationship. Anyway I want to hang on to the pictures until I find out why they're so important.'

She sighed. 'I don't know. I have passed my days in the shop, little knowing the drama and excitement going on around me.'

I could have told her about ducking the identification parade. I could have told her the story of my life, but I decided against it.

'So what *are* you going to do?'

A woman was explaining to a man why he could climb off any appropriate cliff, any time, as far as she was concerned. I stared at them. What was I going to do? I had considerable difficulty in answering. The year was dying, I had almost no money and was embroiled in a seemingly fruitless and unprofitable venture. Yet I couldn't drop it: perhaps there was gold in there somewhere . . .

'Well,' I eventually replied, 'I'm not sure. But there are two things you could do for me.'

'What?'

'You could give me Astin's address, and you could get hold of those books you lent your ex and let me have a look at them.'

'That's easy. 'She took an address book out of her bag. 'Astin lives, lived, at 12 Romford Court, Tulse Hill. The books are easy, too. He came round on Saturday and brought them back along with a few other things he had borrowed over the months. I think he wanted an excuse to come and shout at me.'

'Did he get it?'

'No, he did not. I took the stuff and sent him on his way.'

I wrote the address down. 'When can I see the books?'

She looked at her watch. It was ten to ten. 'You can see them now if you want.'

We looked at each other warily.

She lived near Mornington Crescent in a flat in a terrace. Two rooms full of fairly successful colour supplement design tips on how to make a fun place out of two rooms in Mornington Crescent. There was a poster blow-up of Virginia Woolf looking old and gloomy, a Sony stereo, a Dolly Parton album on the floor and an untidy desk with an open typewriter. By the gasfire was a cardboard box crammed with the aftermath of a relationship, books, a couple of 45s and a saucepan.

She took off her coat and put it in the bedroom. 'Tea or coffee?' She gestured to the box. 'The books are in there.'

I wanted tea. I squatted in the corner and began to work through the box. There were a couple of Margaret Meads and some women's movement titles, which seemed unlikely material for Astin or a thesis on Mosley. Then I found five books with an elastic band around them. She returned with the tea and leaned over the box. It was the closest we'd ever been. Some people look great from a distance and you lose them in close-up. With others, the character shines through only at five inches, the clouds drift from the terrain and you catch a fleeting glimpse of their souls. She looked good either way. 'The bastard,' she said. 'I never knew he'd taken half of these. I was looking for that Margaret Mead for ages.'

'You had a really fulfilling relationship.'

'He was full of himself. He talked as if he was lecturing an audience of two hundred most of the time. I wound up conducting dialogues by heckling his speeches.'

'Political?'

'He always *said* he was. He never belonged to anything. He was always setting up discussion groups. They would read five pages of *Capital* and then go back to the pub.'

'If he was such a slob, why did you get off with him?'

She sat on the floor, rearranged her dress and crossed her legs. 'I would ask myself that question regularly, post coitus, at about three in the morning, with a matinee summary of the salient points at the shop. He would come out with a lot of crap about the women's movement and his deep sympathy with the struggle despite its essentially apolitical nature.

I, like many a poor woman before me, fell for his honeyed words.' She laughed. It was like her earlier smile.

I pulled out the books. The first was *The Greater Britain*, written by Mosley in 1932, and his 1937 *Tomorrow We Live*. There was a little bundle of pamphlets, some of them were written in Dutch I thought, and there was a yellowing duplicated magazine called *Gothic Ripples*. Lastly there was a fat, dark green volume with an embossed cover, *Fighting For Paradise*. I opened it. 'Have you looked at these?'

She shook her head. 'I saw them in the shop one day and told Greg, my, uh . . . associate. He asked if I could get them for him, I asked Astin and he said go ahead, said he wouldn't be needing them anymore. I had a look at the Mosley. The rest seemed to be in Dutch.'

'This one isn't.'

She leaned over my shoulder. On the flyleaf was a handwritten dedication in purple ink of the sort used on French menus. It said: 'To Selwyn Astin, for past struggles and future successes, Alexander.'

'He must have had some friends, even if he had to die to find them again. Who is Alexander?'

I flipped to the title page. The book was by Alexander Paradise, published in 1924 by some apparently one-off operation, Bartholomew Books. The author stared out from the photograph opposite the title page, a man in his mid thirties with lank light-coloured hair. There was another dedication too, but this was set in gothic type: 'My Father, Sir Gaynor Paradise, Member of Parliament for the New Forest North Constituency, 1898-1918, born 1850, died 1920.' I thumbed on. It had the ring of a G.A. Henty boys' story, but wasn't. 'The Seeds are Sown,' was one chapter; 'The Reckoning', 'The Struggle', 'Friends in the East'.

'OK,' she said, 'so he wrote a book. Who else was he?'

I let the book slide to the floor. 'Don't ask me, some old right winger, with another right winger for a father. Wait until I've read it, Watson.'

'You don't make much of a Holmes, kiddo.' She stood up. 'Do you want a smoke?'

'Why not?'

She went to the desk and pulled out a black snuff box. I returned to Alexander and his dad. The early part was a eulogy of Sir Gaynor's efforts in the Empire, followed by his successes in the New Forest and Parliament, which seemed to have had little impact on the subsequent evolution of our island home. Later it dwelt at length on Sir Gaynor's campaign to stem immigration, treading a path that many were to follow.

'I can never get the thing to stick together, that was one thing that Greg could do.' She paused, and re-licked the side of the joint. 'About the only thing. It's Colombian, a friend from the States gave it to me. After you've smoked it, you know why the Colombians haven't been doing too much lately. Go easy with it.'

She lit it and handed it to me.

'You don't sound very sure.'

'Oh, it's all right, doesn't do all that much damage. Anything in the book?'

'Not much. Sir Gaynor was an MP and he didn't like immigrants, a familiar tale from a long time ago.'

'Anything about Astin?'

'Not that I can see, it would have been before his time.' I found the 'Friends in the East' chapter. 'Ever heard of the British Brothers League?'

'This is your damn country, I don't know. I'm a Daughters of the American Revolution freak.'

I read from the book. 'When the hard pressed and diligent MP for Stepney, Sir William Gordon-Evans set up the British Brothers League, he found a ready ally in my father. He spoke at many packed meetings in support of their cause. Indeed my own political development as child, youth and young man springs from those gatherings twenty and more years ago. My father was distressed by the decline of the League in the years before the Great War and fought long and hard to preserve it. It is a cause which I still regard as crucial to the preservation of our race and empire. In my own humble way I intend to continue with the work that he began.'

I passed the joint to her. It may have taken Broadway by storm but it was leaving me unmoved.

'Well he didn't do a very good job, did he?' She sat on a chair. 'You've never heard of it.'

'But Astin must have done. You said you didn't know Astin's politics?'

She wrinkled her nose. 'Well, we didn't discuss them. He let out odd hints from time to time, mainly connected with his time in the colonies.'

'Which colonies?'

'I think he was in Australia for a while. Look, I really don't know; ask his wife.'

I put the book back in the box. 'Yes, I will. Do you mind if I borrow these?'

'Suit yourself. They aren't mine anyway. The way your flat seems to be, someone will rip them off anyway.'

'I'll probably take them round to Ferret.'

'Who is Ferret? Or what is Ferret?'

I told her.

'Hmm,' she said. 'He's political, you're not.'

'I wouldn't say I wasn't political. I suppose Ferret thinks of me as a woolly liberal. When I was at university, there were always the people who were in things like the Socialist Society arguing about the Vietnam War or fighting against rises in the price of the canteen chips. I suppose they were political and some of them still survive, but if that was political I didn't want anything to do with it. Well, Ferret is a genuine working-class militant, and the other kind sit round in his reflected glow, it seems to me. They developed phony proletarian accents kept quiet about their degrees and went on the building sites. They talk about a new society, but most of them are well buried in the worst aspects of the old one. And I don't fancy standing round selling papers at half past seven in the morning to people I don't know who don't want to see me. If they want to have a bloody revolution, then let them get on with it. I'm all in favour, I'll be right behind them.'

'Will you? I don't know why this Ferret doesn't just tell you to piss off.'

'I sometimes wonder myself. We get on. He's an interesting guy. I suppose we take holidays in each others' heads.'

'Well, what does he find on his vacation?' She was curious in a cold way, as if finding the essential emptiness within the pit of my soul. I suggested it to her.

She didn't laugh. 'Some people in this world go off and make money, hustle, build a home, buy an auto, assemble the world's greatest stereo system. Some people get smashed to pieces.' She took a long drag. 'Some people get like your friend Ferret. But what do you do?'

I shifted uneasily, she passed me the joint. 'I dunno. What do you do?'

'As it happens I go off and talk to five women every week and sometimes wonder what the hell we are doing. We have gone through lengthy personal biographies, contemplate how we can get involved in local politics . . .'

'Study your souls.'

The comment was unwise. 'No, we don't! We also talk about what men do to us and what we are supposed to do about it. The fault, dear Raven, is not in our souls but in our lives.'

'Sorry about that.'

'So you should be. We also say that we really should understand why the Western economy has gone down the trash-can, why Margaret Thatcher keeps winning your elections, and that we should get a reading programme organised. Two of the group thought of joining the Communist Party and one is having thoughts about joining up with the Bhagwan Shree Rajneesh, one is doing EST, and those are two reasons why I got out of the States. But I asked you first.'

'I have a male version of that, I think. Except that I do it in a pub, on my own.'

'Oh, how sad.' She laughed. 'Haven't you got some nice young woman to tell your troubles to?'

'I did have. Maybe she felt a bit like you and uh . . .'

'Greg.'

'Yeah, Greg. Except that I didn't lecture her, I don't think. I didn't do anything really. She went off to Italy. Isn't this getting a little heavy?'

'Heavy?' She sounded incredulous. 'This isn't heavy. I

was just asking you what you do. I was wondering why you've got involved in this crazy thing with Astin. In the absence of any hard information, I decided that since you were drifting fairly cluelessly through the world, you found a little drama like this an ideal way of having an apolitical political cause. Nader for beginners.'

I winced, and inhaled some more of the Colombian. I had been wrong about it. My brain was beginning to function like a projector with a lens out of focus, the sound out of synch, and the projectionist off having a cup of tea. I listened to my voice. It was some way off. 'I suppose that isn't inaccurate. In theory it was just because of the book I'm supposed to be doing. I haven't *done* anything, things have just happened to me. All I've tried to do is find a way out of the thicket and all I've got is more trouble.'

I unsteadily negotiated the vast open space between us and handed her back the burning remains. Most of my grey matter had been sucked into it, I thought. The only sound was the hiss of the gas-fire which she had turned up.

'Back in the 1960s people kidded themselves they knew what they were doing,' she said.

'They weren't kidding themselves. Some of them did.'

'I think a lot of them were kidding themselves, at least in the States. Maybe I'm wrong. I was still in high school. I watched a lot of guys burning their draft cards and talking about the revolution. I knew they were ass-holes, most of them.'

'Well,' I observed incautiously, 'there aren't really any American reds.'

'Yes, there fucking are!' she shouted. 'My old man was a party member through the 1930s. The only way he managed to hold a job down after the War was because he was a doctor. Christ, he couldn't leave America for years. It was crazy, the only guy he hated more than Stalin was McCarthy.'

'Sorry about that, good to know a WASP family like the Marchants . . .'

'You can cut the WASP crap, too. My family were the Mankiewitzes until my grandpa decided to make a bid for the golf club. He blew that, too. Anyway, what the hell,' she dragged on the joint. 'Those guys, a lot of them, were rich kids playing games; some of them were serious, now they're demoralised, a lot of them. Though the nuke thing is getting them on their feet. I suppose you people were the same, I heard about marches you had on the embassy and that kind of thing. Now we've got a lousy government, you've got a lousy government, and a lot of demoralised socialists.'

'They aren't all demoralised. Ferret isn't demoralised. He was delighted when Mrs T marched in with St Francis. Shake the buggers up, he said, cut the flab away. He sounded like a Glaswegian Tebbit.'

'Well, I don't feel like that. I got out of the States because I was bored, and had some illusions about this place, culture and fields, all the usual East Coast intellectual myths. Now I find myself on a crummy little right-wing island floating in a cold grey sea, inhabited by poor people and racist cops. It's amazing, the US and Britain are both going down the pan. You try to sustain some parody of our life style, and we can't afford it ourselves anymore. You've got your North Sea oil as an old age pension, I guess. Christ knows what we've got. We bail you out, who's gonna bail us out?'

'We aren't being bailed out. The people who own this country are. Anyway I didn't think you knew about economics.'

'I don't. And I thought you didn't believe all that stuff about a ruling class.'

'I didn't say I didn't believe it. Merely that there is sod all I can do about it.'

She stared at me through the cloud of smoke. 'All this stuff about the ruling class is a big switch-off as far as everyone apart from your friend Ferret is concerned. I'm a rarity, my old man used to go on about it, if I was lucky I got blank looks from the kids on our block, otherwise it could be nasty. But Christ! The way the left goes on here, and the way you all think! It isn't just the ruling class that's in a slump over here, it's the whole goddam country, left included, in one big morass . . .' She laughed. 'Still I can't go on, the only good thing in the States are some of the feminists, the US left are the biggest bunch of crazies, and all I do is sit round wondering what to do next.'

Things were getting worse in my head. The projectionist had returned and seemed to be tearing the film up. 'What are you going to do next?'

She shrugged her shoulders. 'I don't know. I only got the Astin job with some careful footwork. I don't think I can benefit from your wonderful welfare system. I might become one of those people your papers are always warning everyone about. Anyway, what the hell. What would you be doing if you didn't have all this Rip Kirby stuff to worry about?'

'The same, really. I would be trying to get on with my book, keeping my nose clean, doing a bit of work here and there. People like me didn't really used to exist in this country, thanks to the class system. I mean you had all your stories about from the log cabin to the White House, we didn't. In the old days the rich got educated for a life of leisure and then went back to their estates and sat in their East Wings and gazebos. They had the money for it and their education programmed them for it too. The kind of education people here like me got in the fifties and sixties wasn't all that different to that, only we haven't got the money, or the gazebo, or the East Wing.'

She abandoned the chair for the carpet, and smiled again. I wasn't sure if it was dope, or affection, or interest. 'I'm sorry, I shouldn't interrogate you.'

The projection room was now stripped down to the floorboard joists. I could feel myself on the verge of falling. I vaguely remembered what I had said, what she had said. She did have a very good figure. I wondered if she would fall through the floor. I wondered if she already had. Where had the projectionist gone?

What was the bloody film?

'I taught a bit,' I said. 'I went to France and taught English, taught at a school in Hackney. Did some freelance writing . . . worked two years in an ad agency . . . hated that . . . I was a trainee copywriter. I trained so long I lost interest. I was a bit of the 1960s stage army. I went on the marches. Never quite knew why. They all shouted "Victory to the NLF" . . . I didn't know what that meant. I thought the Americans should just stop bombing. Peace, an easy life for everybody. That is my slogan . . .'

She buried her head in her knees. 'Well, you're out of luck. You've chosen the wrong century.'

'Centuries? They're all wrong centuries. Anyway, I didn't choose, I was drafted.' My voice trailed away. I could feel myself slipping through the joists. I looked for flickering castles in the gas-fire. None appeared. The evening had not gone the way I wanted. I was interested in Astin, but she had done quite a good job of undermining my motives about that. I was interested in politics, I thought, but perhaps I wasn't. I was interested in Moira, or maybe it was just the grass that was interested. It was twenty past eleven and it would be a cold walk home.

'So late, isn't it?' I observed chattily. Then I closed my eyes. Yes, I was through all right, sliding and rolling down. How unlike the stuff that Ferret got from a friend who grew it near Heathrow airport, I thought.

'It certainly is.'

I thought about whether I should attempt to stand up. I rocked to and fro. 'Perhaps I should go.'

'Perhaps you should.'

I didn't want to go. 'I wouldn't mind staying.'

'Why?'

Yeah, why? It would lead to unnecessary complications, sour a professional relationship. I was extraordinarily stoned, and she was very attractive, and the marijuana made her more so every second, and every second endured for a long time. I could almost see the blue in her dress coming alive. I was very attractive, this was clear, and she was very attractive and aware how attractive I was and . . . Clearly she was waiting for me to fling my arms around her yielding person. I was falling in love, I was falling down the stairs, out of the projection room, what was the bloody film? I was a man, not a mouse. In love? Me with her? The only sound was the fire. She was looking at me. I thought she was amused, or maybe as far away as I was.

'I find you very attractive.' I sounded like a dignitary launching a ship. God bless you and all . . .

'You find me very stoned,' she replied and flopped out on the floor. One of her knees, a blue shrouded mountain, towered up into the red glow of the room. I reached out a hand and grasped her ankle. I was surprised it was there and surprised that she didn't move it.

'Well, this won't bloody do,' I said.

She retrieved her ankle and lurched inelegantly to her feet, smoothing her dress down as she did so. 'Well, I've just gone back on the pill for someone else, actually.' She paused, and repeated 'actually' syllable by syllable. 'You could be a trial run.'

'How fucking charming.'

'Fucking charming or charming fucking.' She smiled pleasantly. 'Suit yourself.'

We stumbled arms round each other's shoulders into the bedroom. This was as much a question of stability as of lust. My clothes were curiously heavy. She took off her dress in a single movement. Her bosom was even more impressive. 'You're thin,' she said.

'Well, I've been ill.'

Our passion was intensified by the grass. I scrutinised her face on the pillow, in the faint light. We stared through each other but hung on to each other. We made a hurried routine tour of registered erogenous zones. Impressed by her breasts, I set up camp there. It was a long and frenzied journey, visiting a strange and exotic land, but I never met her there, she was somewhere else, in another land that I had deserted.

We joked about it afterwards. Where were you? we asked each other, holidaymakers back in the office swopping experiences.

Later still she spoke. 'You're cynical, you know. You make me cynical too.'

Me? I brooded. Me?

8.

Spizzichino settled into a prolonged coughing fit. Simultaneously he attempted to squirt condensed milk from a tube into his coffee. 'Unless you want to be an office boy, you are out of luck, Raven. Nothing is happening this week, except we argue this week with the *Economist* about this picture they want and for which they do not wish to pay what they are going to pay.' Some of the milk dropped in a globule into the saucer.

'I'm too old to be an office boy.'

'Yes. And we are too poor to be a branch of the dole office.' I had visited Spizzichino the morning after Ms Marchant. I was broke enough to be worried.

'Why don't you write some articles?'

'Because nobody wants any articles.'

He belched. He was large and fat. He wore a brown waistcoat, hornrimmed glasses of the kind that Ernie Bevin would have felt at home in, and a pair of cavalry twills of the type popular with middle-class youth in the early 1960s. His three hairs were flattened across his head, but one made sporadic advances on his forehead. He had left Italy in 1938 and spent the remainder of his life selling photos to picture editors and abusing them down telephones. 'Well, I don't really even want an office boy this week,' he said. He contemplated his coffee; the milk was refusing to mix properly.

'Ever heard of someone called Astin?'

He shoved a pile of pictures of tennis players into a tray. 'There are doubtless many Astins in the world but I have never heard of any of them.'

'How about someone called Paradise?'

'Are you trying to make money or waste my time?' He looked up and his spectacles slid down his long flat nose. 'Or are you doing both? I do not run an information service. There is a *Who's Who* over there.' He pointed his arm at a stack of newspapers with a cat dozing on them.

I walked over and prodded the animal. The book was concealed behind it. The creature waved its paw lethargically, but with a degree of ill-will. The *Who's Who* contained no Paradises. I asked Spizzichino if he had any old copies. He didn't. He told me to go to the British Museum and stop wrecking his business. I did.

There was an entry for Sir Gaynor, but not one for his son, apart from a mention that he had one. By then it was lunchtime. I drank a bitter lemon in the Museum Tavern and decided in the absence of job prospects to continue the investigation, if that was what it was. I looked up Astin's number in the phone book.

It was thirty seconds before the phone was answered. Mrs Astin's voice was querulous. I began to feel a slob, or a grave robber, or both. 'I'm an acquaintance of your husband. I wonder if I could come and see you.'

'Is that Fuller?' She sounded angry.

I played bemused. 'Fuller? No I'm not Fuller. I don't know any Fullers. I want to talk to you about some of your husband's property I've been left with.'

'Why?'

It was a fair enough question, to which I could think of no very satisfactory answer. I decided on a modified form of honesty. 'I had a bit of a dispute with your husband, I'm sorry about it, I wondered if I could clear it up . . . or try to.'

'You do what you like.'

'Yes, well I wondered – ' I was speaking into electronic thin air; she had hung up. I walked down the pub staircase steps. A couple had taken over my seat. The bitter lemon was nestling next to the ashtray for company. The man was dressed in the style of an England footballer off to get pulverised by Luxembourg. The girl was small and dark and convulsed with amusement. He didn't sound that amusing to me. I finished the bitter lemon.

I dislike leaving pubs at lunchtime. It was misty in Bloomsbury. It would be nightfall before I made Tulse Hill. A few people were drifting back to the British Museum, adult versions of snail-like schoolboys dragging themselves back to the Reading Room and anything from Chinese painting to the Hungarian Rising of 1919. I don't know why they haven't opened a drinking club at the BM, it might bring people together.

I walked to Leicester Square, got a tube to Waterloo and a train to Tulse Hill. The electric service threaded through those wide flat expanses of goods yards and highrise blocks. I always think that south London highrises look like leftovers from *The War of the Worlds*: mighty machines gradually edging towards the Thames, away from the boredom south of the river and towards north London where the action should be, were there any action. In between the highrises were the little corner shops and terraces, survivals of 1930s England, full of people eating Sunday dinner and reading the *News of the World*, unchanged since Dad dumped his kitbag and put on his demob suit back in 1945.

Tulse Hill is like that. But you have a faint feeling that the place would like to pack up, shift down the road nearer to Brighton, get itself a bit of class. The Crystal Room of the Railway Tavern offered entertainment on Thursday, Friday and Saturday evenings plus lunchtime on Sundays. The rest of Tulse Hill offered a Wimpy Bar and a traffic jam down the main street.

'Romford Court? Left on the main street, fifty yards down.' The West Indian ticket collector shivered. It had started raining and was in training to turn to sleet. I walked down the road.

Romford Court was a pre-war block. Once it would have had ambitions to be a cut above council house design, but it had been overtaken. The windows had metal rims around the panes to let in the draughts and collect moisture for the rust. The grass outside was primarily mud. The entrance hall reeked of rancid cooking oil, the beige walls were dirty. Number twelve was on the third floor. Twilight was dying, it was almost dark. Somebody on the ground floor was playing an old Spike Jones record.

'The story is told
Of the fool and his gold,
Behind the swinging door-or-or
Behind the swinging door.'

I climbed the stairs. Number twelve had a green door with scuff marks where somebody or everybody had used their feet to gain admittance. There were no lights showing. I rang the bell. It didn't want to be rung, made a coughing noise and lapsed into silence. I flapped the letterbox. Nobody answered. On the third attempt, a light came on somewhere in the recesses of the flat. Someone shuffled towards the door. A chain was connected, the door was pulled ajar. She didn't put the light on, so all I could see was a white blob, with a dark scar where her mouth was.

'Mrs Astin?'

'Yes?' It sounded like a question but I took it for an answer.

'I rang earlier. About some stuff of your husband's. You said to come and see you.' My voice faded after this half truth, and I waited for a response.

It came more briskly than I expected and was loaded with animosity. 'No, I didn't. I didn't invite you, I didn't ask you to come to my *home*.' It sounded as though she had just christened Twelve Romford Court after years of uncertainty.

'I'm sorry, I thought you did. It won't take a minute. I wonder if I could explain.' I wondered a lot if I could explain. I wondered if she would give me a chance.

'You're from Fuller, aren't you?' She was emphatic.

'No, I am not from . . . from Fuller. I don't have anything to do with Fuller. I have never met anyone called Fuller, although I have heard the name. That's one of the reasons I've come to see you.'

Her hand reached up to the light switch. A faint sour smell of alcohol drifted past me. She looked at me, up and down, slowly, unsteadily.

Her age was difficult to tell, sixty to seventy, I guessed. Her hair had been blonde, but was grey now, with streaks that might have been a tint, but looked as if she had used nicotine. She had bright grey eyes which accentuated the sense of lost youth. She looked distracted – she had plenty to be distracted about – but it was deeper than that, as if she had been distracted for the last forty years, about as long as she had known Astin, I thought. She wore an ageing blue twinset, a shapeless brown skirt, flat shoes and socks. There was a wet blob on her cardigan and a cigarette stub smouldered in her right hand. She was wearing a lot of powder and unnaturally red lipstick. Looking at her didn't cheer me too much.

'I don't know you.' She said it slowly, like a child introduced to one of her parents' more dubious friends.

Let's take it from the top, I thought. Whether she registered anything I had said was questionable. *So go through it one more time. My name is John Raven, I come to smoke pipe of peace . . .*

'My name is John Raven. I have some pictures that I bought from your husband's shop. We had a bit of a disagreement about them afterwards, I'm sorry to say.'

Why am I sorry? I thought. *Never apologise, never explain . . .*

She looked over my shoulder. 'It is cold here.' She said it like a weather forecast. 'You must come in.' She turned her back to me and shuffled down the hall.

It was a small hall. She looked over her shoulder and beckoned me as if auditioning for an all-female *Hunchback of Notre Dame*. I rather expected her to shout 'The Bells!' She didn't. I followed her into the living room.

There were books around the shelves. Some had fallen off, and no one had picked them up. The news was showing silently on an ancient black and white televison. On a formica table was a half empty bottle of sherry and a glass, elegant, with a long fluted stem. An old standard lamp did the best it could to disguise the decay of the room. The wall-to-wall carpeting was in retreat.

She poured herself a drink, sat on a metal chair and looked at me. 'I'm sorry.' She emitted a girlish laugh. 'Silly me! Drink?'

She had forgotten I was a suspect visitor. It was as if I had called to collect her for the Junior Primrose League Ball.

'No, that's all right.'

'Don't be silly! Have a drink.'

I wasn't silly. I had a drink. She fetched a glass from a tray on a bookshelf. The drink was in theory a rich golden

Oloroso; but, like the House of Astin, it had fallen on hard times.

'It's very good of you to see me,' I observed.

'Yes,' she said. 'What do you want?' She didn't know who I was, what I wanted, and quite possibly wasn't too sure who she was either.

'Well, there has been some trouble over the pictures. I bought them due to a misunderstanding, and Mr Astin wanted them back.'

'He is dead.'

'I know, I'm very sorry. The pictures seem to be of a family, taken abroad – in the colonies – and some Edwardian shots, and some old newspapers, *Tribune* and *Action.* The pictures abroad seemed to be of big game hunts, and some general travel shots.'

She looked sly. 'That was a long time ago. From Selwyn's family album.' She made 'family' sound like something from *The Godfather.* 'So he gave them to you, did he?'

'Not exactly. I bought them when he wasn't there. Apparently he didn't want to sell them. That's what he told me.'

She shrugged. 'I can't think why, should have been glad to get rid of them. Should have got rid of them years ago.' Her voice rose a few pitches. 'He should never have got involved.'

'Involved in what, Mrs Astin?'

'That lot. I told him. You're nothing to do with them, Selly, I told him. They'll use you and kick you out. They don't give a damn. I told him!' She wound up sounding like I had introduced the unhappy Astin to the big game hunter and it was my fault.

I decided to pursue my own line rather than escort her down Memory Lane. 'Fuller does come into it, Mrs Astin; the girl who works at the shop said that your husband – well, implied – that your husband may have been anxious to get the pictures back after he had spoken to this Fuller person, whom I've never met, and that is why . . .'

'Fuller is a swine.' It was another weather forecast statement, but she said it with rather more confidence than the average weatherman.

'Who is Fuller? Did he ask your husband to Wales?'

'Oh yes, he asked him to Wales.' She poured herself another drink, drank half of it and fortunately didn't offer me any more. She must have been sitting there pickling herself ever since Astin had passed on, or before.

'Whenever they said get out, he got out, snivelled off and whined to me about them, that he'd never go back. Then they would whistle and off he would run.' She snorted and started giggling. 'You can't teach an old dog new tricks, especially a cur, and that's what Selly was. Wasn't he? A whipped cur. They ruined his life. They haven't got me. They rang and said how sorry they were – Fuller rang – said how sorry he was. I told him, you don't give a damn, I know *you.* I told him, you probably did it, so don't come sympathetic to me, I know you lot. I told him I'm not like Selly. I'm not your property, even if Selly was.' She started whimpering.

The style was pre-war Somerset Maugham. But she meant it. She was ideally suited for that little house in a clearing in Burma drinking and reading old copies of *Illustrated London News* while Selly consorted with undesirable native girls.

I tried once more. 'Who is Fuller?'

She slipped out of her chair and stumbled across the room. There was a portrait on the wall. A photograph. She ripped it off, put it close to her face and stared at it. Then she raised it above her head and threw it against the opposite wall.

It fell on the record player. I went over and picked it up. The subject didn't resemble my idea of Fuller. It was an old picture. The man was wearing a wing collar in the Neville Chamberlain style. He had a broad fleshy face and fair hair. From his expression it seemed that the photographer had just expressed doubt about his parentage.

'Is this Fuller?' I asked.

She had lost interest. She was renewing her friendship with the Oloroso. She sat the bottle in her lap after pouring out another glass and falling back in the chair. She stared at the spot on the wall where the portrait had been and started humming to herself.

'He never gave a damn, not a damn,' she observed and

scratched her chin with the edge of the bottle. This at least solved the mystery of why she had wet blobs on her cardigan. 'All those years and Selwyn would say "Yes sir, yes, anything you want, it's all for the cause, sir, wonderful to be able to contribute sir, can I clean your boots sir?" Stupid fool!' She shouted the last word and fixed her eyes on mine as if I were reckless enough to offer her my own footwear.

I went back to the picture. Old fleshy face glared at me. Maybe he was angry. I couldn't see how clean his shoes were. 'I'm sorry, Mrs Astin, but I don't understand.' I decided to try the sweet voice of reason once more. 'Is this gentleman here Fuller?'

'Gentleman? Oh yes, he was a gentleman alright. Selwyn always respected *gentlemen*. There's nothing like a tatty public school and two years in the Army to make you respect gentlemen, is there?'

The question was directed at the floor. She took the cork out of the bottle and slopped out another fix. The alcohol overflowed on her skirt. Increasingly painful reminders of the Colombian grass flowed through me. If she took much more, then I could just as well do a highland fling for all the attention I would get from her.

I tried affirmation and it produced a response. 'So this is Fuller?'

'Fuller? No, of course it isn't Fuller.' She gestured at the picture. 'That gentleman has been rotting in hell since 1948. He's probably pleased to have Selly with him to clean his . . .' Her voice trailed away.

'Well, if it isn't Fuller, who is it? Why have you shown it to me?' I was uncertain that her method of display counted as 'showing', but it seemed more diplomatic.

'It's Mr Michael Fuller's wonderful father, isn't it?'

It was all getting too enigmatic for me. I looked at my watch. It was twenty past six. 'Great, Michael Fuller's father, Mr Somebody Fuller.' I stirred in my seat.

'No, no, no.' She replaced the bottle on the table. 'Little Michael didn't want to carry his father's name around with him, did he?'

I don't know, you tell me, I thought. I stared at her.

'It's Mr Alexander frightfully nice Paradise, isn't it?'

Well, they were a long-lasting family. Her expression indicated that I was rated a little above the dumb animal classification. Maybe I was. I thought back to the book of the night before. It was still shrouded in dope smoke.

'So your husband worked for Alexander Paradise and knew his son Michael Fuller.'

'Worked? Unpaid slave.' She leaned back. 'Then slaves always are unpaid, aren't they? And when Fuller called, Selly went running, just like for his father.'

Astin must have known Paradise since the early 1920s if the book was anything to go by. 'So your husband was involved with Alexander Paradise from the 1920s until 1948.'

She failed to notice that I'd inserted my own bit of information; she was well away. 'When Paradise left England because of his little difficulty in 1928, Selly went with him and so did I. We went to Australia together, went to Africa together, we were inseparable.' She laughed, but was not amused.

'Paradise was always going to do something. What it was I never really found out, plans, all those plans! Make more money, make the important deal, take over the world . . .' She eyed the bottle again.

I resolved to hold her on course. 'Why did you go to Africa?'

'Johannesburg was the place to make money, wasn't it? That was what Paradise said and he was always right, wasn't he? That was when he was there and not off on all those funny little trips. It was when they went off to Europe together that I complained. Why don't you marry him? I said. You spend all your time with him. It was all right for Mary . . .'

'Mary?'

'Mary Paradise. She had the nice little house in Jo'burg – Houghton it was – with blacks running round for her and little Michael and little Maud and all we had was that rathole. Then they went off to Germany so they could sit round with cheap little Huns and talk about how they had just missed Adolf. And what did Selly get out of it?' The stream of recrimination against ghosts had left her drained, the bottle was drained too.

'They went back to South Africa?'

'Oh, they came back. It's a wonder they didn't wind up in jail. Then there was all that fuss in 1948. Thank God Paradise died.'

'What did he die of?'

'He died of a car crash. Otherwise there would have been more trouble, what with that German.'

'What German?'

'Some man Paradise was trying to smuggle into the country. Not a high-up, just a Nazi friend of his. I told Selly, thank God he's gone, maybe now we can live our own lives. So we came back and settled down. Then that bitch Mary wrote to us "for old times' sake", she said. It was just so that we could be cheap servants for little Michael Fuller when he came over for school. And then he had the audacity to batten on us! Now! And Selly's dead, for that rotten family!'

'Fuller wanted your husband to do something. That's why he went to Wales?'

'Of course that is why he went to Wales. Selly tried to be firm. Told me he wasn't putting up with it. That Fuller was crazy just like his old man,' she cackled. 'Selly was always good at saying how he wasn't going to put up with it. He always did in the end. He told me he was going to Wales and that it was very important but that he was only going to get it cleared up once and for all.'

'What did Fuller want Sel . . . your husband to do?'

'Something to do with money, I think. I don't know.' She looked at me keenly. She was wondering who the hell I was, and why she was talking to me. 'Why do you want to know all this?'

'I was just interested. Because your husband wanted those pictures back and I think Fuller may have wanted them back, too. You wouldn't know why that might be?'

'I don't know anything. Why do you come here? Why don't you get out? I don't know you. Take your filthy pictures!'

I got up. 'Well, thank you, Mrs Astin. I'm very sorry, I'm sorry to have bothered you at a time . . .'

'Get out of my house!' She stood up and the bottle clattered from the table. I made for the door fast. 'You can go back to Fuller,' she screamed. 'He doesn't frighten me!'

I got out of the front door rather faster than I had entered. I heard the sound of crashing glass as I walked down the stairs, and the sound of her screaming. She hadn't finished with her ghosts. Spike Jones wasn't playing anymore. Who needs Spike Jones when you have got Mrs Astin two floors up?

The Crystal Room had a magical charm after the saga of Astin and Paradise. Then I caught the train back to London Bridge. It was cold. I was cold, and confused. I went home. There were no late night visitors, just Pedro practising his riffs. I made a cup of tea, drank it and collapsed. It was only ten o' clock.

9.

Mrs Astin had cast a chill which remained with me the following morning, I woke up to a grey flat and a dead life. I stumbled downstairs to get the paper.

Gold had made the front page, a little box towards the bottom. 'Martin Gold, the 25 year old engineering worker charged in connection with the alleged bombing of Conservative MP Raphael Hales's north London house, appeared at Hampstead Magistrates Court yesterday. Bail was refused and he was remanded in custody.'

I made some toast and settled down with a cup of tea. The phone rang.

It was Ferret. 'You've seen the paper?'

'Yeah. Great isn't it? Have you found out anything about him?'

'Not very much, a friend of friends; I think I met him a while back. He was one of the people pounding in and out of Hales's life during the last few months.'

'Is he a bomber?'

'I don't know if he's a bloody bomber.' Ferret was irritated. 'I don't care if he's a bomber. If I thought he was, I wouldn't go on about it on the phone. Frankly I don't think his shower could organise a piss-up at a trade union conference but that doesn't matter. The poor bugger has been picked up and the press will have a field day with him, and Hales will have a field day with him, and it's partly to do with stupid buggers like you.'

'No, it isn't,' I shouted. 'It's half past nine in the morning, and you've nothing better to do than ring me up and lecture me.'

'OK, OK, take it easy. I rang to give you a bit of information. You asked me if I had ever heard of Fuller before, right? Well, it so happens I was talking to a mate – well, a man I know – called Courtney. He's a strange guy, spends half his time wandering around with fascists telling them what a good Nazi he is and the other half wandering around with reds telling them what the other lot are doing. He says he's infiltrating. Personally I wouldn't give him the shit off my boots, I don't think he knows whose side he is on any more, if he ever did. He's a weird guy, I used to know him when he . . .'

'Anyway.'

'Yeah, anyway, he was telling me about this meeting they are having this week.'

'Who?'

'The British Alliance, the popular front for Nazis and right wingers with marital problems. Now apart from this fascist punter Lee, they've got some thrusting businessman to represent those forces of capital being held back by the alien financial conspiracy and the dirty reds within the unions.'

'And?'

'His name is Fuller, I think. Courtney mentioned this bloke, couldn't get his name right, said Fulton or something, but when I suggested Fuller he said that was right. That was the one he said, Fuller.'

'That is interesting. He must be back from his holiday in Wales, if it's the same Fuller. You won't need to worry about Astin anymore.'

'Why?'

I told him about the passing on of the bookseller, and about my meeting with Mrs Astin, and a modified version of my night out with Moira Marchant.

'Raven, you should watch out. You may get politically committed and wake one day singing the *Internationale*.'

'I'm more worried I might wake up one morning flying off a cliff. When is the meeting?'

'Tomorrow. Some hall in Victoria, it hasn't been well publicised. Not by them anyway.' He chuckled. 'I think they want it to be a number for parents and friends. We're going along to give them a cheer when they go in.'

I wasn't happy about that. 'You, the Wircs and me. Wonderful. I'd just like to see what Fuller looks like.'

'Well, if the reds don't stomp on you on the way in, then the Nazis will probably pass you over their heads through the window. You shouldn't get too curious. We're trying to keep people out, not let daft liberals in.'

'Thanks, Ferret. After meeting Mrs Sunshine yesterday, I felt like packing it in.'

He laughed. 'Oh, come on now, John, it's the vicarious alarm of the petit-bourgeoisie. Anyway, there is another thing I wanted to tell you about. A defence group is being set up for Gold. I know some of the people in it, you might be useful to them.'

'Oh Christ,' I moaned. 'I'm popular enough already. I don't want to address meetings of your friends about the iniquities of the law.'

He swore down the phone. 'You hypocrite, you play detective for a bit of package holiday glamour but when you are asked to do something,' he thrashed around for some appropriate piece of moral blackmail, 'something *positive* to see some people who might be able to prevent this Gold bloke going down for twenty years, you skive off. The least you can do is come and see them.'

I thought about it. 'All right,' I sighed. 'I don't promise anything.'

'No one is asking you to promise anything. They live in

this place in Wapping. I said I would be down about eight.'

'All arranged, was it?'

'I told them I might have some trouble, but that deep down you were, at least, a decent, confused liberal.'

'That's big of you, Ferret.'

'Yeah, I thought you'd like that. Liberals always like being called decent. It's about all they can manage. You know Commercial Road? There's a pub down there called the Star of the East.'

I didn't. We arranged to meet at seven, exchanged random insults, and I went back to my toast.

I had some freelance work that day in South Kensington. It was a sunny day, pleasant as I walked down to Arsenal tube. I had no change so I queued for a ticket. The periodic hiccup of passengers came through the barrier. A few old age pensioners, a couple of shoppers . . . and Anorak.

I thought that if he was going to turn the flat over, I should perhaps accompany him to suggest modifications to his style of interior design. I was undecided. He was on his own, had combed his hair and looked almost respectable, and preoccupied. I didn't have to do much thinking, I was through the barrier and looking back at him. He stood at the entrance, surveying the scene, looking for Raven, looking for me . . . He turned back and saw me.

He didn't recognise me straight away I walked down the passage. There are metal grilles along it to make the football supporters feel wanted. I moved as if I had all the time in the world. At the bend I looked back. I heard shouting; he was arguing with the ticket collector. He had a way of getting on with people, did Anorak. I waited just off the platform.

He ran down the platform, missing me as he did so, and paused at the other end. He kicked a coke can angrily on to the line. I decided on the upfront tactic and strolled up to him. 'Found Raven yet?'

He stared at me, cold, uncertain. 'Oh yeah, you . . . I don't think I have yet. I don't think I have.'

'No,' I said, 'nor have I. I've just been up, but he wasn't there. I wait for the money, you wait for the pictures.'

'Pictures, yeah. That's right, I'm still waiting.' He stared at me. He wasn't sure, but he was getting surer.

'What pictures are they, by the way?'

'Like I said, just pictures. He took them off a friend.' He looked me in the eyes. 'Old pictures, very valuable, history.'

'That right? Who is it you are working for?'

The train came in. Which was just as well, as Anorak's double vision about my identity was beginning to clear. We got into the tube and sat down. 'I work for this top businessman,' he said, in the language of American Express ads. 'He's very annoyed about it.'

And when big Louie is annoyed, everybody is annoyed, I thought.

He turned and looked at me, his arm resting on the carriage window ledge. 'I'll tell you one thing, though,' he said.

'What's that?'

He poked me in the chest with a half formed fist. 'I'll tell you that if you see him, you'd better tell him to take them back where he found them pretty fast or he is going to get so well trampled he won't be doing anything for a very long time. Know what I mean?'

I decided it might be wise to change trains at Kings Cross, but waited until the doors were about to close. 'I'll tell him if I can find him,' I shouted over my shoulder. 'You might mention the tenner, too.'

The doors closed. The train pulled out. He was looking back at me, his stubby fingers drumming on the ledge. It was the safest place for them. The rest of the morning and afternoon were peaceful, and lucrative.

It was unlikely that the pub in Commercial Road had ever seen many better times, but seven in the evening on a cold winter night was definitely one of the worst. An old lady chewed over the implications of the *Crossroads* episode she had just watched. Most of the drinkers were solitary and miserable. I made a choice from the limited selection of the juke box and worked at a sour pint of beer. Ferret was late. He arrived with Odgers, whose moustache seemed droopier than ever. They bought three pints and came over. We exchanged grunts.

Odgers stroked his moustache.

'You met Cal? John, Cal, Cal, John.' Ferret gestured vaguely.

'We met in the Norfolk, Ferret. Drink must be rotting your brain.' I thought I would try a little politeness. 'Hello, Cal, are you involved in this defence thing?'

'I'm not sure. Of course if the group leadership think we should get involved, well, I suppose I'll go along with that. I think we have to think about it *politically* – before we make any interventions, that is – I mean the people involved are a bunch of anarchists if you want to know what I think. I don't think we should just get dragged along in some adventurist fashion . . .'

'Yeah, well, it is just a preliminary meeting.' Even Ferret, I thought with satisfaction, did have the power to be exasperated with the rambling debates that Odgers staged in the tatty Comintern building within his head. The Scotsman pulled out his Number 6 and handed them around. They tasted foul, particularly with the beer.

'Most peculiar, Mama,' sang Lennon out of the juke. The old lady tapped her foot.

Ferret blew smoke across the table. 'It's round the corner, where they are. In a squat, so if we drink up . . .'

I groaned. 'The only thing worse than sitting in this dump will be sitting in some chilly squat. Why can't they come here? Anyway, I thought you were keen on security. I bet the police are keeping a watch on the place if they are friends of Gold.'

'He's got a point there.' Odgers had agreed with me; maybe I was wrong after all.

'Gold didn't live round here. He had a place in Wandsworth. Anyway, there's no point in spending all our time fretting about whether the cops are watching us, that way lies madness.'

'I don't know about that,' pontificated Odgers. 'I don't think you can be too careful. The trouble with the British left is that we've got no sense of security. They are watching us all the time; look at Agee, look at ABC, GCHQ . . .'

'Oh, for Christ's sake, man,' exploded Ferret.

I regretted my rash words. God help any cop who had to follow Odgers's peregrinations.

Ferret looked at his watch. 'It's ten to eight. We'd better drink up and go over.'

It was raining, fine light rain that crept around you like mist and soaked you in ten minutes. Insinuating rain, whining and miserable. We walked to the junction, and Ferret led us into the backstreets behind the Limehouse parish church. 'Hawksmoor, that church y'know,' said Ferret, gesturing at the gloomy pile.

'That so?'

'Aye, it is.'

The streets had never been cheery, I suspect. Once they might have had character, though, the romance of the Victorian slum, or at least romantic in retrospect. Now most of them were knocked down, the buildings that housed all the poverty and misery and murder and beatings. Tower Hamlets council had provided their own follow-up to the Blitz and left a land of tin cans and garbage for a few cats to roam.

Our destination was one of a group of six terraced houses left standing in a narrow street. Light poured through a hole where a letter box had been. Ferret banged his fist on the door.

A woman answered, about thirty, with streaky blonde hair, a wide face, and a big forehead. She wore a poncho, grey shirt and green jeans. 'Hello, Ferret.' She gazed at Odgers and me as if we had come down with the rain. She hadn't picked up her accent down Wapping way, but she was working hard at it.

'Hi, Alice.' Ferret introduced us, and we entered the hall. A smell of fried onions hung heavy in the air.

We followed her into the kitchen. A sharp-faced man about the same age as Alice was toying with a plate of chilli con carne. Or I thought it was chilli con carne. I hoped it was.

Little pink lines on his face indicated that he had spent some time in the nearby pub or one of its rivals. He smiled; he had a good smile, open. Any smile was welcome after Alice's layer of frost.

'This is Mike Cutter,' she explained. 'He is a good friend of Martin Gold. He's setting up the defence group.' She introduced us all in the style of a clerk of the court swearing in a jury.

Cutter spoke between mouthfuls, waving his hand to lend emphasis to his muffled utterances. 'Alice has done most of it . . . she spoke to the bourgeois press . . . she's the one who's been around . . .' His voice vanished with a mouthful of beans.

'Well,' said Ferret, crouching on a stool by the gas cooker, 'this here reprobate John is the one who saw what happened.' Ferret wasn't very happy. Long words and laboured phrases usually indicated a desire to be off and back to the pub as rapidly as possible. With no offence of course.

'What did you see?' Alice asked.

I told her about the police and the identity parade, but not the rest.

'Well, you did Martin a lot of fucking good,' she observed when I had finished.

'Yeah, yeah.' I had anticipated that she would try the sanctimonious bit. 'I've had all this out with Ferret. I don't need to go through it again. I'm a dumbo, right? I'm a friend of Ferret's and I didn't want to get involved, but even less do I want to see your friend go down for something he probably didn't do.'

'There's nothing probable about it,' exclaimed Mike Cutter. 'It's a fit-up.' He glared at me.

'How do you know?' I said.

'I've known Martin for years. We were at college together, in the International Marxist Group together, out of it together. Our politics have been running on more or less the same lines for years.' He toyed with his fork, balancing it on his little finger and periodically glancing at me. 'Yes, very boring politics, and you aren't into that sort of thing, you want to sort out your head, etc., etc.'

I was rather hurt. Cutter had seemed an open sort of bloke. Why pick on me?

'Anyway,' he continued. 'I know what I would do politically and one thing I don't do is get mixed up with bombs and nor would Martin. I *know* he was fitted up.'

'How?' I asked.

'Look,' said Alice, 'I don't want to get heavy and all that, Ferret, but are you absolutely sure that these two are all right?' She waved in the general direction of Odgers and me. 'We need a plant now like nobody's business.'

I was gratified that Odgers had been lumped in with me as a potential undesirable. He started to reply but Ferret interrupted. 'Yes, they're OK. If I bring people down here I don't bring fuckin' SBs with me.'

'Just making sure,' said Alice.

Mike finally laid the fork to rest. 'Want a lager?' He actually included me in his invitation. 'Tennents it is, Ferret, remind you of your homeland.'

'Oh aye.' Ferret had pulled out his Number 6, and the atmosphere was moving a shade away from freezing point. Cutter brought out the lagers. I pulled mine open. There was a picture of Ethne smiling at me from the can, whoever Ethne might be.

Mike Cutter rested his feet on the table, one heel brushed against the side of the plate and a kidney bean affixed itself to the side of his shoe. He took a swig from his can. 'The reason I know that Martin was fitted up was because I was at his place in Wandsworth that afternoon. I answered the phone to this guy who wanted to speak to him, so I passed him over. When he hung up he said that the caller had been put on to him by someone who is in our group. I checked it later and this guy had never heard of him. Martin said that there was a picket of Hales's house that afternoon and he had been asked to go over. It was a special thing because of some new vigilante patrol that Hales was planning – or so Martin said – we had been there a couple of times before. I told him it was a bloody waste of time. There's never anyone in Regents Park Road. If you're lucky you might get sworn at by the evening traffic jam and see a few kids coming out of the Zoo. He asked me to come, but I refused.'

'So he went off on his own?' I asked.

'He had to borrow a quid off me to get there. Tell me

something,' he looked up at me, 'was there anyone else with Martin that day?'

'Not that I saw. Just me and the woman and the people who lived round about, no sign of any pickets.'

'He was always unlucky,' brooded Alice. 'He walked right into it, on his own. Why him?'

'Why anybody? He's a goer though.' Cutter was thoughtful. 'If there was one person that Hales should know by face, it is Martin. He spent most of his time chasing Hales, as if it was a two-man class struggle. God! The day that Hales had that south London squat busted up . . .'

'Could it have been Hales on the phone?' I suggested.

He laughed. 'Not unless Hales had taken elocution lessons down this way. No, it wasn't Hales.'

We fell silent. Odgers began to whistle between his teeth. Ferret screwed up his beercan. 'Well,' Ferret said eventually, 'where's the action?'

Alice tilted her chair, put her hands behind her head and started reciting. 'We've contacted the groups – and a fat lot that bunch of bureaucrats will do – we are trying to tap them for some money, an appeal, you know the routine. We've got Fowler to represent him; he may be a Stalinist but he's the best we could get. He has actually got in to see Martin, which is more than the cops would let any of us do. Apart from you, that is.' She glared at me as if I had put the handcuffs on Gold.

'We're going to get a newsletter out on it. Mike, you'll have to go and see *Socialist Worker* and the rest of them and see if they'll print it, and we're holding a meeting next week.'

Odgers's insensitivity went well with her arrogance; they made a lovely couple. 'That's all very well, but how are you constituting the committee?' he asked. 'You can't just have a random bunch of trendy middle-class lefties and squatters. You should have some delegate basis to it. Send out an appeal to trade unionists, write to Denis Skinner . . .' He trailed off, quailing under her gaze.

'That's your idea of proletarian action, is it? Write a letter to Denis Skinner and get a collection of Trots to sit round and squabble about who stuck the last pin in the Blessed

Trotsky's head. I'll tell you who'll be on the committee. People who will get up off their arses and do something and not sit round yattering on all the time. If you want to be on it, fine, come along. Otherwise you can shut up and piss off.'

I nearly presented her with a medal. A sterling performance.

'Hmm,' grunted Odgers. 'That's what I thought –'

Ferret interrupted him. Odgers rarely finished what passed for a thought without either provoking or being a diplomatic incident.

'Well, all right, love, when you've got the meeting together let us know and we'll send someone along from the group. I'm pretty sure I'll come.'

'Less of the "loves" too,' she added.

I felt it was my turn to contribute. 'That's about it, then.'

Cutter sighed 'That's about it for about half an hour. Will you come to the meeting?'

I agonised. Devoid of an alibi I agreed.

'Well, that's fine, maybe you could say a few words.'

'What about contempt?' I mumbled, '*Sub judice* and all that.'

Most of the contempt was being generated in my direction. 'Possible,' said Mike Cutter, 'but I don't see how.' He turned to Ferret. 'Are you going to this meeting tomorrow? The British Alliance?'

'I thought you would have had enough on your plate without a bunch of right-wing nutters to shout at,' said Ferret. 'Why bother with them?'

'Because Hales is going to be there, of course,' said Cutter. 'We'll certainly warm that bastard's backside.'

10.

It rained again on Thursday, all day. I gave myself an excuse to do nothing and sat round waiting in the British Museum Reading Room for 1930s books that I hardly looked at when they arrived. I sat and smoked in the awful tea room. Smoked and thought.

Since Hales and Fuller had been foot-tapping through my subconscious for eight days, it was hardly surprising that they should make a public appearance with their song and dance act. The affair crowded out work, tedium of life, sex . . .

I thought of Moira. We had said little the morning after. The grass, or at least the clippings, were still flying through our brains, I suspected, and thanks to it we had been like two strangers on holiday together, saying goodbye at the airport. Two cups of tea, telephone numbers, keep in touch, let me know what's happening.

There was the usual queue by the phones at the entrance to the Reading Room, the usual 'out of order' notice on three of them. A lady in tweeds was being articulate and lengthy on one of them, to the fury of a Frenchman, an Indian, two Americans, and a woman in orange trousers and a Genghis Khan style woolly hat.

I tried an out of order phone, carefully lifting aside the notice.

'It's out of order,' said Orange Trousers. The removal of the notice clearly interfered with the natural order of the universe.

I felt guilty, and gazed at the notice as if someone had just planted it on me. 'Yes,' I smiled apologetically. 'Well, I'll just try it.'

She stared at me stonily.

'Just to see what happens,' I added. I dialled, the tone worked, and Moira answered.

'Moira, John.'

'Hello, John.' She sounded pleased to hear me. I was gratified.

I asked her what she was doing in the evening; she wasn't doing anything, so I suggested she came to the meeting. It made a change from a night out at the pictures as bait.

'What do I want to go to some boring lefty meeting for?'

'It isn't a boring lefty meeting. It'll be a lively righty meeting. Fuller will be there and so will Hales.'

'Hales?'

I realised I hadn't told her about Hales. 'It's very odd, Moira. If you come along I'll explain.'

She agreed. We met in the pub where I was meeting Ferret, at seven. Ferret wasn't due until quarter to eight. All the pubs round Victoria are horrible.

Rain dripped off her hair and on to her check lumberjacket. She wore jeans and a resigned expression.

'So.' She said.

'So, want a drink?'

She reached into her purse. 'Let me get them. Old Mrs A actually paid me off today, three weeks' money.' She brought the drinks back and sat down. 'I read about Hales and this bombing thing in the paper. What's it got to do with you?'

I told her.

She laughed. 'Well, your very own conspiracy theory growing by leaps and bounds. I'll tell you one thing, I don't want to get involved in any brawls.'

'Who does?'

'A lot of your pals, probably.'

'No they don't. And anyway I didn't come to get thumped. I think it is important, and I want to know why.' I looked at her, attempting to be both imploring and noble at the same time. From the stare I got back, it didn't seem to have worked. 'This Gold guy has been done – almost certainly wrongly – it is connected with Hales, possibly with Fuller, and I'm the man in the middle.'

'People in the middle get knocked down by the traffic going both ways.'

I waved my hand in the air, vaguely looking for a branch to hold on to. 'It's almost a civil liberties thing, isn't it? I don't want to see him sent down.'

'That's pretty lame. Scratch John Raven, inadvertent leftist, and what do you find? John Raven, human rights activist.' She sipped at her drink. 'Still, I wonder why I came. I don't suppose idle curiosity is a very good reason either.' She picked up the evening paper and turned to the entertainments page. 'Just think of all the movies we could have gone to.'

We chatted aimlessly. Ferret was late. He shambled across the bar looking for me.

'We're gonna have to go,' he said. 'It's ten to eight now.

Getting really noisy out there.' There was a note of relish in his voice. 'We're going to eat them.'

I gestured at Moira. 'Ferret, this is Moira, Moira, Ferret.'

'Hello, Moira.' He sniffed. She nodded, unsmiling. He rubbed his hands together. 'Well, like I said, we should go.'

'I'm not happy, Ferret.'

He looked at me as if I were saying that after all I didn't think that the First World War was a good thing and, upon mature reflection, I had decided against going over the top. He asked me what I meant.

'I'm not going to fight fascists. I want to get into the meeting, see what Fuller and Hales look like and what the set-up is. I haven't come for a punch-up.'

'That's fuckin' great man, really helpful. We all want to get into it, don't we? But why don't you take a bucket round for the Hess old age pension fund while you're at it?' He glared at me and scratched his ear.

'Well, that's why we're going. You weren't all that keen yourself last night . . .'

'That isn't true.'

'OK, maybe not, I don't want to argue about it. Moira worked in the bookshop where I got the pictures, that's why she's here.'

The Scotsman pushed a roll of *Workers Speak*s back into his pocket, from which they had been attempting to escape.

'Your certainly know how to stay inconspicuous, Ferret.'

'Oh yeah, I should take lessons from you. You're the invisible man. Well, if you can get in, which will surprise me, I hope you have a wonderful time, but don't blame me if they trample all over you. If the left don't do you by mistake, the right probably will. See you.' He nodded curtly at Moira and stalked from the bar.

She drained her glass. 'Wonderful friends you've got.'

'He's fine, just gets on his white horse occasionally.'

'Any trouble, John,' she said, looking me in the eyes; 'and yours truly is off.'

'Quite, me too.'

We left the pub and walked the two blocks to the hall. I knew the way, but had I been struck blind I would still have had little difficulty. The shouts of the crowd echoed down the alleyways. The hall was just off Victoria Street, designed presumably for a church with a booming congregation. The police, or television, had rigged up arc lamps. There were about five hundred demonstrators from the left, a central phalanx shuffling against the police line, and an uncertain periphery wondering whether their commitment stretched to a cracked skull, courtesy of the Special Patrol Group, and a night in a cell. In and out of the second group weaved paper sellers like sheepdogs. You could have done a lot of reading if you could have found the time.

The police had vans behind the crowd. Their reinforcements were filing out of them and forming a line behind the demonstration, which was well on the way to being encircled.

'They're trying to cut us off, comrades.' A small dark haired man in a dated Guevara beret waved his arm at the crowd and dropped his papers in the process.

'I know that man,' said Moira. 'That's Don Southcombe.'

We were standing back, under a street light. 'Who's he?'

'Teaches maths at the South Bank. He is a friend of my . . . my ex. He's a creep.'

'Well, he's going to be an arrested creep in a minute.'

He was. Having made the fatal error of exhortation to action while isolated from the masses, Don Southcombe was grabbed by three cops and levitated into a little green bus before he had spoken another word. One of the policemen rammed his knee into the mathematician's groin, and Southcombe screamed in pain.

I felt sick. 'The bastards.'

'What do you expect?'

What neither of us anticipated was to be swamped by the crowd. The left had used some sense of tactics and from behind us a wave of demonstrators washed over us. I grabbed Moira's arm, but was uncertain which of us was supposed to be doing the protecting. The wave hit the police line, and it shuddered. The cops were getting in from both sides. Having thrown the cordon around the main demonstration, they had run out of reinforcements. A child wailed. A woman screamed. A cop lost his hat, and then his feet. A young black girl bled from a cut on her forehead.

There was a lot of dust. That rainy night it blew into my face, acrid. I smelt bodies, farts, dirt, even some aftershave. Moira shouted. She was falling. I pulled her back to her feet. The police formed a wedge and were cutting through the crowd to relieve their colleagues on the cordon, but they were having difficulty. Another policeman went down, his helmet flew through the air. He couldn't have been more than twenty, with long fatuous sideburns and a droopy moustache. Someone hit him on the nose and he blinked back tears. Stupidly he lost his temper and dived at his principal tormentor. A second later an old cop pulled him out. 'You rotten little sod!' the younger cop screamed into the melée.

I was fleetingly back in the playground. A silence fell over that section of the crowd, and an opening appeared. Perhaps the young cop and his unknown opponent would square up and fight it out according to the Queensberry rules. A figure broke from the mass of bodies, his hands raised in a boxing stance. *Threatening behaviour*, *three months*, I thought. Hit the bugger and you could be down for a good year. The crowd closed again, and the man disappeared.

I was still clinging to Moira, and we had been swept on to the police cordon. I remembered my conversation: '*Any trouble and I'll be off*,' she had said. I couldn't even turn my head to see her. *Oh Christ I'm not going to fight these so-and-sos*. The cops pushed me back. I tried to give an appearance of shoving forward while sliding back. Behind me the cries grew louder; the police line snapped. Four of us were through it, two bewildered East Enders holding a 'Dockers Against Racism' banner, Moira and myself. One of the dockers went down under three cops; the other, using his banner as a club, battered the police, and they fell back.

The line had re-formed behind us. Apart from the three fighting the dockers, the police were concentrating on the people across the cordon. There was an alley, and we fled into it. There were a couple of cops standing by an entrance to the hall, and a glow from a cigar butt. A tall man in a blue striped suit was talking to the police. Light from the hall flooded across him, and his four companions. They looked like bookies' runners, apart from one who looked like the bloke who persuaded punters to pay their debts. I wouldn't have wanted bad debts with him around.

'Jesus,' said Moira.

'That must be where they are letting them into the meeting,' I whispered. 'If we just walk quietly down there, as good as gold, we should be all right.'

'Be all right?' She was nearly crying, not with pain or hysteria, just anger. 'You bloody fool. I want to get out!'

'You can't. We can't go back through that lot again. The only way out is through that door, as far as I can see.'

Again a crowd, but of a different persuasion, made up our minds for us. About eight men had come through the side of the cordon. 'Christ, we'll mash those red scum,' shouted one of them. He had waited until he was on the right side of the cordon before giving his opinion.

'You don't need to wait,' said another. 'There's two here.'

'Don't be daft,' I heard my spirit of improvisation saying. 'We're all on the same bloody side, all we're trying to do is get into the meeting.'

The red scum masher smiled. He looked tough, but as if he spent a fair amount of time sneaking to the teachers. 'That's all right then. Come on!' We hastened down the alley.

'. . . And a first rate job you've been doing officer,' Blue Striped Suit was saying. 'I'm just sorry that you have to do it, that's all.'

'Just the job we're paid to do, sir,' said the cop.

'And not well enough paid, either. That's another thing we're going to have to change. I can tell you that.'

I missed the remainder of the mutual appreciation. We stumbled through the door. A middle-aged blonde woman was standing by a fold-up card table, checking tickets. She wore black boots and a neat little black twinset and skirt, like a close friend of Eva Braun. 'Well, I know you lads!' She laughed. She didn't know us and clearly wanted to, but we didn't give her the time. Hanging on to the convenient coat-tails, we swept into the hall.

It was packed out, despite the counter-demonstration. About five hundred people made up of that curious new alliance at the right of the political spectrum – blink once and it was a Tory meeting, twice and it was Labour – but with that strand of young Burton-suited fascist heavies, a sprinkling of black leather, mainly men and mainly people resigned to a life of gloom and phone-in programmes until the British Alliance came along.

'At the back,' Moira pointed to two seats at the end of a row, 'let's go there.' We kept our heads down and shuffled to the seats. An old lady sitting next to us was reading a newspaper called *Britain Free*. 'Don't betray us, Maggie!' said the headline.

A steward bounced on the tips of his toes to our left, neat black beard and leather jacket, clearly a veteran of many a street corner.

It doesn't matter who meets in England, an air of tattiness hangs over the proceedings. In the battle between resurgent Britain and the decaying Anglicanism of the hall, the Church won easily. Two union jacks drooped across the platform. Tables, clearly relics of a thousand jumble sales, were arranged across it. At the centre of the tables sat a man in late middle age, with a face of perpetual schoolboyhood, his hair white but in a style of 1920s St Dominics. Beside him sat a thin Zapata-moustached young man, with the 1964 Beatle cut which now passes for respectable rebellion on the far right.

I asked Moira if that was Fuller. It wasn't. She pointed at the other two speakers who were coming through a side door. One, the man in blue pinstripe, was clearly Raphael Hales. The other, she said, was Fuller. Fair hair neatly parted, an ad-agent's suit with a rather dated kipper tie.

The man with the white hair was the chairman, an Air Vice Marshall Causley, he informed us. Having spent the war bombing hell out of Germany, he seemed to have come round to the opinion that he had been knocking off the wrong people. He shuffled some papers, the conversation in the hall began to dwindle, he coughed and wished the audience a good evening. Chants from the crowd outside drifted through the closed and guarded doors. Causley was the totem pole of authoritarian respectability for the three faintly dubious speakers. He delivered the appropriate oration, 'Hour of crisis . . . men ready to come forward . . . Spanish Armada . . . betrayers . . . Falklands . . .'

Then he launched the speakers, and the first off was Fuller, 'A man in the prime of his life who was willing to speak out.'

Fuller made a fairly clean take-off too, but it was familiar enough stuff. He had a punchy delivery and was clearly not new to the art, even if he pleaded inexperience.

'I'm a small businessman, and we aren't too popular these days,' he said. 'We are profit hungry blood suckers. If we stand up against the big conglomerates or the finance houses we're pushed aside. If we face up to the reds in the unions, then we are troublemakers. Not them, us. Why? Because we want to make things, and we want to make money, not just for ourselves – although I'm no saint –', he laughed deprecatingly at that point, and the audience gave a discreet sympathetic chuckle, '– but for the good of all of us. And by all of us I mean the native Britisher. The people who have been through two wars, depressions, lying politicians, privations, oil crises and now see their savings disappearing, their companies robbed by asset-strippers, their jobs taken by foreigners, their taxes used to prop up foreign demagogues and dole queue drop-outs . . .'

He sustained it for ten minutes. 'I used to say I wasn't political. "Stuff the politicians," was my attitude. Well I've changed, because this country has been made political, by the politicians, and I don't just mean that Labour lot – those crypto-Communists – that the people in their righteous anger cast out. I mean no disrespect to our distinguished colleague from the Mother of Parliaments . . .' Hales bashfully acknowledged the round of applause from the hall '. . . but many of his colleagues who, I fear, would be equally at home with the gang still trying to wreck this country today.'

Hales smiled.

'And if this government still insists on submerging me as

an independent businessman with fatuous little forms, and still lets the unions get away with telling me who I can employ, preference given to two colours, red and black, and tries to prevent me succeeding against all the odds in getting a return on my capital, well, I won't take it! The powers that be aren't just spitting in my face, they spit in every Briton's face, and they do worse than that. They create the conditions in which we are all brought up against Big Brother in Whitehall, we are all outcasts in our own society, in our own nation. They have created a climate in which *we* are made out to be the sinners, the minority – although we are the majority – suitable to be pilloried, overtaxed and the target of the thugs on the streets. And you know where they are!'

Fuller was quite excited. He gestured in the direction from where the, now feebler, shouts of 'Fascists out' were coming. The audience gave him a big hand.

'It means that people like us can not only be bullied and physically assaulted, it now seems pukka – if I can use an *immigrant* word – to bomb people who stand up for right, despite the efforts of the police to keep some sanity in this land. I've realised that right isn't just a word with a small "r", I've realised and I hope not too late that I have to stand up for the Right with a big "R". That's why I'm pleased to throw what little weight I have behind the British Alliance. I've had enough!'

The audience hadn't. As Fuller sat down, it rose to its feet. Fuller rose and waved his hands above his head like a Tory candidate after a surprising upset in Slagley West.

Lee, the fascist, was next. The technique was also not new, but different. A slow build-up, an abrupt change of gear into declamation, followed by another build-up. Early Cilla Black really, with a hint of the black country. But if Fuller sought to portray himself as the aggrieved entrepreneur, then Lee went directly to the point. They called him a fascist, lies; a racialist, true; but a man of good will . . .

'We don't all agree, that's part of being British, but we share a concern for the race, for the nation, whether we are workers like you or I, a brain worker like Mr Fuller here, or a parliamentarian like Mr Hales. The party I am proud to represent here has had more than its share of lies, violence from the reds, vituperation from little men . . .'

He wasn't very good. My eyes strayed around the hall. The leather-jacketed steward was still rocking on his heels, and stroking his beard. The old lady gazed dreamily at Lee. A couple of kids fidgeted alongside rapt parents. Then I saw her.

Mrs Avis was in the middle of the row, two blocks up from me. She was turning her head and caught my eye. My stomach moved slightly. 'Christ!' I muttered.

'So be it. If they are going to bomb patriots, if they are going to attempt to drive us from the streets and by-ways of our land, then perhaps it is time we said enough. We don't want violence, but the good old British fist is the only cure for this sort of bullying tactic,' Lee suggested.

Yeah, but who are you going to start with? I brooded.

'What is it?' whispered Moira. I told her. She raised her eyebrows. I looked straight ahead. Mrs Avis had turned away.

'Now, I don't agree with Raphael Hales on every point, but I don't need to. I can assure him that as long as he maintains his own splendid patriotic record, then we'll back him, and as long as reds and blacks pollute our streets, then we'll oppose them.' Lee's content was becoming more virulent but his style remained pedestrian Birmingham.

My eyes drifted again. Shock number two was more alarming, because they had seen me first and there were three of them. It was Anorak, without his anorak, and his two young friends.

I pulled Moira's arm. 'We're getting out of here.' She was looking bored. 'It wasn't my idea. It's easier to read the *Daily Express* anyway –'

'It isn't that. Hurry.'

We got up. I tried to look casual. The three had been near the front. They were walking down the side aisle. We beat them to the back central exit.

The two stewards on the door didn't like early leavers.

'My friend is ill,' I said. I smiled at the older of the two who was wearing a grey cardigan with a cigarette burn that matched his hair.

'Bit early to leave, there's a lot of them trash outside . . .'

'I know. It couldn't have happened at a worse time. Still . . .' I glanced behind me. Anorak was talking to the leather-jacketed steward. They stared at me, and all four began to move towards us. Grey Cardigan had partly stepped aside and the door swung open. He looked suspiciously at me.

His young companion, seeing the action in the hall, stepped in the doorway. He had a nice line in Gene Vincent quiff. 'What's your hurry?'

I pushed Moira ahead of me, I'm always gallant on these occasions. He let her into the foyer. 'I'm sorry, my wife is pregnant, we must go.'

My excuses were getting feebler all the time. Quiff was most unimpressed. 'I don't think you need go.' The four were moving in from the hall. 'I think you should stay and hear what Mr Lee has to say, you might learn something.'

'Well, I think you are wrong.' I smiled again and pushed him very hard. He fell back against the doorpost. A cardiganed arm reached for my cuff. I dodged, a boot hit my leg, but I was through the door. Moira was by the entrance talking to a cop. I made it to her in something less than a second.

'That lot out there will tear you apart,' he was telling her. I glanced back; my six new acquaintances were in the doorway. So would the other lot.

'Thank you, officer,' I said, and gestured at the stewards, 'but these gentlemen said that this was the only way out.'

The gesture worked. Anorak and his associates pulled the door of the hall shut, with them on the inside.

The policeman shrugged. 'Once you're through that door you're on your own.'

I pushed it open. The police had ringed the hall, but they were no longer linking arms; it was the quiet part of the evening. Until we came out. I suspect the cop was given a lecture later on the inadvisability of his move.

'There they are!' shouted a Nazi-spotter. 'Fucking fascists!'

The cops started re-forming, but the line broke. Three of my – or Ferret's – comrades were through.

'You bastard!' He was a fast mover was Odgers, on occasions. His boot hit my crutch just about the time that realisation dawned.

'Thank you, Odgers.' I groaned and collapsed. I watched the blue trousers sway like a drunken chorus line from the horizontal. The police grabbed Odgers. Moira looked down at me. I felt like throwing up; shock waves ebbed through me.

'Ha bloody ha,' she said.

11.

'I think he got away,' Ferret buried his nose in his beer. 'I saw him break loose and he was going for a gap in the police line. He dived between their legs.'

'Stupid bastard,' I thought he didn't believe in provocative and adventurist – that's one of his words isn't it? – behaviour. I missed castration by about an inch.'

'It was bloody brave of him. It's your fault, if you go to a thing like that you can expect the consequences.'

I sighed. 'Well, it isn't everybody who can get done over by the fascists and the left in successive minutes.'

We were back in the pub. Ferret had seen me go down, and he dragged me through the crowd.

He scratched his nose. 'Your uh . . . lady friend was none too pleased.'

'She didn't have to come. I'm fed up about it, all she did was complain.'

'I don't blame her. It's the difference between stupid liberals and sensible liberals. You either come for a purpose or you stay away. You got the worst of both worlds as usual.'

I looked at Ferret. A trickle of blood oozed from a cut on his chin. He was down to one *Workers Speak*, extremely dog-eared, with a torn front page. 'Fight' was the only word of the headline left.

'I can see you did all right,' I said.

He pulled out his Number 6. 'I did all right, *we* did all

right. It puts off all the parlour Nazis. They don't like it when they see what it's really like.'

'I wasn't too keen myself. The only arse that got warmed was mine – or rather crutch – Hales is probably still sitting there on the platform.'

Ferret smiled. 'Isn't all over yet, is it?'

'It is as far as I'm concerned. Anyway, you're wrong.'

'What about?'

'You say I didn't get anything out of it. I did, so did they. You know the woman I told you about, the one who identified Gold, Mrs Avis?'

He nodded.

'She was at the meeting. That was one reason why I got out. The other was the three I met at Highbury on Sunday evening. The ones who turned over my flat. They were there as well. I decided I would be better off outside. I didn't allow for Odgers, of course.'

Ferret was impressed. 'Very interesting,' he said in a German accent as poor as his Italian one. 'It proves it was a fit-up.'

'No it doesn't, but it's pretty odd. And it also links those three with Fuller. The whole thing that happened that day slots together into a nasty plot.'

He screwed up his face. 'I don't know. The world doesn't run on conspiracies. That is what the right always thinks. Do you want a drink?'

'Not only does the right think the world is made up of conspiracies. They act as if it is. They conspire. I'll have a pint.'

He managed to slop the beer on my knee when he returned. 'You've still got the file?' I asked.

'Oh no, man, I flogged it to some rag and bone man in the street.'

'Yeah . . . Maybe that would have been a good idea. Can I crash at your place tonight? I'm not sure tonight would be a good time for Highbury.'

'It doesn't worry me.'

I swilled the beer around my mouth, I was aching.

'And you've got the books I gave you?'

'Yeah, I got the books. Always wanted to read the collected works of Mosley.'

Ferret was losing interest. His thoughts were drifting back to the demonstration. I thought about Fuller, and his father, and his grandfather, and Mrs Astin, and Mrs Avis, and when I was going to meet Anorak again.

We drank like two old age pensioners who had run out of conversation around 1945. 'It's your round,' Ferret said at last.

I opened my wallet. I needn't have bothered. 'Not unless you lend me a couple of quid, it isn't.'

'Christ, Raven, you should be making a fortune with all your pictures and that.' He sighed and dug into his pocket. 'Here you are, a short-term loan from the paper sales.'

I went to the bar. The early evening revellers from the offices were beginning to drift off to Victoria Station and the delights of life in Bromley and Beckenham. A few resolute junior executives were plying bored secretaries with gin. The replacement drinkers were locals and what looked alarmingly like right-wing refugees from the meeting. I wasn't happy.

A fat, bald-headed man in a check suit was talking to a friend. 'I've never seen anything like it. There's this screaming mob of the unwashed shouting their heads off, and the poor bloody police trying to hold them in line. I mean you can't even cross the road to go and have a drink. They looked at me as if I was something with two horns and a tail.'

'You are as far as they're concerned,' said the friend. 'I don't see why they can't hold their meetings in peace. When it comes down to it, the trouble starts with all these Socialist Workers and Commies and what have you.'

I looked at Ferret. He was ostentatiously reading his paper. God knows why, he had probably written half of it himself anyway. Who was he converting? Clearly not the great washed of Victoria, but he continued, oblivious of the inhabitants of the lounge bar.

'I don't think you're winning too many hearts and minds here, Ferret,' I told him, when I got back to our quarter of a table.

'Middle-class nothing in particulars. When do they ever appear on the streets?'

'That fat bloke just has. Didn't like what he saw.'

The Scotsman dipped his nose back into the beer. 'That bunch spend their lives in pubs whining. They passively follow any daft right-wing politician who offers them tuppence off their income tax, and then if a Nazi paratrooper lands in their back garden they get all surprised.'

'Well, I'd get all surprised if a paratrooper landed in my back garden.'

'You know what I mean.'

We relapsed into silence. Ferret kept glancing at the doors.

I decided to revive the conversation. 'Funny about Fuller,' I said.

'Didn't seem all that droll to me.'

'No, it was just that for someone with such an immaculate right-wing pedigree, he came out with an ordinary "I am a worried businessman" speech, "lately come to politics".'

'Politics is a dirty word. It belongs to some rich bastards somewhere else who are screwing you. If you pick it up, you get the clap, too. It's a kind of pass the parcel. What, me political? No, officer, not at all, I gave it to that wee man over there. Politics means dirty deals, the top seven per cent . . .'

I yawned. 'Who own eighty-four per cent of the wealth.'

He glared at me. 'It's mainly concerned with the people who've got it ripping off those who haven't and coming out with a lot of blather about the good of the nation which nobody really believes. If your mate Fuller is half way smart, which I assume he is, then the Now Is The Time For All Good Men routine is the best way to get round it. Makes everyone feel pure and clean. You can run a political movement for years on self-righteousness.'

I refrained from suggesting that he should know. 'The point is that Fuller must have a reason for starting up now. It's funny he went on about people employing people and keeping the wheels spinning, but from what I found in Companies House all he's doing is sitting on top of a property company.'

Ferret snorted. 'It's simple enough. Fascists talk about the division between finance and industrial capital. The first is bad, the second good, they say. In practice, it's just a different bunch of flash Harries filching from the till and doling each other out back-handers.'

'All right, but why now? He doesn't seem to have done anything political before.'

Ferret shrugged. 'How should I know? I'd never heard of him until you struck up this warm relationship. The trouble with you is that, now you've got your conspiracy, you keep wanting to add new bits to make it more dramatic. Watch out for my drink.' He disappeared into the Gents.

The meeting was definitely over. I recognised people from the hall coming in and wondered how they had made it past Odgers's friends. It was becoming an increasingly unhealthy place to be drinking in. There was a howl of laughter from a corner of the bar. Three of the junior executives were doubled up with laughter. One was prodding the small blonde girl he was sitting next to in the ribs. Bright pink. She slapped his face. Bright pink, the trio stopped laughing. The slapped man's friend made an unsuccessful attempt to mediate and show that everyone was still good friends. The girl pushed away his hand and stood up. So did the subject of the slap. Slowly he collapsed across the table, glasses crashed to the ground. Ferret stepped delicately between the puddles.

'Bunch of piss-artists,' he sniffed.

'I love the way you combine Calvinism and drink so obliviously, Ferret.'

'Yeah, well, I don't go round getting my face slapped by wee girls.'

The blood had dried on his chin. 'Might do you less damage if you were.' I shifted my legs. My crutch ached where Odgers's boot had landed. 'It would help if your friend would lay off too, or pick on her for a change.'

The landlord ushered the demoralised junior executive and his party from the pub. As the door swung open, I caught a flash of red. I prodded Ferret hard.

'For fuck's sake, man! D'you want to spill my beer?'

'I've just seen who I don't want to see. Look over there.'

Anorak, still with his mates, was edging towards the bar. It wasn't really his kind of pub. But it wasn't really my kind of pub either, particularly then.

'What?' Ferret gazed disbelievingly at me. 'Those miserable little weeds? Are they the front line stormtroopers assigned to hunt down John Raven, agent of the Comintern? You must be putting me on.'

I was hurt. Seen in the smoky red plush surroundings, they didn't look too impressive as fascist heavies. They shuffled uneasily to the bar and stood in a semi-circle with their backs to us. Another figure emerged from the gloom and headed towards them. I indicated him to Ferret. 'How about that one?'

Ferret turned up his collar. 'Jack Moyne, west London postal worker, Irish mother, English father, smashed up a gay bar once. He's a crawling little moron.'

Moyne was the bearded bouncer in the leather jacket. He started chatting to Anorak. They laughed.

'Odgers has done enough to me for one night,' I said. 'There's four of them and two of us. Let's get out of here.'

Ferret finished his drink. We got to our feet and lurched unsteadily to the door. I looked back. Moyne was staring at me, and he tugged at Anorak's sleeve. They both stared, and put down their glasses.

I didn't need to whisper, the pub was pushing towards maximum alcoholic decibels. 'They've seen us, Ferret. I think they're developing an interest.'

Ferret can move fast when he wants to, and so can I. We were at the next corner before they had emerged from the pub.

Ferret spat into the gutter and coughed. 'I'll have to pack in smoking, I'm absolutely knackered. Come on, we can pick up a thirty eight from the station.'

Moyne knew the area better than one would have expected. As we dived down the street we met them head on. They must have gone round the other way.

One of them let out a howl. 'That's the bastards!'

As the first blow hit me I felt that familiar surprise. Why

was I there? Why not at home? In bed? Reading a book? 'No!' I shouted, not a denial, not even fear, merely disbelief. I grabbed at my assailant's leg. He fell forward across me, and caught the edge of Ferret's boot as it swung into Moyne's face. There was a hideous crunching noise that indicated that he would be visiting a dentist shortly. I staggered to my feet. Moyne was still down, spitting blood, swearing, crying. He tried to get up. I couldn't bring myself to repeat Ferret's effective tactic; the spark of hate wasn't there. Perhaps if I chat to him, he'll go away, I thought dreamily. Ferret was pinned back across a Cortina by Anorak and one of his youthful friends.

'What the fuck you doing, Ray?' Anorak was shouting at Quiff and pointing at me. 'That's the fucker we want! Get him!'

Ray was little more enthusiastic than I was. He gazed stupidly at the scene. Moyne didn't present much of an advertisement for the virtues of good old British fists. I swung my shoe into his rib cage. It wasn't much of a shoe or much of kick, but it was enough to send the poor sod back on the deck. I flung myself on Anorak and in a replica of the technique that had yielded me little success twenty years before at junior school, attempted to twist his neck off. Anorak grunted, his head stayed on his shoulders, but Ferret broke free of the double hold. Ferret swung his right hand into his other tormentor's face, who replied by ramming both fists into the Scotsman's stomach. I felt an arm winding round my neck and realised I had forgotten Ray.

'Cal! For fuck's sake, man!' Ferret shouted.

The bad language was beginning to open windows and attract the attention of the locals. This was more of a Dalston scene than Victoria, I thought stupidly. A touring violence show.

Ferret had seen Odgers, who had, for once, shown up at the right time. He was stumbling down the street. He looked drunk. I couldn't free myself from Ray, so settled into kicking his shin. Across the road was a police Panda car. A cop sat, window wound down, observing the clash between the forces of progress and reaction. His mate was talking on the intercom.

Ray kneed me in the kidneys, I grunted. Ferret was putting on the performance of his life, but I was uncertain whether he was inflicting more damage on himself or his intended victim. He smashed his head into his opponent's face. The youth's face was streaming with tears, intermingled with the slower drip of blood.

Odgers pushed Anorak back across the car, grabbed his legs and toppled him head first over the bonnet.

'Ferret! The cops!' My voice came out as a high pitched squeal.

The police were out of the Panda and were strolling towards us. Ray was more impressed by their leisurely progress than by my efforts on his shin and was half way across the road almost before they had closed the car door. Odgers looked round. Then he and Ferret started running. The cops were nearly on us. They would have got me had it not been for Moyne. Blinded by blood, and infuriated by Ferret, he stumbled finally to his feet and, deciding that the world at large was his enemy rather than any particular section, took a swing at the driver of the Panda. He made contact, then fell heavily against the intercom man, and all three subsided into the gutter.

I felt the sickly taste of my own vomit and spit and ran faster than I had for some years. We just made the bus. Ray didn't, we overtook him outside a Wimpy bar nursing a twisted ankle. His interest in us, the cops and his companions had vanished. He mouthed four letter words into the void as we leapt on to the bus.

12.

I looked at my watch. My arm was shaking. 'It's only twenty-five to ten now. It seems like a bloody endless night.'

Ferret snorted. He has an irritating habit of snorting outwards rather than in and retaining the contents just within his nostrils, visible to the world. The bus was stuck in a jam half way up Shaftesbury Avenue. Odgers rested his feet on the front window rail of the bus. We were upstairs. The conductor asked him to move his feet.

'What's the bloody difference?' Odgers asked the conductor.

'Give it a rest, man, he's only doing his job.' The conductor echoed Ferret's words before he had finished uttering them.

'Jesus,' sighed Odgers, and removed his feet.

'Well, we'll have time for another pint before the night is over.' Ferret rubbed his hands together. 'Might be a bit more peaceful, too. Old Moyne is going to have to pack this lark in if it goes on like this. He loses four teeth every time he pokes his head out of the door nowadays. How d'you lose the cops, Cal?'

'Went between their legs. I was half way across the road before they knew I'd gone. Heavy lot, the way they went into me . . .'

'You didn't do too bad on me.' I rubbed the battered area. My neck throbbed where Ray had wrenched it, my hands stung from where I had hit the pavement, and my kidneys weren't all they might be.

'Look man, if you come out of a fascist meeting you can't be surprised if someone lays one on you. It's your own bloody fault for being there. You shoot first and ask questions afterwards in that situation. Anyway, I'd like to ask you where you would be now if it wasn't . . .'

'I know, I know. I'm grateful. I'd run out of ideas about five minutes before you showed up. If Moyne hadn't spent his time looking for his teeth, God knows what would have happened.'

'Knock off the central committee first,' observed a satisfied Ferret. 'Leave 'em directionless. Once he was away, we were in there with a chance.'

We changed to a seventy three at the Angel and rattled into Stoke Newington. I didn't want a drink. Ferret and Odgers wanted a lot of drink. We sat and listened to a tuneless post-punk band on the corner of Stoke Newington

High Street. Ferret was hitting the chasers while Odgers gave his views on the state of play between the Socialist Workers Party, and the Communist Party and Militant. At least, that's what I thought he was talking about. An occasional phrase would penetrate my brain between the rapid thuds of the drums. Ferret started waving his hands. To him, an argument about the SWP and the CP was like knitting to a Women's Institute cadre.

I brooded about the evening. I had made myself too many enemies that week. The cops, Anorak, Jack, Ray and friends would doubtless be happy to have another, more private meeting. Mrs Avis was the sort who didn't forget a face. And Moira had been unencouraging.

'Just what I said,' she told me as she went off to the Victoria Line after Odgers's first intervention. 'You muck around with things and you don't really have a clue what you're doing. Thanks for the evening.'

Why was Fuller so anxious to get the pictures back, what was such a big deal? Or was it one of the cuttings? I hadn't looked at the file since Sunday.

I felt terrible, my beer was untouched.

'That's the whole bloody point, Ferret, we've never given it a try!' shouted Odgers. The band was between numbers and he was orating to most of the surrounding tables.

'Tell him the truth, man,' murmured an ageing West Indian with a sub-Rasta hair-do. 'Don't tell him the lies.'

Ferret made a drunken effort to put his arm round the reluctant Odgers's shoulder, and nearly fell from his seat in the process. 'I've seen it all before, Cal, and I've seen all these so-and-sos before, too. Half of 'em were expelled from the Young Socialists with me when we were with Gerry Healey, and the other half were expelled with me from IS, and those who weren't expelled with me were people I voted to expel from IS. There are revolutionaries and parasites. That lot are parasites and no-hopers. You get in the Labour Party and you'll find, once the fuss is over, you'll be sitting there with a bunch of deadbeats on one side of the room and a bigger bunch of Trot deadbeats on the other. You'll all be discussing the young persons' disco and the jumble sale the week after next.'

I had little idea what they were arguing about. 'Shall we shove off?' I said.

'C'mon man, there's time for another,' said Ferret.

'Well, I'm off,' Odgers stood up. 'I'm going to bring it up on committee.'

'The way you are, you'll probably bring it up two yards outside the door. You're all mouth and no trousers.' Ferret veers to truculence when drunk, combining it with sporadic visions of the starry future of humanity under socialism.

'You won't get another,' I told him. 'They shouted time five minutes ago.'

'Well, fuck that. I'll get a take-out. What'll it be?'

'A glass of milk.'

He never heard. He struggled to the bar and returned with a quarter of Teachers and a six-pack. We made it to the flat. The remains of the Sunday Hemingway turnip stew were still strewn around the room. A copy of the *Morning Star*, well sat upon, was on the old brown armchair. The curtains were, as is usual with Ferret, pulled. His home was like a dark cave from which he would sally forth with the light of revelation. He walked over to the television and switched it on, with the sound turned down.

A man was giving snooker hints. The balls ricocheted across the baize, and an off-white one dropped into a pocket. The camera cut to the audience, who were wearing dinner jackets and resembled a group of shady solicitors with their East End clients.

'Used to play a lot of snooker in Glasgow.' Ferret had prostrated himself on the floor, cupping his chin in his hands, and was staring at the screen. 'Nice little game.'

The image flickered; then, as a player lined up a cue shot, he and his field of battle slid off the screen. Ferret swore.

I walked over and picked up the envelope containing the pictures. Ferret had heaped the books on top of them. 'You really should get something done about the horizontal hold,' I said. 'I've never seen more than fifteen seconds on your set without the cast getting waist amputations.'

He reached his hands to an old candlestick, crawled forward and tapped the tuner. The picture was restored, but snow began to drift down on to the baize and flicker on the players' black waistcoats.

He pulled the six-pack within his reach, extracted two cans and tossed me one. I opened it almost without thinking, collapsed in the chair and drew the pictures out of the envelope.

They looked the same.

I dropped the copies of *Tribune*, *Action* and *New Weekly* on the floor, together with the launching of the *King George V*, the hunger marchers and the Hyde Park demonstration. I was left with what I assumed was the Paradise family on tour.

Ferret leaned across and turned up the volume. 'A tricky shot but with the Rest of the World so far ahead it may be his only way out,' boomed the commentator. 'It worked, lovely!' The audience stirred, Ferret snorted.

The first picture was of the woman with the swastika badge on her bosom. She looked like Unity Mitford. There were some drinks on a low table in the background: wine. It was an album shot, not a press pic. I tossed it to Ferret. 'Who do you think this is?'

'Put this away and that'll be it,' said the television.

He scrutinised the woman as if she had made an unwelcome suggestion. He scratched his nose. 'My back hurts like hell where that little bastard got me,' he announced. 'I don't know. Some woman.'

'Look at the badge.'

'Oh, aye. Some Nazi bitch.'

'Unity Mitford?'

'Could be. There were a lot of blonde ladies wandering around with swastikas on their front fifty years ago.' His eyes wandered back to the snooker match.

I went back to the other pictures. There were four shots of the family group with dead animals. I scrutinised the man, the Sanders of the River figure, and thought back to my meeting with Mrs Astin, and the portrait on her wall. Was it Alexander Paradise?

He looked healthier than he had done in her portrait, if it was him. The hair was white, or maybe just bleached by the sun; he was tanned. Since he was evidently surrounded by tropical wild life, this was unsurprising. There was a little puckered scar beneath his right eye, which probably showed up quite distinctly in real life. I would have thought that it was a blemish on the print, except that it was present on all the pictures.

What did he do? What was he doing there surrounded by the dead animals, and his family, in the heat of the sun? I remembered the sound of cicadas, emphasising the still summer heat in the south.

I looked at the woman. In one shot she was holding a dead monkey up by the ears. It was gruesome, the skull seemed to be decomposing, or perhaps it was the light. She was smiling, unconcerned, squinting into the sun.

I kept thinking about Mrs Astin and the sherry dripping down her cardigan.

The pictures would have been taken any time between 1920 and 1950. The clothes were archaic, but they had persisted through the dying days of Empire. Russians still wore them now as they plodded around Africa, bush shirts and pith helmets . . .

I looked at the children. The girl was about eight, but most of her face was covered by a white cotton hat, the same hat in all four of the dead animal pictures. The boy was younger, not more than four, with cropped fair hair. He wore shorts and a military style shirt, with a neckerchief made of leopard skin.

'Here John . . .' Ferret's voice tailed away. 'You want a shot?'

He had opened the Scotch and produced two milky coloured glasses.

'For God's sake, Ferret, haven't you had enough?'

'What are you getting so fucking sanctimonious about?' He glared at me. 'If it wasn't for me, you wouldna be here.'

'In the state you're in, I'm not sure you still are.'

He unsteadily poured two large measures. I took a swig and examined the inside of the glass. Small globules and streaks of milk floated in the alcohol. The spirit tore at my throat. I nearly threw up.

The kangaroo shot was taken earlier. The boy was absent and the girl not more than three years old. If Mrs Astin had said they had gone to Australia first, then the later shots were probably taken in South Africa.

Was the son Fuller? It could be, it could be anyone, a child with fair hair like millions of others. In one picture the child sat astride a dead deer, or wildebeest, smiling toothily.

'Poundstretcher fares can reunite you with your loved ones', said the television.

The deer picture was taken with a lot of sky. The family had gathered in a row, with the deer and boy in the middle. They occupied the lower half of the picture. A group of blacks, out of focus, stared at the curious white ritual. There was a motorcar behind them, a big 1930s Packard, I thought. That dated it. Say it was about 1938 . . .

The solo picture of the man revealed nothing. It was presumably taken around the same time. He was in hunting gear with a gun crooked in his arm.

Nor did the dog picture. It was just a dog, an evil looking animal snarling for the party shot, with a crooked ear. As Ferret had said, animals are timeless. Only the curling of the photograph and the sepia put forty years between us. There was a picture on a quay. It might have been Sydney, it might not. A couple of dockers were looking on, laughing at some long-gone joke. Husband and wife were unsmiling, not amused.

There was only one other shot of the family. They were on a riverboat. There was forest in the background, and they sat beneath an awning with lunch spread in front of them on a long bench-like table. The inevitable black waiter hovered in the background. The two children were sucking drinks through straws, while the adults raised their glasses in a toast. Husband and wife as usual, but there were two others as well, and I knew them. I had seen them in the previous few days. Neither shared the rest of the party's enthusiasm.

Astin had a shrivelled smile, and his wife looked as if raising her glass would be her final act. She was scowling. So that clinched it. Alexander Paradise, Mrs Paradise and children, plus uneasy retinue.

I sifted the remaining three pictures. Another family, but definitely Edwardian. A stern patriarch, the withered wife, a son, the governess. The son was about ten, fair hair once more, but not smiling in the tropical sun. It was a studio shot, with everyone neatly arranged by some Edwardian flash expert. The father had cropped black hair, well macassared. The wife wore a white dress; the son, the inevitable sailor suit. The governess seemed quite jolly; perhaps they fired her soon afterwards, because she was the only one who did.

The other two were of public meetings, clearly patriotic occasions, for union jacks were much in evidence. One was in the open air, dotted with the boaters of Edwardian England, the other was the picture in the silver frame.

The first photograph was of a man stabbing his finger into the rhetorical wilderness where hack patriotism draws its succour. It was a small crowd in a park. A low hill sloped up behind the speaker. A little boy was clutching a cat and holding the hand of what I assumed was his little sister; they had no shoes, and were staring at the speaker. Most of the crowd was clearly poor. It resembled one of those pictures of poverty in the London of eighty years ago.

I looked closely at the man. It could have been the patriarch, but it might not. His hair was flying across his forehead.

A cigarette I had been smoking had burnt to its end, and burnt my finger. I stubbed it out on my shoe and dropped it on the carpet.

'What are you doing with my carpet?' Ferret had stirred from his obsessive television viewing.

'Sorry, Ferret, I didn't realise you took such an interest in domestic order. You could have fooled me.'

The snooker had ended. I passed him the pictures. 'Alexander Paradise on tour of the Empire with family.' I explained, and filled him in. He wasn't very interested. Too drunk, I thought.

I retained the picture in the silver frame. It was of a long hall and was taken at night; it was dark and ill-lit and mainly of the back of people's heads. A few faces stared at me from the past, illuminated by gas lamps, framed by more union jacks. It resembled an earlier version of my evening's entertainment. At least I was in no danger from that lot, I thought, they were long in their graves. I looked at the platform, at the speaker; there was no hair flying this time, it was short, neat, the hand was still prodding the void. It was the same speaker and I was pretty sure it was the patriarch. But so what? An ancient meeting, once again attended by the poor, in some now demolished or bombed, or derelict hall . . .

'What a charming family,' muttered Ferret. His interest was reawakening. 'They've got a lovely way with monkeys. What a nice little group of people.'

He moved on to the riverboat shot. I pointed out Astin and his wife.

'You're sure it's them?' The fog of alcohol was clearing from his eyes as he looked up, and from his voice.

'I'm pretty certain. They look miserable there and they certainly looked miserable when I saw them. They had a lot to be miserable about from all accounts.'

'What do you make of this lot, Raven?'

'Not much. You've got the Paradise Family Robinson, and I've got a silver framed picture of a public meeting. It hardly seems worth the effort that has been put in. Christ, my neck hurts.' My head had begun auditioning for next day's hangover. 'Where can I sleep? I'm tired of this.'

Ferret pointed to the wall. 'There's a camp-bed in the hall, but hang on.' He was squatting by a low table he had constructed from stolen bits of iron and the wreckage of what had once been an SWP speaker's stand. It still had torn pieces of *Socialist Worker* pinned on it. He laid the last pictures out on it and gazed at them blankly.

I looked again at the silver framed shot. I felt as if I was going to vomit. I had eaten nothing. The picture revealed nothing. Perhaps it was Alexander's old man, what was his name? *Gaynor*, Sir Gaynor. So what? I glanced at his biography in the corner, yellowing and old, like me.

I rose to my feet. 'I'm going to get that camp-bed.'

'Hold on, hold on, let's have a look at the one in the silver frame. You can always melt it down and live off the proceeds. Perhaps you've got the Paradise family fortune.'

I tossed the picture to him. He reached his hand out to grab it, missed and it flew through the air, and bounced off the wall. As it did so the glass shattered. He picked it up. The picture was slightly shifted in the frame, I noticed as I looked over his shoulder. Ferret's grubby forefinger poked at it. It slid sideways and half folded. He drew it out, and there was a faded white sheet underneath.

'I always liked it when we changed the lino in our flat back home,' said Ferret. 'You'd have all the old copies of the *Daily Record* from way back when. Most of them were what my old man put on the floor in 1945 when he came back from the war. So you'd get all this stuff about Celtic and how they were all getting together again and how things were looking up and what the government was going to do and all that . . .'

He pushed at the sheet. But it wasn't paper, it was the reverse side of another photograph. Ferret turned over the frame. It was covered in brittle brown paper. He crossed to what passed for his sink and picked up the bread-knife. It was smeared with Marmite and margarine. Very fond of Marmite was Ferret. He wiped the blade on a tea cloth.

'I used to like that, too,' I said, as he slit the brown paper from the frame. 'You used to get the same in drawers too, when they were emptied out. My parents kept the most amazing old junk. The only thing of interest was the newspapers buried at the bottom of it.'

The frame was held by a clasp in one corner. When shifted, it fell apart. The picture fluttered out.

Both pictures fluttered out. The public meeting landed near the table. Ferret caught the other in mid-air. We looked at it. It was grimy with age, and there was a rectangular brown mark where the silver frame had been.

It wasn't a professional shot. None of your Edwardian studio jobs. Clearly done with a shaky camera and not in very good light. But it was clear enough who was in it. There was the patriarch, who was a shade dishevelled, his son, and another man.

'Interesting variation on the family hunting shot, eh?' said Ferret.

'It certainly is.'

As with the picture of the wife with the monkey, the boy was in the centre of the picture. He was holding his victim by the ears, and he had a proud smile on his face. He was sitting in a chair, must have been in his mid-teens, I guessed. The victim was dead all right, there was a great dark clot from his neck down to his chest. But it wasn't a monkey this time. It was a man, whose eyes were still open and stared lifelessly out of the picture.

There was a mark on the boy's cheek, just below his right eye, which could have been a blemish on the picture. But I didn't think it was.

13.

I can't say the camp-bed was comfortable. I can't say it wasn't. The night before had ensured I was incapable of making an accurate assessment. I awoke into a grey morning with my left ear flap roughly folded against the pillow. I observed Ferret's hand putting down a cup of coffee. He has spectacular powers of recovery. I had seen him on some nights lying insensible, with egg-size bruises on his forehead, dead to the world, and insensitive to the insults of hosts and hostesses, yet the morning after, lively, spritely even, he was the virtuous soul pursuing his daily round.

That day he was silent, thoughtful. It was more than I was.

'I don't like coffee in the morning,' I mumbled. 'I like tea.'

'Then go pluck yourself a tea-leaf,' he replied. 'I'm off.'

The night before floated back. Crowds, violence, Moira, Moyne's face spewing teeth.

'Christ.' The nicotine fought to throw itself out of me. 'What the fuck am I going to do?'

'Lead a life of leisure, take up golf, I dunno. I'm off to the site.'

'I've gone off Highbury. Can I crash for another night?'

'Suit yourself.'

I repeated my question. 'What the hell am I going to do? Obviously it was that picture that Fuller is so anxious to get his hands on. So what is it? Fuller's old man in action? And who is the dead man?'

He shrugged his shoulders. 'Someone who has been six foot under for about eighty years. What do you want me to do? Dig up a few graves?'

'Do you know anything about . . . about that time?'

'What time do you mean? We've got a nasty picture of a corpse from a long way back. We don't know where it was taken, by whom, why, and what happened. Everyone in it is long gone.'

'Not all reds are in their blooming youth. There must be some people who remember . . .' My voice trailed away.

'Do us a favour, Raven. There are a few old guys who remember the twenties. There aren't many around who go back before the First World War. Anyone who was our age then, say . . . well they would be pushing about a hundred by now. It's a really nasty picture, the making of a million bloody stories, and none of them you'll ever prove. Suit yourself, but I'm going to work.' He put on his donkey jacket and walked to the door. 'Why don't you make yourself useful if you're squatting? Buy something to eat tonight.' He left.

I got up, ate a slice of bread and jam, sifted through the pictures yet again. I was supposed to be a picture researcher, among other things. I should know how to look at pictures, I thought. I stared blankly at the three pictures of the first family, and the picture of the murdered man. I was sure that the patriarch featured in all four, and since the son had graduated from his sailor suit in the photograph with the corpse, that it must have been taken at least five years later. But where and when any of the pictures were taken remained a mystery.

I thumbed through the book again. Paradise had worked for the British Brothers League in Stepney. Perhaps the picture came from that time, perhaps they didn't. I sat in the room, stared into space.

After a while I thought of Spizzichino. He was an old man, he knew about photographs. I went down to Covent Garden, with the four pictures. I decided he wasn't going to see the key bit of evidence, but perhaps he could date them. Perhaps.

He was hunched over a pile of press cuttings, muttering to himself. He wasn't pleased to see me. His eyes glared at me above his spectacle frames.

'I haven't come for work,' I said hurriedly.

'I know you haven't. I told you I have none this week. So you, being a rational man, would not come to me for that. But maybe you just want to waste my time like so many of the . . .' his still flawed English vocabulary searched for some suitable epithet and settled on those first years in London '. . . jackasses who come to me.'

'I wanted to ask your advice.'

'I'm not interested in marriage, sex, motor cars, money . . .'

'How about photographs?'

He looked up. 'What photographs?'

I pulled out the family group, and the two crowd pictures, and laid them on top of the cuttings.

He glanced at them cursorily and made a token gesture of returning to his cuttings. He could be a peculiarly cantankerous and obstructive old man, could Spizzichino. 'So? Old pictures, what about them?'

'I just thought, doubtless wrongly, that since you know rather more about photographs than I do, and, I must add, have been around rather longer than I have, that you might, just possibly, be able to give me some idea when they were taken.'

He picked the family group up, and fingered it. 'How am I supposed to know that?'

'I don't know, it was just a naive hope, based on my deep confidence in your innate genius. The clothes, I suppose, or the type of paper used, style of the print.'

He scratched his bald dome.

'There are a lot of old photographs around. How am I supposed to date them?' He muttered under his breath in Italian and held the picture up. 'Probably about 1914, maybe earlier. It looks like your typical English family. Your imperial family.' He laughed and asked me where I got them. I avoided a direct answer but didn't lie. He examined the others.

'Any idea where they might have been taken?'

'In God's name, Raven, how am I supposed to know that? I come to this awful country forty years ago, these were taken when I was a boy in Roma, we didn't go on trips to England in those days, and I don't spend my days roaming round this city now. I look at pictures. I try to *sell* pictures when I have the time and people don't come in asking me questions.'

'Yeah, well thanks very much, Spizzichino. I'll keep in touch.' I reached over to pick up the pictures.

He was looking at the picture of the open air meeting and picking up a magnifying glass, scrutinised the corner of the shot. 'I must say, John that for someone who knows this city, you are somewhat ignorant.'

'How so?'

He pointed at the photograph and tapped it. I stared over his shoulder. The speaker was still on his grassy knoll, the crowd was still listening. 'Well, what am I looking at?'

'What you should be looking at is the building.'

I did so. It was a interesting design, somewhat blurred and out of focus, and I had no idea what he was talking about. 'Well, so what?'

He made a hissing noise. 'Oh come, come, John. And you such a keen student of photography, such an *artist*. You know that building.'

'No, I don't.'

'It's the Whitechapel Art Gallery.'

So it was. It was quite obvious, even without the magnifying glass. 'My God, Spizzichino, so it is. Now why didn't I think of that? Do you know when it was built?'

He spread out his hands. 'I don't know when it was built. What more do you want? Probably about 1912, a fine building, rare in this country. So now you know it was taken after 1912, and in Aldgate.'

It was progress. I asked if I could use the phone, and rang the gallery.

It was built in 1901. That gave me another thirteen years to play with. Spizzichino returned to his cuttings and I arranged the three pictures in a row and surreptitiously pulled out the fourth. I didn't want Spizzichino to see it, I didn't want anyone else involved. The patriarch looked much the same age in the open air picture, and in the shot in the hall, as he did in the murder photograph. So maybe they were taken at the same time, anytime after 1901 . . .

Spizzichino looked up. 'Are you staying?' The tone indicated that I wasn't, so I left.

I went to a pasticceria off Cambridge Circus and had a coffee. It was nearly time for lunch, and I couldn't afford one. So someone had been murdered sometime after 1901. Perhaps in the East End, perhaps the body had been dumped, perhaps it was mentioned in the papers. Whatever the papers in the East End were in 1900.

When at a loss, try the British Museum, or the Museum's newspaper library, that 1930s concrete time machine on the edge of north London. There, after about half an hour of old papers, one enters a world of long-gone political scandals, crises, vicars caught in compromising situations with now respectably retired chorus girls who have long since buried their past. Until the reader, as time travelling vagrant, unearths their history. I flipped through the card index, tracked the local paper through to the 1900s, and started reading.

It took the afternoon to get past 1903 in the *Hackney Gazette*. Periodically the attendants would pad across with a dusty volume. They were like a lower order of priests for some British quack religion, such as the lost Tribes of Israel. They prowl the rooms, snatching stacks of the *Cawnpore Times* from the desks of researchers foolish enough to leave the room and fight the tea dispensing machine downstairs. There's always some guy reading the *New Musical Express* of sometime in 1963, for some never to be completed thesis on the role of Bootle in the rise of the Mersey Sound.

The bell went at ten to five, and I was in February 1904. The lay-out of the paper was different, but the stories weren't. Strikes, suffrage demonstrations, the alien menace, anarchists, prostitutes, a couple of drag queens arrested in the Commercial Road, deserted children, plenty of murders, but not the right one. A man had had his throat cut and been found in the Stepney Highway. It momentarily stirred my interest, but he was Chinese, and that wasn't my bearded corpse.

'We're closed,' said the attendant, and grabbed the newspapers. I walked in the dark to the tube, made my way back to Stoke Newington and did some meagre shopping. There was no sign of Ferret. I ate half of a tinned chicken pie, gazed at Ferret's television and went to bed early. I heard Ferret, smashed once more, stumble in at midnight. I feigned sleep and he was gone before I woke up.

I went back to the library, which was crowded since it was a Saturday, fought for a seat and read on, forcing myself to concentrate on corpses. It did my mood no good. I stifled thoughts of the futility of the search and of ringing Fuller. 'OK, Fuller, I give up, your old man was a killer, just tell me who the corpse is . . .' I had to be one up on the spokesman for independent businesses.

But I wasn't. I was haunted by missing some death, or by misinterpreting those I found, or having the wrong paper, the wrong time, the wrong place. My corpse had probably met his end in Ruislip, or Manchester, or Sydney, I brooded. But I didn't think he had. I didn't want him to. Five o'clock came, and again nothing had been revealed.

Ferret was at home watching the television. 'Party tonight, Raven. Get yourself out a bit, eh?' He was in good spirits. I slumped on to the camp-bed, and told him where I had been.

'You'll do anything to avoid work,' he said. His bonhomie passed me by. He reverted to the party, only it wasn't a party, he explained, but a social, down at a trades club much used by Ferret's comrades.

We went to the club. The bar was small and crowded. A man with a stutter pointed out Ferret to an angry fellow countryman. 'You take him, he was an *organiser* for your lot. And look what happened to him!'

'What did happen to me, pal?' asked Ferret.

'You left. Come and explain why to him.'

Ferret clutched his pint. 'I'd sooner not just now.'

I said, 'Is this the social?'

He glowered at me, shoulders hunched. 'No, man, it's a bar. The social isn't on for another hour. It's upstairs.'

We went up two hours later. An old Stones album was played repeatedly on a flashing but arthritic disco. It wasn't crowded. The Stones record did nothing to cheer a small party of post-punks. A man with a 'Drunks Against the Nazis' badge was sipping an orange juice. Odgers danced with a small belligerent girl, Ferret became passionately involved with a Chilean, and I lost an argument about the correct position towards the Second World War with a self-assured daughter of the middle classes who explained that I should have joined up and argued for soviets within the army. The amplification exploded in a cascade of flashing lights and white noise. A drunk wandered in and harangued the thirteen revellers. The self-assured woman resisted my attempts to move the conversation away from the War. Ferret had fallen on the Chilean girl, and both had collapsed under the table.

'In many ways, they had a worse problem in the First War,' said my companion. We had slid along the room and were half leaning against the window.

'What?'

'In terms of organising. I mean the pressure against the conchies . . .'

'Conchies?'

She was deliberately amazed by my ignorance. 'Conscientious objectors. Now that wasn't really an initiative based on a *deep* class analysis, not in Britain, anyway. But when you talk to the people involved then, well, you begin to see some of the problems.'

I became interested. 'You've . . . uh, talked to people who were active during the First War?'

'Well, in a way.'

'Before the First World War?'

She frowned. 'How old do you think I am? Most of them were only our age' — she looked at me critically — '*my* age in the War. It's a long time ago.'

'Yes, well I'm very interested in that period just at the moment. I don't suppose you know anyone you could put me in touch with, uh . . .'

'Diana, Diana Passingham. I told you my name earlier.' She frowned again.

'Yes, I'm sorry, terrible with names. I wondered if you could put me in touch with anyone you might have met from that period.'

She looked slightly uncomfortable. 'Well, I haven't actually done much fieldwork in that area myself. Still, there is a friend of mine, a woman called Hazel Brill, she did some interviews with old activists in *Spare Rib*. You could ask her.'

She didn't know where Hazel Brill was, and her interest in me was dwindling. We edged away from each other. Ferret remained buried under the table. I decided it was time to leave, and another night in Stoke Newington might be a mistake. Anorak and his pals couldn't be on duty at that hour of night. They weren't. The flat was undisturbed. I went to bed.

Sunday passed uneventfully. On Monday I decided to give the library one more chance. On the way up, I rang *Spare Rib*. There was no-one there who knew where Hazel Brill was to be found. By mid-afternoon, any lingering hopes I had had for a lead from the *Gazette* had vanished. I flitted through a few other papers, filling in time. Then I left. On the entrance to the tube I bought an evening paper, and glanced through it. There was no mention of Gold. Someone had written a feature denouncing the continued tide of extremist violence.

There had to be some evidence somewhere. A man had died, his remains were buried somewhere, or strewn around in the dust. The British are good at files, reports, photographs. The tube was almost empty at Colindale but began to fill up at Golders Green. I congratulated myself on having a seat, and was cheered that there were no one-legged geriatric mothers who would have a moral call on my seat.

A railwayman was sitting opposite, and idly flicking

through the pages of some north London local paper. 'Patrick Jenkin Dreams of London in the 1990s' said the headline. I dreamed of London earlier.

He turned the page. 'Inquest Says Accidental Death', I read. Inquests. People who die in mysterious circumstances get inquests, the least the state can do for them . . .

If their bodies are found.

And if their murderers are found, they are tried. But there was no mention of any trial in the book, no scandals, no murders, just the long struggle.

Inquests are official, with coroners, and expert witnesses, and juries.

I bought some food at Highbury and went back to the flat. There were no callers, no disturbances. Perhaps Anorak had lost interest, or been called away.

A couple of years ago, some pictures I had taken had been used by a magazine. The magazine went bust, as magazines do, and I had got myself a lawyer. Well, I had known him before, when he was selling the *Morning Star* and abusing Trotskyists for their incorrect views on Leonid Brezhnev. It didn't stop the Trots from going to him when their debut court cases came up. He had been impressive in the brisk little interview with the magazine proprietors. There's nothing like a good Communist to put on an impressive performance of middle-class legality. His name was Pointer. I rang him the following morning.

'Yes,' he said, 'they have records. I don't know where they are. There's probably some old man somewhere, just waiting for someone to go and look at them, surrounded by old archives. Each district should have them. Each borough.'

But what borough? Tower Hamlets? Hackney? City of London?

I scanned the telephone book. It came down to Poplar, Hackney, City of London. 'I wouldn't know, love,' said an old lady from Poplar. 'No one's here, I'm the caretaker.'

Hackney was a dead end too. 'Yes, squire, we've got records,' boomed the voice down the phone. 'When? 1900? No . . . Only back to 1922.'

The City of London was better. 'Well, you can't read them

really before about 1880, the handwriting is so bad. Well, different anyway. Yes, we take in bits of the East End.'

They have a pleasant records office. Well, there's money in the City, it adjoins the Guildhall. It is a strange part of London. There are still those narrow streets tucked in behind the skyscrapers, forgotten alleyways.

Two women were copying from old ledgers into the new ledger. Some academic was reading parish records. Occasionally his head jerked; perhaps he had got up too early. I asked for files from 1901. They came in two separate sections, the verdicts and the depositions. I ignored the depositions and began working through the verdicts. I had started at eleven, and by three was up to 1905. It was depressing reading, more so than the papers at the British Museum. There, at least, there was life, people arguing, going to the Music Hall, being born. In that office, it was the time machine once more, but it took me to the ends of lives, the closing hours of warehousemen on their way to deaths in the River Thames, a youth depressed after becoming lame who took his life and was found floating off Swan Pier by a lighterman. Where was that? I wondered. Buried under some highrise car park?

There were few murders. Presumably the reports would be sent on as evidence to higher courts, if the culprits were discovered. Some macabre inquests on murderers duly hanged after trial. A couple of women hanged for murder of a child, but no man with a beard, or not my man. There were even a few photographs of the corpses of people washed from the Thames; unknown faces made brutish by poverty, and hideously distorted by the water. By four, a depression, born of the hopelessness of the search and compounded by the succession of drownings, shootings, poisonings and infanticides, drove me off for a coffee.

I was back twenty minutes later. By quarter to five I had just disposed of a 1907 murder of an overweight Italian organ grinder, stabbed to death by some youths dressed in the style of costermongers. I settled into 1908.

My technique was becoming sophisticated. I could get through three suicides, an accidental drowning, a fire in

Queen Victoria Street, and a bridge building disaster in as many minutes. Then, at five to five, I paused and pulled out the fading blue document.

'A Man Unknown, wilful murder against some person or persons unknown,' it said.

'Before Frederick Joseph Waldo Esquire, coroner of our lord the King . . . on view of the body of a — ' at that point the official type was replaced by the handwriting — 'A Man Unknown . . . as to his death those jurors whose names are hereafter subscribed upon their oaths and affirmations do say that on the 18th day of October in the year aforesaid in the Parish and the city aforesaid' —

My eyes raced down the document.

'And the jurors do further say that the man was feloniously, wilfully and of malice aforethought killed and murdered against the peace of our sovereign lord the King, his crown and dignity, by some person or persons unknown.'

I didn't have the depositions. Just the verdict. I asked the woman by the door for the documentation.

She smiled. 'It's too late, we're closing. You'll have to come back,' she said.

14.

'There is a spot on the wisdom tooth,' said Mrs Walter. 'That's why you feel the pain.'

I had thought about it all night. That and the inquest report. My teeth usually hurt in preparation for a visit to the dentist. It was mid-morning, and the cotton wool in my mouth made me want to throw up.

She smiled. She was blonde with a unplaceable accent. I was impressed by her as a dentist; she was straightforward.

'You could come back or I could take it out now.'

'I don't like novocaine.' A hatred of needles will ensure I never become a junkie.

'Well, you'll have to have it out. Now or later, and you can't get it out unless . . .'

I wanted to get back to the records office. I didn't want to dread a return visit to her. 'Take it out now,' I said.

She put two shots of novocaine into my jaw. She plunged something else in and then waved it at me. It was a thin needle, a spike really. 'There, I put that all the way into your jaw and you felt nothing, did you?'

'Nothing, amazing.'

I closed my eyes. I heard her searching in one of her trays. A huge piece of metal was thrust into my mouth. Tears streamed down my face, I stiffened, felt the sweat breaking on my brow.

'Feloniously, wilfully and of malice aforethought . . .' There was a ripping noise as if a tree was being torn out of rock. And I could feel it as well as hear it. I choked.

'It's over,' she said. 'Look, keep it, it is a wonderful tooth, a truly wonderful tooth. You should wear it for luck.'

It was, too. A square top with a root composed of long fronds of bone pointing like fingers, with the remains of my gum and blood still adhering to it. It looked quite disgusting.

By the time I arrived at the Guildhall, I had a foul taste in my mouth, and the cocaine was beginning to wear off. I surreptitiously spat into the gutter, and glanced at the accumulated globule of saliva and blood as it drifted with the rain water into the drain.

The academic was still there. He seemed more awake than the day before. I sat at the table, half-reading the paper and waiting for the file, for the depositions. Each one was numbered to correspond with the verdicts. I sat with them spread out before me. There hadn't been many murders, just the organ grinder, the occasional dead child. It had to be the one . . .

There were three depositions. A house surgeon from Barts, a policeman, and a man called Loskonoff. Each was hand-written, in a clear hand. They looked almost contemporary.

'I am James Laing, and I am a detective sergeant in G Division,' I read. Laing had found the body in the Thames at Old Swan Pier, wherever that was. It had been bobbing against the shore, and he had dragged it on to the beach. The victim hadn't died of immersion in the Thames, and had stones in his pockets. The body had been taken to the station and later examined by a surgeon, Hervey John Gavain.

'The man died,' Gavain had explained to the twelve honest men, 'in consequence of a wound originating behind the neck, of a haemorrhage due to the severance of the vessels of the neck, inflicted by a weapon at the hands of some person or persons unknown. The posterior avicular artery was severed. In my opinion that wound might have been produced by some instrument such as a slightly curved knife or bayonet. It may have been caused by some person just behind the deceased or to the left of him holding a weapon in the right hand; a stab in fact.'

A gruesome, but predictable statement. But Loskonoff's wasn't. He had a bookshop near Houndsditch. He had been to see the police after a fight outside the shop. 'Deposition of Nathan Loskonoff through an interpreter.'

'I am the proprietor of a bookshop in what is called Frying Pan Alley. On the 10th day of October at about seven in the evening I was visited by a man who said he had recently come from Russia. He told me that there he had been involved in socialist activity, that he left that country because he feared for his life as a result of the recent upheavals in that country. He was a member of a social-democrat organisation. He had no money, he told me, and said that he had been wandering the streets. He was scared. He said that he had been in a fight the day before and had nowhere to sleep. I told him that he might stay with me for one night. He said that he had met a man in the Whitechapel Road who had taken him to a club in Jubilee Street. This is a club much used by people from our country and from Poland. It is run by a German. It is true that many people who go there are of an anarchist or socialist persuasion, but it is a peaceful club. No drinks are served there. There are readings, discussions . . .'

By the sound of it, Loskonoff had encountered difficulties with whoever had taken his statement. Much of it was taken up with a rambling defence of the club.

'. . . He told me that he had met a man there who told him that I would be able to put him in touch with someone who could offer him work. This was true. I know a man called Seeler, who is the proprietor of a small workshop that makes clothes. It is near my shop, in Goulston Street. I told him to go there. I gave him a note of introduction. It was dark, I saw him to the door and pointed out the way that he should proceed. Then I went back into the shop. I heard a shout and ran out of the shop. The man was at the end of the street. I did not know his name, we sometimes do not say these things. The man was struggling with other men, there were two or maybe three. I ran down the road. Then I tripped. Someone had tripped me. I was hit on the head. When I woke up the men had all gone. My daughter found me. She is nine years of age. I was lying on the pavement. She was very upset. She said the man had been taken, she said she saw a knife in one of the men's hands. She had a doll in her hand that the man had given her. It was a Russian doll. Later that evening I told the police. They took a statement. Then later Mr Laing came to see me. He asked me to see this body. I think that this is the same man. The water makes it difficult.'

I turned over the page. There was the list of questions the coroner had asked the jury. Murder, they had said. Then on the next page was a photograph, to complete the set, the last picture of the man, with the medical details scrawled on one side like some post card from a friend in Hell. Presumably he had been in the water for a week when Laing had dragged him out, and the Thames had worked on him, but he was still quite recognisable. The blood had been washed away.

The ache in my gum was developing into a stabbing pain. I could taste the blood. I closed the books and stumbled out into the grey light. It was strange, I thought, almost the same time of the year. I walked out of the City. Where was Frying Pan Alley? Do what Loskonoff had done, I thought, ask a policeman.

There was little of it left, just a street with a car park, no bookshop, no Loskonoff. I felt half mad. I passed down Goulston Street, turned left at Aldgate, and walked down the Whitechapel Road. Jubilee Street was much further down, an old woman told me, between Whitechapel and Commercial Road. There was an old block of houses left, but much of the street was council houses, 1950s highrises. There were no clubs, no Russian emigrés. It was getting dark. I was lonely, and scared, as if murderers from three quarters of a century before could return to those streets.

I decided to ring Moira. I hadn't seen her since that night. The phone rang on, there was no answer. I had to get out of the East End. I climbed on a two five three bus, hardly knowing where it was going. I watched winter night-time London glittering in the rain from a top-deck window. I had found my man, and his unknown murderers.

I got off at Stamford Hill, and went into a pub. Perhaps it was the sense that I had reached the end of my trail, plus the tooth, and the chill of the old death, that depressed me. The bar was deserted apart from the landlord polishing glasses. I drank a half of Guinness and stared at the woodwork. I was near Stoke Newington, I suddenly realised. Ferret could share my discovery, if he was in.

He was. 'We're out,' he said almost as soon as he opened the door. 'Could be for weeks. We bloody walked into it, too. I think the gaffer wants us all off the job. Well, he won't bloody get us. Cup of tea?'

I told him while I dug tea bags from his inadequate larder. His mind had long since moved on from my obsessions, but his interest flickered when I told him that the dead man was a socialist, and a Russian as well.

He put the cups down. 'You should join Scotland Yard, Raven. Or do some bloody work getting Gold out of nick. You know the defence committee is meeting this week?'

I didn't. That side of the affair seemed less important than the dead Russian. Yet Gold was sitting in Brixton Prison.

I skated around the subject, agreed to go to the meeting, fidgeted.

'Do you know somebody called Hazel Brill?' I asked.

He looked up from his tea. 'Yeah, I know Hazel. Daft bugger. Why?'

'That social of yours last Saturday.'

'Aye, it was great. Met this girl called Alma, from Chile she is . . .'

'Yeah, I'm really pleased. I hope you'll be very happy. Now I met this woman called Diana Passingham, and she told me that Hazel Brill did interviews with some old socialists. They might have been in *Spare Rib*. I haven't looked it up.'

'Aye, she did. I read one.'

'Well, why didn't you tell me?'

'You never bloody asked, did you?'

'I asked if you knew anyone . . .'

'Well, I bloody don't. But I know Hazel Brill. She asked this old woman she was interviewing all these fatuous questions about consciousness raising. As if they had time to sit round and raise their consciousnesses!' Ferret was appalled at the very idea. 'They had about three ha'pence between them, those people. What fighting they did was against the bosses . . .'

'Yeah, yeah. Well, where is Hazel Brill?'

'What does it matter?'

I sighed. 'I'm not sure. She might be able to tell me something, put me in touch with some of them. Perhaps they would remember. I'd just like to see if I can follow the thing through.'

'You're flogging a dead number, Raven. You really are. Let's go and have . . .'

'Oh Christ, Ferret. We don't keep out for more than half a bloody hour.'

'Cool it, cool it, man. I'll ring Ms Brill on the way, honest.'

I bought the drinks while he made the call. He came in looking perplexed. 'I really don't know what's up with the world these days. I never thought she was great shakes when she was in the organisation, always going on about feminism and all, but really. You know what? The stupid bitch has gone off politics now, she says. She's into the Bhagwan, whatever that is.'

'What did she say?'

'She told me that half the people she interviewed have died off since. There was an old bloke called Arthey who knew Hyndman apparently, and he's kicked it, and Mannie Kovacs who was big in the Party in the 1930s and started before the First War apparently. I met him once, marvellous old man, even if he was a Stalinist. She didn't use those in *Spare Rib* but she did ones with about four others, women, I think. I saw about three of them myself, not that I remember the names . . .'

'All you've done is give me a list of corpses. What about the women?'

'Two of them are dead. The other two are Enid Pye and an old girl called Sally Mellon. I read the one about Enid Pye but not the other, but I remembered her name when she mentioned it. Hazel said that she lives on an estate in Islington now. I knew her when she was living up in Holloway, we were in this tenants' campaign, wonderful old girl.'

I swilled the beer around my mouth, attempting to anaesthetise my gum. 'It's a bit hopeless really, isn't it? She probably wasn't alive in 1908.'

The Scotsman picked at his left ear. 'I'm not sure about that, she was getting on when I last met her. I reckon she was around, but probably only a wee kid. What do you want, Raven? An interview with Bakunin? Or how about Lenin? Time passes, people get old.'

I sighed. I wasn't sure what I wanted, maybe just a chance to meet someone from that long ago who wasn't sitting on a cloud following a float in the Thames.

'What about this Mrs Mellon? Did Hazel give you an address?'

'She's no Mrs. She's got principles. They were brought up opposed to marriage. She lived in a free union. Wonderful old people, there's nothing we can teach those folk, they did it all seventy years ago. Of course she's still an old anarchist, never forgave Lenin from what Hazel Brill said. She sounded a great old sort. I told Hazel it was to do with a book you're writing, about the period. She said she would give her a ring and I was to call back.'

After three drinks, Ferret got round to making the call. He came back frowning. 'That woman gets more crazy every day. She says that knowing Sally Mellon made her realise that we've all been barking up the wrong tree for the last five hundred years. If people like Sally couldn't get it right, then we never will, so we might as well pack it in. Search for your soul from within, Jesus!'

Despite his tirade, he had managed to get Hazel Brill to arrange a meeting with Sally Mellon. He had even decided to take time off the picket line to come down with me the following afternoon.

It was a cold clear day in the City Road. The highrises are clustered on the right, a triumph for the politics that Sally Mellon had presumably spent her life fighting. Tall blocks built by Labour reformers in the 1950s under the eye of a Conservative government basking in the warmth of the post-war boom.

There were a scattering of Arsenal slogans, the occasional NF daub and ageing SWP replies.

A group of flats were set aside for old people at the base of the tower. An old man peered out at us from behind a lace curtain. His eyes only half-registered us. Like us he was looking into the past as he stared at the traffic of the City Road.

'Number Five Rohan Towers,' announced Ferret. 'This is it.'

Appropriately it was a glossy red door with a brass knocker, which showed no sign of having been polished since its installation. I raised it. The thud against the void echoed down the passage-way. Two small boys on bicycles stopped to look at us. An old woman opened her door two flats down.

'You looking for Mrs Mellon?'

'Yes,' I said. 'She lives here?'

'Oh yes. Of course she might be away, she goes up to Liverpool quite often.'

The advice on Sally Mellon's whereabouts would clearly have gone on for some time had not the occupant of number five opened the door. She gazed at us and then poked her head round the door at our informant.

'I am *not* Mrs Mellon,' she shouted. 'I am Sally Mellon. Not Mrs Mellon, how often do I have to tell you, Lisa?'

Lisa looked hurt and shrugged her shoulders. 'Well, you suit yourself. I was only trying to help.' She went back inside. The door slammed.

Sally Mellon had a wide face with a broad nose and blue eyes. It was an old face but her eyes were bright. She wore a grey jumper and a pair of shapeless fawn trousers. Her hair was silver and cascaded down her back, as if she had brushed it after taking it out of an Edwardian coiffure following some exciting night on the town. She fixed her young blue eyes on me. 'That woman is stupid, and always has been stupid I would say. Nothing ever happens, no matter how stupid, and she is poking her head round the door.' Her accent had traces of Eastern Europe in it, overladen by East End Jewish and cockney. 'You are Mr Ferret?'

'No, I'm John Raven. This is uh . . . Mr Ferret.'

'Hazel told me you were coming.' She ushered us into her living room. The sun shone across the table. There were some flowers in a bowl and a shiny apple. She motioned us to a sofa in a corner.

'Tea? Would you like some tea?' She leaned against the table. A budgerigar twittered in a cage by the window, and a pendulum clock ticked to provide the bird with a backing.

'Well, I don't want to cause any . . .'

She coughed. 'If I did not want to make any tea I would not have asked.'

Ferret coughed back. 'Well, that's very nice. Yes we'd like a cup of tea.'

She went into the kitchen. Ferret clasped his hands together and cast his eyes around the room. 'You're always apologising, John,' he muttered out of the corner of his mouth. 'The chronic English liberal disease.'

There were a lot of books. Politics mainly, a vast selection of the battlegrounds of the century. Dirty, yellowing orange Penguins in neat rows; Emma Goldman, John Read's *Ten Days That Shook The World.*

A heap of magazines littered the top of the television. Anarchist papers, a *Labour Weekly*, a *Socialist Worker* and some *Spare Rib*s. She kept in touch, did Sally Mellon.

She returned with a tray. 'Stupid woman. I went to Liverpool three months ago and she thinks I spend my life in the place. She has nothing to do, nothing to think . . .'

She rested the tray on the table. Three mugs, a pint bottle

of milk and some biscuits. There were no concessions to china tea sets. 'You take sugar?'

We didn't.

'Very wise. Everyone takes too much sugar. They lived on it all the time. They still do. Sugar and grease, that is what the English live on, that is why they are so dull.'

She spoke as if she had recently arrived in the country. 'Have some biscuits.' She pointed at five ginger nuts and some little Jewish pastries.

She settled in an upright chair and rested her hands in her lap. She was out of breath. It was the first sign, apart from the venom of her opinions on her neighbour, that she wasn't unaffected by the years. 'So, Hazel tells me you are writing a book about anarchists, Mr Ferret. Why are you doing that?'

Ferret dipped his biscuit into the tea. 'I'm not, Mrs uh . . . Miss Mus Mellon. John here is, and it isn't what he's writing about that we've come about.'

We had deliberated about what to do before arrival. In the event of Sally Mellon being fragile, the prospect of brandishing pictures of half-decapitated Edwardians at her had struck us as a bad idea, but she wasn't fragile.

I told her that I had bought some pictures, and I wanted to know if they meant anything to her. I didn't tell her about the picture in the silver frame, or about the inquest.

'Have you brought them with you?' She asked.

I pulled them out of the envelope. It was becoming frayed after its travels around London. I gave them to her, but hung on to the photograph of my corpse.

She crossed the room, pulled out a spectacle case and balanced a pair of half-moon spectacles on the tip of her nose. She flipped through them and then looked across to me.

'I am not a big game hunter, Mr Raven.'

'John Raven. No, but if you keep going, then you'll see some pictures that were taken before the First World War.'

She laughed. 'How old do you think I am? That is a long time ago, I was a little child, only thirteen when the war started, and I hardly spoke English. You know where I was born?'

I reddened. I knew very little about Sally Mellon, and I suspected that she had seen us as part of her world. Ferret's political credentials may have been dubious but mine were even worse. I knew next to nothing about her.

'I was born in Russia. I was a babe in arms when my parents came to this place, to London. I may be very ancient, but I am not that ancient, Mr Eden, and I was watching what went on in my street, not what happens in photographs. Are these pictures about politics? I was political when I was a child because my father, and my mother, they were political. But at that age I was not the most political person. Not like I was later.'

She shuffled through the stack. I walked across and looked over her shoulder. She was looking at the picture taken opposite the Whitechapel Gallery.

The budgerigar sang louder. The shouts of some children ehoed through the room. Ferret took another biscuit and went back to the sofa.

'Does it . . . does it mean anything to you?' I asked.

She shrugged. 'As I said, it is long ago, an old picture of people at a meeting. Well what is it?'

I pointed out the Whitechapel. She laughed. 'You forget these things, maybe my eyes. Yes, I know that place. But as for the meeting, who knows?'

I tried a long shot. 'Have you ever heard of someone called Paradise?

It went out of court. She hadn't.

I thought back to the book, to Paradise's book.

'Or something called the British Brothers League?'

She bounced it straight back. 'Pigs,' she said.

I was faintly surprised by her vehemence. 'Pigs?'

'Yes, pigs they were. The first of many poisonous organisations in this century, in that place.' She waved her hand at the window. I guessed she was talking about the East End. 'Racists, fascists, call them what you like. England got off to an early start. I heard about them, my father even warned me, but they were fading after 1906. It was just like now. They grew up, cheap little street corner thugs, then government gave into them and passed an immigration act in 1906. They were not so strong. They didn't like us, they didn't like Jews.'

She sat down, the picture of the meeting still gripped in her fingers. 'We used to fight even then, you know – well, not me – a little girl, but my father, and the older ones. Mind you, my father used to tell me that the Jews fought amongst themselves as much as anyone.' She laughed. 'The anarchists, they fought the socialists – they were a dry lot – all they could do was sit round and talk, they organised nothing, and there were Jewish anarchists and Jewish socialists and Polish Jews and Russian Jews, and orthodox Jews and atheists and Zionists, the lot. There was one time, about 1900 I think it was, when it was the sacred day for the Jews, the Day of Atonement, and the arguments between the atheists and the orthodox Jews had been really bad. So when they were coming out of the Synagogue, it was in Brick Lane on that awesome day, all the Elders saw this group of young Jews – atheists all – marching up the road. And you know what they had?'

I didn't.

She was shaking with laughter. 'They all marched up the road with a ham sandwich in one hand and a cigarette in the other.'

'What happened?' asked Ferret. I had almost forgotten he was there.

'The Elders picked up clubs and staves and battered the atheists off the streets. It took them years to recover.' She crossed to the table and poured out more tea.

'But it was difficult in those days,' she continued. 'Many of the immigrants could speak no English, like it is now with the Asians. Many of them didn't even know why they were being attacked, apart from having come from the stink of the pogroms and the Black Hundreds . . .'

'Who were they?'

'Nikol'ski and his mob. The Union of Russian Peoples they called themselves, that and other things. They were Russian fascists, they followed the revolution of 1905 as it died like jackals, and in this country there were the British Brothers! Cheap little imitators. But some people were fighting back even then. My father fought. There was a boy I used to play with, Manny Kovacs, he only died about five years ago. He was about five years older than me. He went into the Communist Party – the stupid man – in the 1930s. He was as brave as a lion. I remember him being chased by those people – or people like them – there were about twenty of them, after he had thrown this big piece of earth at one of their meetings in the street. Could he run . . .' She smiled at the memory.

I stood by the window, thought of her memories, and my pictures. 'Do you remember any of the names of these British Brothers?'

She rubbed her chin. 'There were a lot of them. An MP started it you know, some military man.' Her voice trailed away.

I thought back to the book. It was Ferret who remembered. 'Major Evans-Gordon.'

She was surprised. 'Yes, that's it. A name I haven't heard in many years. Not a name I wanted to remember.'

It was interesting, but it wasn't getting me anywhere. I pulled out the photograph I hadn't shown her. 'I have this other picture, Miss Mellon. It isn't nice. It was taken in those days, I believe.'

She took it and winced, but it meant nothing, if I was to judge by her expression. 'What is this?'

I showed her the patriarch in the open air meeting, and in the hall, and in the family group. 'Very nasty,' she said briskly. 'So is it the same man?'

'I think so.' I told her about my days in the reading room, and my days at the records office. I told her about Mr Waldo the coroner, and Mr Gavain the surgeon, and Mr Loskonoff and Detective Sergeant Laing.

What was left of the sun was shining in on her face, that was blank, impassive. 'I know Loskonoff,' she said. 'I know him.'

'You know him? Who was he?'

She smiled. 'My father.'

15.

'I changed my name,' she said. 'It was in the twenties. I thought it old fashioned. Someone said I looked like a melon, so I said I would call myself that as a joke. I couldn't spell very well, which is bad since my father sold books, or did until he died. He was a social-revolutionary, a great bomb thrower in his day, but that was back in the 1880s. He denounced Lenin and his crowd almost before he had got off at the Finland Station. My father was a *Narodnaya Volya* man – the People's Will. They caught him in a library one day after a bombing.' She laughed. 'He had always been very conscious of security, he was famous in the organisation, but that day he was writing a letter to some girl, and he dropped some pamphlets. They caught him and sent him to Siberia. Everyone thought he was dead, but he wasn't. He escaped, lived underground in St Petersburg, lived with this woman . . . my mother . . .'

'The girl he was writing to?' I asked.

She smiled. 'No, a different one. He said the other one was no good, she had been a mistake. Anyway, that is not what you want to know. When was this trial, this inquest?'

'October the 18th, 1908.'

She paused, and looked again at the dead man. 'I remember something. It is so long ago. There was this evening that I ran out into the street after my father, because I was scared for him. He would get into fights sometimes, more than once I had helped him home.' She screwed up her face.

'Do you remember the visitor?'

'It's too long ago.'

I racked my brains for a hook, a memory.

'*My daughter found me. She is nine years of age. I was lying on the pavement. She was very upset. She said the man had been taken, she said she saw a knife in one of the men's hands. She had a doll in her hand the man had given her. It was a Russian doll . . .*'

'Did the man who came to see your father – did he give you a doll?'

She stared at me. 'A doll?' Her face cleared. 'Yes, he gave me a doll. He spoke to me in Russian. I did not understand him very well. I was supposed to speak Yiddish, and Russian, but I didn't speak them well. English was taking over. Of course! It was much later, when he was dying – my father – he spoke about it one night they were taking him to the hospital, it was after the war. He was very old. He told me about that night. I think you block it from your head because it was unpleasant, so unpleasant. I don't remember anything of it except my father lying in the street. But that evening when he was going he said to me "It was the Okhrana", and I said "What was?" and he said "That night when that man came, it was the Okhrana".' She stopped again.

'What was the Okhrana?'

Ferret rushed in to cover my ignorance. I think he was dismayed that my cover as a researcher was being blown. 'The secret police, the Tsarist police.'

She didn't notice, or hear. She was lost at her father's death-bed. 'He said who the man was too, he was a Social Democrat, "not a bad one by all accounts," he said. He despised them really. He told me his name, said a woman had come by, about 1918 it was.' She stopped again.

'Do you remember the name?'

She rubbed her chin, and pushed the hair back from her forehead, like she must have done when a child in Frying Pan Alley. 'Anstein? No that wasn't it . . . It's a common name, a common Jewish name . . .'

'Goldberg? Bloom?' My mind raced through a limited list of Jewish patronyms.

She laughed. 'No that wasn't it. Abrahamson? No! Abramovitch. Piotr Abramovitch. that was it.'

So now he had a name, my dead man, and it meant nothing to me at all. She handed me the photograph. 'So he is called Abramovitch,' I said.

'It was all so long ago,' she said. 'How many faces do you remember from your childhood? How many people have died and been murdered and thrown in trenches and rivers since then?'

We didn't leave until after five. She talked about the 1920s and 1930s. She had a curious and rare ability to remain enthusiastic and dedicated without sinking into that slough of sectarianism which Odgers and his multitude of look-alikes had so joyfully entered on the day they were born.

The sun had long gone. A light drizzle blew down the City Road. It was dark. The Angel was crowded with people going home. We walked down Upper Street.

'A wonderful woman,' said Ferret in a voice which he kept for major historical events and potential new recruits. He had tried to monopolise the conversation after the identification of the corpse. As a concession to age – but quite probably out of a sense of self preservation – he had avoided extolling the virtues of the Leninist party to the old anarchist, and they had warmed to each other.

We stood at the bus shelter. 'Vote NF and make Britain normal again' suggested the graffiti. The queue huddled under the concrete and corrugated iron. Cars splashed mud across the edge of the pavement.

'Well, there you are, John. Case solved,' he said. 'Now you know who your victim is, and who knocked him off. The Tsar and that nasty old man. In the end the Almighty got 'em both.'

I was irritated. 'Is that all you can say?'

'What d'you want me to say? It was very interesting. She was a wonderful old woman, and I can tell you what you've got to do right now.' He prodded me.

'What?'

'Do something about poor old Gold. He's the one that needs the assistance now. Help get him out of nick. The meeting is tomorrow night. You said you'd come.'

'It isn't as simple as that.'

He asked me why not. A shot of the romantic past after a suitable five minute pause only spurred Ferret to fresh endeavours in the present. A commendable attitude, I supposed. I pointed out that even if Ferret had lost interest, others hadn't. The photograph was still in demand. He looked bored. I suddenly thought that maybe now I was evens with Fuller. A bus splashed towards us, and the queue began to shuffle forward, jostling for sneaky advantage. I reached into my pocket. I had a fivepence piece.

'I've got to make a call.'

'Oh, for Christ's sake, man. This will be the only bus for the next two hours. I'm not waiting around.'

'Where are you going?'

'Down the Norfolk.'

'Well, I might see you there.'

I thought that maybe they would have gone home, but the bright voice answered soon enough. 'Wakely Investments.'

'I wonder if I could speak to Mr Fuller.'

'I'm afraid not, sir.' She made it sound like she was telling me to have a good day.

'He's gone home, has he?'

'Who is that, please?'

'My name is Butcher.' It was getting stupid. I thought I would have to change my pseudonyms or they might begin to add up two and two. 'I rang the other day.'

'Oh yes, Mr Butcher. No, Mr Fuller hasn't gone home. He has gone to Wales again. Sorry. Do you want to leave a message?'

'Sirius, Rhydd-ddu, eh?'

She was suitably impressed. 'Quite possibly, sir. You don't want to leave a message?'

I didn't. I went home instead. Fuller was keen on his Welsh hideaway, I thought. Maybe Ferret was right, just let it rest. See what happened with Gold, perhaps it would all fit together. Meanwhile I resolved to leave Ferret with his pub and his comrades.

It was raining with renewed intensity as I walked down Highbury Hill. I felt for the file, which was stuffed inside my coat. It was too wet even for Anorak, I thought.

I was wrong, or maybe the rain had been light in Highbury until I arrived. The house was in darkness. What was left of my room's decor had been further re-arranged, with the mattress now propping up the wall. There was an envelope on the table. I opened it.

It was a sheet of paper. The words had been arranged from cut-outs from the papers. It looked like an early Sex-Pistols ad with an excessively wordy copy writer.

'You stupid bastard,' it said. How true, I thought.

'The cops will dislike you a lot soon, because you cause too much bother, but you will not be seeing them. We dislike you already and next time we'll be around when you're in. Post the file to Mrs Astin and make life a bit easier for yourself. Your room stinks of piss,' it concluded.

They were right. They had urinated on the mattress. The arrangement of the letter and state of the room gave a faintly surrealistic air to what hadn't been much of a flat, but better than nothing. I felt sick. The door swung open. I started, and immediately felt ashamed. I was fine as long as my victims and my enemies were well buried, well in the past. I wasn't too good with a couple of cheap little hoods from down the road.

There was no one there. They had just removed the lock and the door was swinging in the draught. It was a badly insulated house, I thought idly.

I tugged the mattress to the window. I didn't make a serious attempt to clear the room. I felt sick and afraid. But I was angry. I was furious. Furious with them, furious with my fear. I wasn't sure what I was going to do then, but I had an idea. I sorted through the rubbish and packed a small hold-all. It was back to Ferret's that night but, I thought, just for one evening.

He was in the pub, discussing the strike. Odgers for once wasn't there. I didn't know the other three, they were clearly from the site. They weren't very happy, but then neither was I. After an hour in which I read the paper and they discussed their work problems, I got a word in. Drink had boosted my resolve.

'Got any mates in Wales, Ferret?'

'Wales?' If he had an inkling, he sidestepped it. 'We're trying to get a branch going in Swansea. I've never been up there but there's a bloke called Mike Rose.'

'How about further up?'

'There was some girl around Milford Haven. She bought a paper once and filled in the form asking for further information. I dunno how she got it in Milford Haven, anyway. Perhaps Rose travels the valleys, hawking the paper.'

He would probably have given me background on all the group's paper sellers had I given him the chance. An amiable man with a beard put down his glass. He was one of the people Ferret had been talking to. 'Whereabouts in North Wales?' he asked.

'Around a place called Rhydd-ddu.'

'I know someone,' he said.

'Keep away from this punter, Bry. This is my mate, John. He's well on the way to being a head case if he's thinking what I think he is,' Ferret muttered.

'I'm looking for somewhere to stay up there.'

'There's a guy I used to know in Manchester,' Bry said. 'He teaches, I think. Name of Cutler, Caradoc Cutler. He lives in a place called Nantlle. I went up there once. Lovely country, I think there was a place called Rhydd-ddu near there.'

'Yeah, so do I.' I asked him if he wanted a drink.

Ferret waved his empty glass at me. 'Watch out, Bry.'

'Oh shut up, Ferret.' I told him about my room.

He was not greatly moved. The saga of lodgings was becoming a part, albeit changing, of the scenery. I bought the drinks.

'Thanks, mate.' The froth settled on Bry's beard, and gradually began to sink into it. 'Do you want to go up there or something?'

The drink, and Ferret's derision, finally got to me. 'Yes, I do. I need somewhere to sleep. I won't be any bother.' I glared at Ferret. 'I'm getting jaded with Ferret's camp-bed.'

'When?'

'Tomorrow night, maybe the night after.'

The Scotsman exploded. 'For what possible reason d'you want to go up there, Raven? We've got the meeting, we've got things to organise, and all you want to do is hare round the country!'

I ignored him. 'Any chance?'

Bry shrugged. 'Well, I could give him a ring. Since you're a mate of Ferret here.'

'No pal of mine,' muttered Ferret.

'I'd be grateful. I thought I would get a coach up. I think

you can go up to Bangor, and I could probably get down from there, or Caernarfon.'

Bry disappeared to the phone.

'John, what the hell has got into you?' asked Ferret.

'Drink, probably. Like you.' But there was more to it. *I am obsessed*, I thought. The drizzle, the turned-over room, the darkness stretching back to the man with the severed windpipe stared out at me from some dirty pit seventy years ago. The country stank of corruption, of an old festering Empire that soured as the years went by and the boys came home from the bivouacs under trees in strange hot places. And that curious family, deaths long ago, dead fascists, a live property shark mouthing obscenity to the flotsam after the ship had gone down. I wanted to meet Fuller, tell him I knew, tell him we all knew. Make a scene. He wouldn't dare, specially after I'd had five pints.

'That guy's home ground would be a semi-detached bunker in Bavaria from what you've been saying about him,' said Ferret. 'It's your phony heroics.'

I thought of Astin and his miserable wife, soaked in bad sherry. She must have been reintegrated into the family. I would walk in, flourish the picture; here's what you want, you bastard . . .

'I just want to follow it through, Ferret. I just want to see what it's about for once. I want to *know*. We never know anything, not even you with all your revolution. You are so busy trying to recruit an army you never get near the trenches.'

'Don't make me laugh. It's what I said it is. Phony drunken heroics. If you think that taking a wee holiday in glorious Snowdonia is going to get Gold out of nick, you're mistaken. If you're very lucky, you might get shoved off a cliff.'

Bry returned. 'He's still there all right. Got married, too. He said you can get the coach through to Caernarfon and then give him a ring. Said it was about time he met someone from the Smoke. Find out what the comrades are doing . . .'

'Oh, aye,' interrupted Ferret. 'Old John here knows just what the comrades are doing. Holding meetings while he fucks off to Wales on his winter holidays.'

We abandoned the topic. The evening ended. The following morning Ferret was still denouncing the idea. The following morning I agreed with him. It was ridiculous. I would go back to Highbury, get the door mended. Give it up, I was broke anyway . . .

I was sick with myself as I went into the front door. There was a brown envelope for me. I tore it open. For once it wasn't abusive. There was a cheque for £150 in it, payment from some German guide for work I'd done six months before and given up on. It was a sign, I thought.

Cashing it at the bank was the difficult trick. I paused on the way out, and went to the enquiry desk. It was a financial matter, I said, I was going away. If I couldn't get back within a week, could they post a letter for me? Oddly, they agreed. Perhaps they were impressed that I passed £150 through their system. I addressed it to Ferret, and summarised the situation. 'Do something with it, Ferret,' I signed off.

I caught the Victoria Line to the coach station. The bus was out of London in an hour. The day was sunny. I could still taste the beer from the night before, but it had lost its cheering qualities. I felt foolish, but relieved to be out of the city. I wasn't sure how I would be returning, or when.

Do something with it, Ferret, I thought, and then caught myself. *Don't be such a melodramatic bastard* . . .

16.

The coach route to North Wales is a dreary journey. It goes through the arteries of industrial Britain, not the real industry but the junkyards, the open spaces of industrial estates, the cheap cafes. The travellers were poor. People returning from unsuccessful encounters with the big city, North Wales seaside landladies back from a holiday with their London relatives, students returning to the isolation of Bangor, itinerant workers departing into the gloom of Birmingham from the oily darkness of the coach station. I drifted into sleep as the coach ambled desultorily from motorway to A road to B road and across the border.

Astin's face loomed in front of me. 'You stole the pictures,' he said precisely. 'It is causing bother, we can't embark unless the pictures are returned. It is very irregular.'

Behind him a boat was moored. The location appeared to be Camden Town, but it was very hot, very bright. The boat was white, bleached. Dead animals . . . there were dead animals around Astin. He picked his way carefully between them. He reached out his hand.

Fuller was behind him. 'We are businessmen,' he announced briskly. 'What incentives are there for us? You tell me that. I blame the blacks, the blacks and you.' He gestured behind him. Black porters were unloading animals on to the boat. There was an untidy heap of carcasses by the table where two children were playing. They tossed a ball to each other. It wasn't a ball, but a head, a bearded head. Blood dripped on to the deck.

I was on the boat. It lurched as my feet slid through the grease. I looked down. The grease was brown-red; the boat was covered in blood.

The boat swung into the stream. There was a row of semi-detached houses on the opposite bank, with palm trees in their gardens . . .

'Conway,' said the driver over the intercom. The woman next to me had stood up and was reaching for her case. I helped her. She thanked me and adjusted her hat. It was a 1950s hat, the type that the Queen Mother specialised in.

The castle at Conway was magnificent but bleak. The coach drove past rows of council houses. North Wales is an area without real wealth. The houses are those of a poor middle class and a working class whose votes have returned a succession of dull Labour councils, who have repaid them with Spartan dwellings set in a grey landscape. In the background rose the mountains of North Wales. Nature is more interesting. Humanity there ignored it and concentrated on making modest sums of money. It was late afternoon. The sun came out as the day began to die and sent shafts of light out from behind the crags.

The sea remained grey. It rolled in on deserted beaches where in the summer the children of Manchester and Liverpool and Leeds would play. The seaside resorts were empty.

By seven we were in Caernarfon. It was a windswept square and deserted. A few people gathered by the bus stop to welcome the remaining passengers. I got out. It was cold but dry. The wind blew from the sea. I asked about buses but there were none, and rang Cutler.

'No, there aren't any now. I'll come over.'

It took half an hour for him to arrive in a neat blue Renault. I put my bag in the back. He was small, dark and taciturn. We said little. It was almost completely dark, but as we drove out of Caernarfon I could see the country becoming wilder, and it enveloped us. Slate quarries loomed on either side.

'They are derelict now,' he said, gesturing into the gloom. 'They were worth a fortune in the nineteenth century. Now it's just a pile of slagheaps.' He asked me how Bry was, and I gave an evasive answer.

'How long are you staying?'

'A couple of days.'

'I didn't quite get why you came.' We were pulling into his village, Nantlle. The moon glinted off a lake down the valley. The village stood at the entrance to a range of mountains. Fuller is down there, I thought, down the valley. On one side of the road were a row of houses that could have been lifted from London. They were incongruous in the mountain setting. Cutler pulled up outside one of them.

'No, well I'll explain.' I thought about it. A story of a picture and my pursuit of a curious family, or just some flannel about my interest in nineteenth century labour history, in the middle of the mountains? I was uncertain.

'Have you eaten?'

'I had a sandwich on the bus.'

'We were just about to eat when you rang. You can have some.'

The house was warm and lined with books in the double room created from some nineteenth century artisan's domesticity.

Jean Cutler was tall, blonde and seemed out of place. She put down a copy of *Radical America* and greeted me with a smile. We shook hands.

I shifted from one foot to the other. 'I'm sorry to spring this on you,' I mumbled.

'No problem,' she said. 'Anyone is welcome. We hardly see a soul up here. You're doing some research?'

She didn't wait for an answer but followed her husband into the kitchen. She returned with a bowl of potatoes and some sausages. We ate and talked of Bry, which was extremely difficult for me, and the trivia of London politics, which was slightly easier.

'I miss it now.' She laughed. 'I couldn't stand it when I left, only too pleased to see the countryside, but now . . .' She glanced at her husband. He munched on obliviously. 'He goes off to Liverpool every day. All I see since I gave up teaching are the bloody sheep across the road.'

He glared at her. A well-worn argument about the limitations of rural existence was approaching. I sidestepped it. 'Did you hear anything about a bloke being killed in an accident down the valley?'

'The other week?' She looked at me. 'Some old man on a walking holiday? Yes, it was odd. People die on Snowdon, but not usually around Rhydd-ddu. The cliffs are high, but you need to take a pretty good run at them to go over the top. Death by misadventure, they said.'

Caradoc Cutler had said little during the meal. He perked up at the talk of the death. 'He came off the top of Carn,' he observed. 'Do you want an apple?'

I took one.

'Just outside Rhydd-ddu, well within sight of Rhydd-ddu,' he said between munches. 'Is that why you are here?'

'Not really. I knew him a bit, met him just before he came up here. It's just a bit surprising to meet somebody one day and find he's kicked it the next.'

'I saw a bloke die at a football match once. In London, Fulham versus Millwall. He was shouting his head off one minute, stretched out the next. Curious, I didn't really feel anything. That was the only surprise, the absence of any feeling.'

'Do you know where the old man was staying?' I asked.

'I think it was at the pub,' she replied. 'That tourist pub in Rhydd-ddu, the Cwellyn it's called. That's what the milkman said, anyway. He is about the only source of information around here.'

The absence of any feeling? Then why do I worry about a seventy year old corpse? I thought. *And why am I unconcerned about Gold, or less interested?*

'Have you heard of someone who's got a house or something around there? Someone called Fuller?'

Caradoc walked over to the window, pulled the curtains and sat on the sofa. 'Oddly enough I have. He's English or colonial or something. The bugger nearly ran me down last year in his Range Rover, just outside. He hit the lamp-post instead. Got out and apologised, flash bastard. He looked like an insurance salesman who had done well. Said that if any damage had been caused, he would make it up. I don't get down the valley much, but I mentioned it to a bloke in the pub, and he said that Fuller had owned this house – called Sirius – for years. It is a kind of English colony, near Llyn-y-Gadair – that's the lake near Rhydd-ddu – and it belonged to his father. I think he just stays there at weekends, but it's a bloody big house. It used to belong to some old landlord, another fucking Englishman. It's always been occupied by the fucking English.'

'I'm the fucking English,' said Jean Cutler. 'And so is he.' She gestured in my direction.

He laughed. 'All right, the idle rich. Which as far as round here is concerned means the same thing.'

He stretched his legs out on the sofa. 'Why are you so interested in Fuller? Why are you so worried about deceased mountain walkers?'

It was evasion time again. I had resolved to keep my obsession to myself. I told them that I had been doing some research, had got into a row with Astin and Fuller and wanted to clear it up, in between 'research' and a short mountain holiday. They weren't particularly concerned. People on short Welsh holidays were understandable enough. It was people coming to live there that worried them.

'Well,' observed Caradoc, 'I suppose it makes a change from London. I'd give you a lift tomorrow, only we've got to go into Liverpool. We were going to stay there tomorrow night.'

'That's fine,' I said. 'Maybe if it's cheap I might stay at the Cwellyn for a night before coming back.'

'If you get up really early we could probably give you a lift,' she said. I declined the offer. I decided to walk down the valley, get myself into the atmosphere, work out what the hell I was going to do. We went to bed.

I heard them leave as the light began to come through the window. They told me to eat a large breakfast, and I did.

It was a good day for a walk. The sun shone and there was a light wind, but the mountains looked cold, and high. Water was pouring off the rocks. It spilled on to the road. Few cars came by. Half way between Nantlle and Rhydd-ddu was a cluster of cottages, with some ruined stone barns behind them. I stopped and sat on the stone wall of one of them and looked up at the face of the cliff. Half way up, a fox sat and stared at me. It didn't look scared, but it looked despairing. Why didn't it run? I thought; perhaps it knows I can't follow it up the rocks. Then I noticed that its brush was stained with blood. Its flank, too. Someone had taken a shot at it, or maybe it, too, had taken a fall. But foxes don't fall. They should know the country. It moved behind a rock, only its brush protruding.

Ahead of me was Snowdon, its summit shrouded in mist. Up the road from the cottages the landscape grew wilder, with an outcrop of rock like some prehistoric lizard, frozen into stone, awaiting a shift in the earth to restore it to life. A deserted barn proclaimed, 'Free Wales Army', and someone had even gone to the trouble to paint 'Up the IRA' next to it.

The sun was going, it grew colder. I reached the summit at the end of the valley and looked back. The lake glimmered in the distance. Beyond, past the mountains, was the sea. Ahead, Snowdon had almost vanished behind a curtain of mist and rain. A few drops fell on me, I was walking into it. By the time I arrived in Rhydd-ddu, it was pouring down. It was midday. The Cwellyn Arms was open. I went in.

The bar was deserted. The barman was shifting crates. He sniffed, he had a bright red nose that almost glowed. I bought a tonic water.

'On holiday, eh? Nasty weather. You never can tell this time of year.'

'It was nice earlier, lovely when I started.'

'Come from Beddgelert?'

'No, along the road from Nantlle.'

'Oh, yes.' He wasn't very interested. I wasn't very interested. He went back to his crates. I went into a small room filled with a pool table and a juke box. A smattering of Welsh ethnic amid the corn of Duran Duran.

After twenty minutes, even the other side of the road was having difficulty in making itself visible. No one else came in. After three more tonics, I got round to a meat pie and a half of bitter.

'You had a bit of an accident here the other week.'

He looked at me slyly. 'News travels. Yes, very unfortunate. An old gentleman. Nasty.' There is a funny kind of sing-song Welsh accent which sounds as though much more would be revealed if the speaker desired, but probably won't.

'Yes, I was talking to some friends I'm staying with in Nantlle about it. Fell off a mountain called Carn.'

He gestured behind him. 'Up there it is. Mr Astin, he used to come up quite regular these last few years. He was up earlier in the season, well it isn't really the season now, is it? But in the summer he was up here.'

'What did he do? Just go off in the morning and not come back?'

'No, no, it was strange. He had been in most of the day.' He put down the glass he had been polishing and leaned across the bar. 'To tell the truth, he had been drinking, as I said to the police when they came. He had breakfast and was in the bar waiting, and drinking Scotch. I was getting a bit worried. I don't really like it when guests . . . you know. We had one old dear who came up, she hardly used to see any of the country, you know? Just used to drink . . .'

'And Mr Astin? He just drank?'

'No, I wouldn't say that. He would get out and around

usually. I think he knew some people down towards Beddgelert. I remember that day, it was about three and I'd just shut the bar when the phone rang, and someone said he wanted to speak to Mr Astin if he was there – which he was – just sitting in the corner of the bar over there.' He pointed over to the window. 'I had served him a chicken in a basket actually. He left it . . . He was really quite far gone. Just sat there drinking the Scotch . . .'

'But someone rang?'

'Yes. He got quite upset. Shouted that he had had enough or something. Slammed the phone down, came back in the bar. I said to him – well I asked him if it was bad news. He just said some trouble in London. Funny that.'

'Why?'

'Because it didn't sound like a long distance call, but it definitely wasn't a Welsh voice.'

'And then he went out?'

'And then he went out. And that was the last we saw of the poor old so-and-so.' He grimaced. 'Until they brought him back in the night. They called me out – the police, that is – to have a look at him, see if I knew him, which I did, of course. There was no need to get him to a hospital or anything. He was in a terrible way, I could only really tell him by his clothes. He must have hit his head on the rocks after he fell down Carn, it is a fair drop. It was just a mass of blood. Horrible it was.'

The rain had stopped. A car drew up, a couple came into the pub. I slipped in a last question. 'Do you know a gentleman called Fuller round here?'

'Fuller? I think there is someone of that name, got a house behind the lake, on the edge of the forest.'

I drank up and left.

I took the road towards Beddgelert. On my right was the lake. The trees didn't begin for another five hundred yards, but then it was solid forest all the way down the low sweeping valley. The air was clean, washed by the rain. I climbed on to a stone wall and stood looking across to the edge of the lake and beyond, where the mountains began. I jumped down on the other side of the wall and walked towards the lake.

Behind it was a slate quarry, long deserted, with its workings strewn across the landscape. I climbed amid the rubble. By walking upwards I got an increasing view of the forest and, just on the edge, a house. *The* house? There was a rough track leading to it, but well used, judging by the tyre tracks which cut across it. I was skirting the edge of the pines, but they dropped behind me as I ascended the mountain. I saw a clump of trees ahead of me and made for it. Over to my right was what I took to be Carn, the mountain where the bookseller had met his curious end. Ahead of me, the mountain swept up, grass-covered, with what looked like large stones scattered across the turf, but they moved, they were sheep. The rocks ahead were not the peak of a hill, merely an undulation before the slope shifted to forty-five degrees. I perched on a rock and looked down. The house was clearly visible, with outhouses just behind it.

It looked close. I felt I could have leapt into the void and flown across those open mountains. There were three cars parked inside the boundary fence. A newly-repaired fence it was, and wired. More than was needed to keep out a few marauding sheep or tourists? Or just normal for the area? There was a Toyota pick-up truck, a Jaguar and a Range-Rover. Nice work if you could get it, and not many of the locals could, I guessed.

A figure came out of the house and climbed into the pick-up. A faint sound of the engine starting carried on the wind. He reversed the truck and set off down the track. It bumped into the trees. I followed it with my eyes as it emerged and set off down the main road to Beddgelert.

Nothing else happened for ten minutes. Then a flock of birds flew out of the pine trees and headed upwards towards the peaks. Down by the pub I could see the bright clothes of some climbers setting out for Snowdon. The sun came out and the wind dropped. I lay back amongst the rocks and gazed at the shifting clouds.

I heard voices, quite close: a shout, then someone laughing. I caught a sentence. 'Can be more difficult out of town,' one of them said. I scrambled between the rocks and poked my head out. I couldn't see anyone. Between me and the house was another outcrop of rocks. The sound was coming from there. A bird's cry sounded above my head. I looked up. It was a big bird, but slow. It could have been a pheasant. Above it was another bird hovering on the wind, a hunter, a falcon or a sparrow hawk. I was never much good at wild life. I hardly know the difference between a robin and a pigeon.

There was a shot. It echoed up the mountain. The pheasant plummetted down, between me and the other rocks. The other bird veered, flew round and headed back towards the peaks.

I waited. I could hear boots slipping on the rocks.

'Further up!' shouted someone. 'Up towards those rocks.'

I was scared, as I had been in Victoria. It was difficult to see why. I was perched on a perfectly respectable Welsh hillside. Below me in the pub the landlord was doubtless still shifting crates. A motor coach proceeded by the road from Beddgelert. The wind was picking up again. The climbers were spread out in a brightly coloured line across the lower reaches of Snowdon.

Another bird took flight. Another shot was fired. The bird arced into the ground and landed with a thud about five yards from me. It was still twitching. It was a pheasant. I looked round the rocks. Two people were approaching. Two dark figures scrambling up the hillside. As they drew closer, their features became clearer. I backed behind the last of the rocks and looked for cover further back. There was another rock about twenty yards along the slope. I half crawled, half ran for it. They couldn't see me as I made the move; the other rocks and the angle of vision obscured their view.

It didn't obscure mine as they hit the outcrop. They were dressed for the occasion, plus-fours and all. One was tall, in late middle age; the other's blond hair was tousled by the wind. The sporting gear didn't really detract from Fuller's urban appearance, but Hales looked more at home in the scenery. He stared out across the valley. They didn't see me. I waited. They sat down and had a smoke. Then they climbed back down the hillside.

They were deep in conversation. Fuller slapped his

companion on the back. They laughed. The noise was whipped away by the wind.

17.

It was about three in the afternoon. I watched them move slowly down into the trees that fringed the enclosure. The entrance was obscured by the forest. A couple of minutes later, they reappeared on the track and walked back to the house. There was no one else there, just Fuller, Hales, and, up on the hillside, me. The traffic was still moving along the Beddgelert road, and the climbers were now nothing but dots on the higher reaches of Snowdon.

The sun was quite warm out of the wind. A jet from some RAF base flew low through the valley. Its noise shattered the stillness. It flew out of earshot across the coast and out over the Irish Sea. Its departure underlined the absolute silence of the mountains. The light was dimming, the colours darkening.

I had arrived at the limit of my safe world. I could dodge, evade, return to London, send back the pictures, emigrate . . .

I could knock on Fuller's front door.

Or I could head down into the forest, along the boundary fence, search for an opening, climb over it.

I looked into my wallet, pulled out the picture. It was curling at the edges. Abramovitch stared at me, lifeless.

If I were careful, and kept to the shadows and the rocks, I could make most of the descent without being seen from the house. There was no sign of movement within its boundaries.

I crawled into a hollow between two ridges, and hopped painfully down the slope. My left leg had lost its circulation. Gradually, I made my way back to the first set of rocks where I had stopped. I scanned the house again, still nothing. I ran down to the rocks where I had first seen Fuller. It was more exposed. I would have been visible had anyone been looking. A sound broke the silence. I sank into the turf, smelling the earth. It was only a sheep. I made my way on down and reached the tip of the forest.

The trees were set closely together, it was Forestry Commission land, neatly regimented rows of evergreens, with dry pine needles, brown and lifeless, cut off from the run, interspersed with narrow bands of water flowing swiftly along artificial trenches. Moss grew round them, strange coloured moss, garish green and pink, unnatural nature . . .

I walked into the trees, pushing my way through the undergrowth. In the distance, a bird sang. I came to the fence. It was a low line of wiring easily surmountable. I crossed it. The forest was just as dense on the other side.

Then I came to a second set of wire. But this time, on each wooden stump there was a circular disc. 'Caution: Electrified Fence', it warned. I made my way along it, hoping for a break. It had to be a small charge, you can't kill off the tourist industry. It was National Park land, or was it? Could you kill off tourists? The forest was oppressive, the moss darkened into a uniform green brown. It was growing darker all the time.

A small creature lay among the pine needles. There was a scorch mark across its back; a dead field mouse.

Across the forest a light showed. It was from the upper floor of the house. Quite a sizeable gap was coming in the trees, where I would be in the open. I moved back along the fence. I guessed I was edging back towards the road, since the forest swept round to what I assumed was the entrance to the grounds.

Then I stopped. I was making a lot of noise. It was so quiet, any sound in the stillness might be picked up, if anyone were listening. So what? I was just taking a walk. *I have as much right to be here as anyone*, I thought. *It's a free country.* But, for some reason, I paused for a minute, two minutes, five . . .

Someone else came moving through the undergrowth on the other side of the fence, whistling.

'Don't it make my brown eyes blue,' murmured a male voice out of the twilight.

I slipped on to the forest floor, just keeping my head up.

Across the fence, not more than ten yards away, I saw in outline the lower half of his body. He had stopped. I waited. He waited. I didn't know if he had heard anything, if he suspected. The remains of the sun left streaks of light through the trees, but it would be completely dark within ten minutes.

He moved on. He was quiet, or quieter than I had been, and vanished into the forest. I'm not used to those places in the dark. The city is my home; I'm safer in Stoke Newington, Fuller's heavies and all . . .

I backed away from the electrified fence and made for the outer perimeter, crossed it and was on the open hillside. Ahead of me was a line of trees running down to the lake. Past it was open ground, leading to the Beddgelert Road. I felt relieved, and let down, and self-disgusted. The lights of the traffic on the road guided me through the periphery of the forest. They failed to prevent me from sinking up to my ankles in the marshland around the lake. I picked the slime from my boots, swore, and headed out to the road.

I was just up from Rhydd-ddu. I walked down the road, fast on the tarmac, and past the car park. There were a few cars there, a touring dormobile, its occupants doubtless still fumbling their way from Snowdon and abusing each other for their bad timing.

There was a truck there, a pick-up truck with a tarpaulin stretched over the back; a familiar one too, a Toyota, *the* Toyota?

The obvious came to me slower than it should have done. Cowardice was delaying me. Not many Welshmen could be driving nice new Toyota pick-ups around. Morris Minor vans were more their style. The pick-up had headed out to Beddgelert, but had plenty of time to come back. I looked at my watch. Five past six; the pub would be open.

I paused. I could go to the pub, have a drink, stay the night, or slip back to Nantlle. I had a key to the Cutler household. The following day I would be able to explain to my hosts my story, and how I had spent the day buggering around on a hillside and been terrified by two dead pheasants and a Country and Western whistler.

I entered the car park. There was no one there. There was a light in the house down the road, but I was invisible in the darkness. I approached the truck. The tarpaulin was fixed by small catches, which opened easily enough. I rolled it back. There was nothing inside, no cause to open it at the other end with no contents, apart from me . . .

I slid into the back. They would notice the catches were undone. I reached out and fumbled with them. It took a few minutes but I sealed myself in.

I was cold. I heard a child cry. The dormobile travellers were returning.

'Thank God for that,' said a woman.

'If you hadn't wasted half the morning, we would have been down hours ago,' said a man. The child wailed. Arguing, they walked across the tarmac, doors opened and shut, an engine revved, the vehicle pulled off and silence returned.

Then I heard footsteps. The truck rocked as doors were opened.

'It's his big night, isn't it?' I wasn't certain, but the accent had a hint of Brum in it. 'We don't want to spoil his fun, do we? Or ours, come to that.' Who was he talking to? I wasn't sure, I heard no one else. The conversation, or monologue, terminated for me as the doors slammed. The floor vibrated as he engaged the gears. The Toyota bumped out across the car park. The driving was not too good.

I could have been going anywhere, over the mountains and far away with perfectly innocuous travellers. I wasn't. The truck lurched to the left as it hit the road, bounced down it for a minute, paused, and then veered sharply right. We were back on the rough, back across country and into the trees.

My head hit the side of the truck with such force that I feared the driver would stop to see if someone was hurling boulders at him. He didn't, but drew up a minute later. Above the vibration of the engine I heard the squeak of a gate being opened.

The truck flung me from side to side as it approached the house; it was cart track now. He paused again, and a door opened. Only one person got out.

Light shone through the cracks in the tarpaulin. The engine was switched off and the door slammed. The driver had left. Another door opened, the light vanished, that door slammed, silence returned.

I lay in the dark and looked at my watch. It was half past seven. I waited until quarter to eight and then slipped out. It took me five minutes to unfasten the catches, my hands were sweating and shaking. I lifted the tarpaulin back into place. A red light glowed by the door, faintly lighting the garage, the sparse concrete, a few empty petrol cans.

My feet squelched on the floor. I crossed to the main doors. They had been locked. The only way out was in the corner by the red light. That door was up three steps, so presumably the garage was in the basement of the house.

In a corner, away from the light, was a water barrel. I crouched by it, removed my shoes and socks, squeezed the muddy water into the barrel, and scraped the slime from my boots. They remained sodden, as I slid them back on to my chilled feet.

The door was close fitting, and no light was visible under it. I climbed the steps and tried the handle. It moved. I pulled the door open and found myself looking up a short flight of stairs. The area was in darkness. I moved into the house proper, there was carpeting under my feet. I reached a hall, with a neat mahogany table supporting a curious chintzy little lamp-stand which cast a dull glow over the surrounds. A pleasant domestic scene in the home of a country gentleman, a pleasant house, but such odd people.

The only sound was a clock by the front door. If anyone came out of any of the four doors or down the wide staircase, then my only hope of escape lay back through the garage. I could not see any lights under the doors.

I padded across the carpet and as silently as possible pushed at the door which I guessed led to the kitchen. It swung open slightly. There was one light on, over a table, and it shone on Anorak. He didn't see me. I swung the door closed. Then I moved back to the stairs, down to the garage, and immersed myself in the darkness. My mind flicked back to my room, and to my drunken confidence in the pub.

Five minutes passed, the silence remained. My fear flickered as I climbed the stairs again. I listened again at the top, in the dangerous dull light. I paused at the door to the right of the main entrance, and pressed against it, but it did not open. Slowly I twisted the cut glass knob, the door opened, and I almost fell into the room.

There was a light in the corner from a standard lamp. It could have been there for fifty years, casting its glow from the 1930s to the 1980s. I eased the door shut and tiptoed across the thick carpet to the windows. They were swathed in dark red, heavy curtains. Only fifty years? The room hinted of the reception chamber in a high class Victorian brothel. There were pictures and souvenirs; souvenirs of dead things and death, animal heads, spears, an African shield, again the bric-a-brac of Empire. The pictures near the light were fairly visible, and familiar, too. The same man, the wife, the children, slaughtered animals.

I glanced at the pictures furthest from the light. They were hard to see in the gloom, just occasional flashes of light amidst the sepia. The images seemed to stir, the white hunter eyed me out of the past. The pictures were different. I wasn't sure about them, I didn't want to be.

I froze. There were footsteps coming up from the garage, and my way out was blocked. Someone laughed in the hall outside. I ran for the curtains, and dived behind them. The windows were recessed. Provided I kept down, I had a two-foot area to stay alive in. I looked out, over the ledge, into the world. It was mercifully dark.

The door opened. 'By that time they were running like pigs.' I wondered who 'they' were. Fuller, out of the wind, out of the hall in Victoria, didn't need to shout.

Nor did Hales. He chuckled instead. 'They usually do, they usually do. They are nothing more than a rabble. I don't like rabbles, Michael.'

Fuller cleared his throat. 'Rather depends on which way they are running, doesn't it? A rabble can be used to tear down the nation, trample on cherished values, or it can be organised, forged into an instrument to excise, cut away the fat, the degeneracy . . .' There was an uncomfortable pause. 'Drink?'

They had scotch. Another light was switched on. Its glow seeped through a crack in the curtains. I shrank back.

'Bit lurid, bright, isn't it?' said Fuller. 'Bright lights don't really go with Edwardiana. I'll turn it down.'

The glow dimmed. *Thanks, Fuller*, I thought, for the only time.

Hales didn't seem keen to pursue the debate. 'Beautiful room,' he remarked. 'Beautiful. Nothing like English country homes.'

Fuller laughed nervously. 'Well, Welsh, anyway. It's a privilege to be in such a *historic* place . . . And it's my privilege to see you here. Mind you, there may have been few guests here in the last fifty years, but those that *have* been, well . . . And times are changing, aren't they?'

There was a long silence. *What are you doing?* I thought. *Padding towards the curtains, discovering me. Cutting my throat.*

But they were still fencing. 'Times are changing,' said Hales, 'but not for the better.'

'I'm not sure of that,' said Fuller. 'Not sure at all. I admire what you stand for, and I think you've been joined by some . . . some interesting colleagues. But we'll never get this nation back on its feet merely through Parliament, will we? Every form of infection that has corrupted the body politic gathers there. And it isn't just the reds; liberalism, laissez-faire, welfarism . . .'

'The fact is,' began Hales, and then stopped.

'Well?' Fuller sounded as if he was shaping up for ideological battle.

It came out in a rush from Hales. 'The fact is I'm none too happy with our companions downstairs. I was none too happy at that damn meeting about it. It hasn't done me too much good with the yellow press. And I'm not too sure it's going to do me – or you – much good here.'

'What's your alternative, Raphael?' Fuller was exasperated. 'What's wrong with them? The accent? Plenty of people, *your* people, have got the right accent, but that's about all they have got. Where the hell would we be without them now? Now that we've started? It's worked in the past, it's working elsewhere now. We have needed them, we are going to go on needing them. It is a question of hammering them into that instrument, providing the leadership, the discipline, and then using it.'

There was the sound of a glass being put down. I assumed it was Hales's. 'An *instrument*? It will break up in your hands. I've gone along with you, yes, it may work, it could be a starting point, but they are cheap little scum, unreliable, likely to break precisely at the moment you need them. Look at that little tyke – what's his name? Enever – did you see what state he was in when he came back from the pub? And that chappie Lee isn't much better.'

So that was Anorak's name.

Fuller put his glass down. 'The trouble with you people, Raphael, is that you've forgotten your own past, *our* past. People like you used to hold these people in line, they looked up to you. That cord has been snapped; it has to be twined together again. In the meantime, most of them are running round in the dark. But some of them, like Lee, even like Enever, are trying to do something. It's a world that has been thrown away, not by people like me, but by people like you. Not you, for God's sake, you are trying to do something. But the British are slow, so very slow. The decay, the corruption, the theft has crept up on us. There is a fire buried in that great sluggish mass, it is like lava, static in this ossified society. Most of them have never noticed, some of them never can notice, they are so inert, but some of them are with us, and we must use them!' His voice was rising. 'They have that fire. They aren't all asleep. We are the master spirits, we have to blast open that rock.'

The silence deepened. A match flared. Perhaps Hales was too embarrassed, or awed, or bored, to say anything. His host sighed, and changed the subject. 'I'm sorry there is no proper meal tonight. It was difficult with the servants, I didn't think it was a good time to get our woman in from the village, Mrs Evans . . .'

'Thank God you didn't bring her in. Some worthy Welsh widow running into those two cut-throats would do absolutely nothing to set anyone's mind at rest. I don't know, Michael. You've got a good deal of talk, I hope you can back it up with action. That makes sense. When is the meeting?' Hales was bored and irritated, as if he had come a long way to buy a dud.

'In twenty minutes. Well, we're all here, almost.'

'All?'

'Well, there is you and me . . .'

'Quite.'

'And aah . . . Mrs Avis, Lee, of course, and Enever . . .'

'Good God, man! You aren't letting Enever into the meeting, are you? I mean Lee is bad enough, but *Enever*?'

'Well, why not?'

There was a clink of glass. I visualised Hales knocking back the remainder of his Scotch as first aid. 'I'll tell you why not. Because I wouldn't trust anything we say tonight not being relayed round the public bars and common doss houses of Hoxton within twenty-four hours, if we let that little footpad sit down at the same table with us. Not to mention what we'll probably catch.'

'God, sense of station, of caste, is one thing, Raphael, but sometimes I think you are just a snob. Half of what we have achieved has been thanks to "little footpads" like Enever.'

'That doesn't mean I have to sit down with him. He stays with the other ranks.'

Fuller sighed. 'We'll see. I don't think that Lee will be too happy.'

'I don't give a penny whistle if Lee is happy or not, and we won't see. Or if we do, I'll be out of here in five minutes.'

'I don't see what makes you think you can dictate terms, Hales!'

'I'll tell you why, Fuller.' The Christian names flew out of the window as the temperature rose. 'Because I have laid my neck well on the line. Because I trusted you, and respected what your father and his father had done. But I am not going to have my head cut off because you haven't the guts to keep order. Who else is here?'

Fuller coughed. I wondered what he had in his throat. 'Well, we have had some difficulties. We were hoping to get our South African representative and this other chap from

Italy who worked with Appleton. But neither of them could get here just at this time . . .'

'What?' Hales was extremely unhappy. 'So who in Christ's name is representing Appleton?'

'Well, I am, of course.'

'*You* are?'

'Well, why not? I know him, don't I?'

'Can you provide any guarantees? Can you provide any money? Any back-up? Can you provide anything, Fuller?'

'Will you have the common courtesy to wait and see, Hales? This isn't the meeting. I can assure you I have everything under control.'

'I wonder if you have. I really wonder. Because I can tell you that I didn't get Mitchell to come all the way up here to meet you and Mrs Avis and Harold Lee. When is Charles due?'

'Any time now. Another drink?'

'I think I need one.'

They both stood up. The two men padded across the carpet. I froze.

'You've got some funny looking pictures here, Fuller.' The MP wasn't happy with them either. At least we had something in common. 'Funny sort of fellow your father, good man of course. Met him in South Africa just before . . .'

If it was an attempt to rebuild bridges, it failed.

'Yes,' observed Fuller. 'He was, he was a good man.'

Behind me I heard the murmur of an engine. A car was approaching through the forest. The headlights flickered in the trees. The lights would swing across the window.

Hales and Fuller heard the car. One of them crossed to the curtains, a hand thrust through the drapes and pulled them back. I shrank back. It was Fuller.

'Good,' he said. 'Mitchell is here.'

The curtain fell back into place. Good thing they are quality, I thought. The light flashed across the window. I sank further into the corner, further into the floor. The two men moved towards the door.

It swung to. Fuller's voice faded as they moved down the passage. I could hear the big, slow, ticking of the clock. I shifted. My circulation had gone and my leg buckled under me. I could hardly move. Fuller had turned the other light off. Perhaps they would not return.

The front door opened. I heard Fuller welcoming his guest. He was effusive. '. . . Got some sandwiches in the pantry, do you want a drink?'

Please God, not a drink, I prayed. *Or make it a beer out of the fridge.* I heard laughter. They were going into the kitchen. Then probably back into the study with its photographs and half paralysed voyeur, and I wouldn't make it behind the curtains for another long session. I was trapped unless I could make it out of the room and down the stairs. I hobbled to the door; it was ajar. I was in the passage. I heard voices in the kitchen. The stairs to the garage were lit and I heard the door at the bottom opening. The only way out was up. I fled up to the landing and made for the first door I saw, lustrous dark wood, a sturdy brass handle. I entered.

It was empty, but it was their room. There was a long table, with folders neatly arranged at each place. They would be coming in; I was just the first arrival.

18.

At the end of the room was a sofa, ornate, covered. Either I hid behind that or took my chances in the wilds of the landing where the strange animals and hunters roamed. It was almost in darkness. I rolled behind it.

The door opened. A chair was drawn back, papers were shuffled, someone was doing early homework.

I was quite comfortable, stretched out in the darkness, my head on Fuller's plush carpet. Snug in a pleasant house in the Welsh mountains, out of the wind and the rain.

The new arrival cleared his throat. I glanced at my watch. It was five to nine. The minutes passed, there were sounds from the hall, voices. Within the room the man turned the pages of his folder. It was curiously soporific, a million miles from the Cutlers' sane little cottage, and their weekend in Liverpool.

I closed my eyes, and fear flooded back. The photographs started slide-showing across my brain. Dead animals, the pictures I had taken from Astin, the pictures under the light downstairs and the other pictures, the pictures almost in darkness, almost . . .

The door opened. I heard Fuller laugh. 'First here as usual eh?' An overenthusiastic housemaster talking to an unintelligent schoolboy.

The Midlands accent was more pronounced. 'Just wanted to see what you had lined up.'

'Plenty, Lee. Don't you worry about that. That's background material . . .'

'Bloody right it is, Harry.' Anorak had come in, drunk and angry. 'You don't know the half of it. This fucker doesn't want me at the bloody meeting.'

'What are you going on about, Johnny?' asked Lee.

'Mr Fuller here says that I'm not sitting in.'

'Look,' said Fuller wearily, 'I've just been talking it over with Raphael and we thought . . .'

'What d'you mean you *thought*?' asked Lee. His voice was quiet, as if asking politely why the monthly back-hander from the betting shop was overdue. 'Why did you think just with Hales? Why didn't you think with Johnny here and *me*? And what *did* you think, Fuller?'

'I'm sorry, it just came out in casual conversation with Raphael . . .'

'Over the claret while me and Johnny were knocking back the lager and scratchings, eh?'

'Not at all. We were just chatting and Raphael said how worried he was about security. He thought it was absolutely crucial that we had someone watching out. You never know who might be around . . .'

'Very true, Fuller, you never do.' Lee was angry, but soft-spoken. 'You never do know who is going to be around. Now Johnny here may not be the sharpest operator around, but Johnny is a very good lad. I rely on Johnny, and sometimes, just sometimes, I rely on Johnny's advice. Like now. And then I pass on the advice to others. I don't believe there is anyone outside we need worry about. I'm more worried about the people in this house.'

How true, I thought.

'I think you've just got the wrong end of the stick, Harry.'

'Could well, be Fuller, could well be. And I might just ram that stick up someone. I want Johnny here, right?'

Fuller sighed. 'Yes, well, you may well want Johnny . . .'

'Mr Enever,' said Anorak.

'Mr Enever here, but I think this is no time to cut the corners on security. This is a crucial time, absolutely vital, and neither Mr Hales nor I want to take any risks about security. Now I know, and I think I impressed upon Mr Hales, that Mr Enever is first rate, and also solid as a rock. Now there is nothing that is going to happen in this room tonight that I'm not perfectly happy for him to hear about. You can provide a briefing for him. I'd just like to be sure that we've covered our exits, that is always the most important thing.'

The door swung open again, and there was more laughter. It was Hales and someone else. 'Michael,' boomed Hales, 'this is Charles. Michael Fuller, Charles Mitchell, and here is . . . here is Mr Lee, and Mr Enever.'

Lee and Enever muttered insincere greetings, Mitchell and Fuller put some effort into it.

'I was just explaining to Mr . . . to Harry and Johnny here how important it was that we had someone to cover security, and that it would be really useful if Johnny . . .'

'Mr Enever.' It was Lee's turn for the correction.

'If he could keep watch for us, downstairs.'

'And I was just explaining to Mr Fuller here,' observed Lee, very deliberately, 'that I didn't think it was necessary. I told Mr Fuller when I came up, when I agreed, that I could provide plenty of back-up. I said I could bring up whoever he wanted from the leadership, and whatever he needed in the way of muscle. He told me it wasn't needed, that there wasn't a safer place to be, so I just came with Johnny here, a reliable lad is Johnny, my friend. Now he tells me that Johnny should kick his heels downstairs and put the cat out.'

'Look, I'm sorry about this,' Hales sounded as if he was apologising to his constituency associates about unforeseen events at the Conservative Fayre. 'I think it's probably my fault. I know we are all honourable men – and women –'

The door had opened and shut again. I guessed it was Mrs Avis.

'. . . But perhaps I'm oversensitive about security matters. The fact is I expect we could all have brought along other people, I'm sure that Mr . . . Michael . . . here wished others *were* here, but I think it is important that each of us represents the viewpoint of each particular group. I'm sure that each of us can. And I am concerned about security. I would take it as a great service, absolutely crucial, if Mr Enever here could provide that. I'm sure that he understands.'

Enever fell for it. 'If you think it's that important —'

'I do,' lied Hales. 'I do. What do you think, Charles?'

'I really have no opinion on the subject.' I was faintly surprised by the crack in the upper class ranks, but then I didn't know Charles, nor did Lee.

'Well, I have an opinion on it, Fuller. I think you're pissing me around. I'm not quite sure why. I'm going to give you the benefit of the doubt, and Johnny can go and man the tail-gun. But if I decide I want him in here, then he comes in here. Is that understood?'

They understood it.

'Well, then,' said Enever, 'I'll be off. I'll be downstairs if I'm wanted, and I'll keep you posted, if . . . anything happens.'

'You do that,' said Lee.

From the corner I could see the shadows of the group, but not the faces; just legs moving to the table, four men, one woman. Mrs Avis all the way from Regents Park Road. They pulled up chairs, there was a clatter of glasses. 'Help yourselves, gentlemen,' said Fuller. 'Maud? . . .'

My knees began to itch. Agony I could do nothing about, the triviality of daily existence elevated to a reason for sudden death. Perhaps it would be off the cliff top.

Fuller tried for bonhomie. 'Now do we all know each other?'

'No, we don't.' Lee was not going to play along. 'I don't know this . . . uh . . . gentleman here, Mr Mitchell.'

'Well,' said Hales, 'I think it might be a good idea if we were fairly discreet.'

'What kind of game is this? I just said that I didn't know who this gentleman here was. Now this is supposed to be a very discreet, private little meeting, where we are all going to be very discreet. I want to know who this person here is, right?'

'I'm Charles Mitchell.' His tone was clipped, military. 'I'm a . . . a . . . civil servant.'

'Well, Charles,' said Fuller. 'This is my sister, Maud Avis. I don't think you've been introduced.'

Maud gave an odd, girlish giggle.

'There are civil servants and civil servants.' Lee was unwilling to be diverted. 'We had a civil servant in our group, Mr Mitchell.'

Mitchell maintained an even tone. 'Interesting to hear that.'

'We believe that it's important to represent all parts of the nation, of the *folk*.'

'Quite so.'

'But he wasn't what he seemed. He made some sort of mistake on his application and said he worked for the post office. Which he didn't.'

Fuller wrestled for the tiller. 'I'm sure this is very interesting . . .'

'Which he didn't. He worked for the filth, or for a little bit of the filth. His name was Elman. Ever heard of Ronnie Elman, Mr Mitchell?'

Mitchell said that he hadn't; nor had I. The atmosphere was chilled.

'Do you know what we did with Ronnie Elman when we found out about the mistake he made on his application form?'

There was another negative from Mitchell.

'Then I'll tell you. We drilled holes for rawlplugs in his knees, and one in his forehead for good luck. Then we screwed him down in a pit in Gravesend. Appropriate place, wasn't it? You see his name wasn't Elman at all. It was Cox. I think it's important to spell your name right, and get your occupation down as well, don't you?'

'I remember Cox.' Mitchell's manner was relaxed, like an officer explaining details to a backward NCO. 'And I know who sent him in. He was a good man, but a fool, they both were. Some people don't see very clearly just who the enemies are. They don't see where the threat comes from, the real threat. But we have to keep everybody happy, we have politicos on our backs sometimes. They can be irritating. I think we all understand who we are, and what our occupations are, don't we, Mr Lee?'

'We are getting away from the point.' Fuller tried the brisk approach. 'We aren't here to recriminate. We are here to plan, and we are here because I have good news. I can tell you I am very pleased to see Mr Mitchell, and I think you will be, Harry. People like Charles are the backbone of what made this country what it is – I mean what it was – and the one thing that you have to remember is that he is beginning to see things our way. Mr Mitchell has been concerned with the security of our nation, or at least what's left of it now the system is riddled with reds.'

'I'm always pleased to meet someone from MI5 on a social basis, or on business,' said Lee. 'But I can't help feeling a little . . . a little uneasy.'

'I can vouch for Charles,' Hales blustered.

'I'm sure you can, Mr Hales. And I can vouch for Johnny downstairs. Only he's downstairs, and Charles is up here.'

I shifted slightly. Inanely I began to sympathise with Fuller. He had brought his harp to the party and they were all clubbing one another, and him, over the head with it.

'This is absurd,' shouted the host. 'We aren't here to bicker. You have my word that we are all here for the best of reasons. Hales, Raphael, is one of the very few patriots in that rotten talk shop of a Parliament who is willing to stand up and be counted. Charles is with us, and can perform a vital role. You, Harry, you and I, all of us, we can and must work together and this is a vital evening. If you would care to open the files amongst other things you'll see a photocopy of a bank transfer in there. It's from Mr Appleton. And it's for a very large sum of money.'

There was a shuffling of papers. Fuller resumed. 'After a night's sleep I hope we can hammer out the details, and I have one or two other little surprises in store for you tonight, and I thought that I would try to explain some of the other reasons why I have asked you to be here. You see I see myself as part of a tradition in my family . . .'

I was getting ready to nod off. The thought of another speech on the nation can bore one at the most inapposite times. I didn't have the chance. Fuller's surprises started earlier than I guessed he expected.

There was a crashing on the stairs, and the door burst open. 'What the fuck's going on?' Anorak had been keeping a watch-out by the bottle.

'Do you think you could knock?' Fuller was put out by an interruption during one of his patriotic orations.

'I'll fucking knock you, mate!' Anorak had difficulty with his words. I wondered if he had hit Fuller's scotch or stuck to a take-out from the Cwellyn. 'You wanted a look-out, right? Well, you've got one. And I looked out.'

'What did you see?' Lee sounded as if he was not surprised.

'Well . . . It's not what I saw. I didn't *see* anybody. It was kind of . . . kind of lights.'

'What kind of lights?' asked Mitchell.

'A red light, I thought. I was just out the front, I saw it through the trees. And I heard some kind of howling noise.'

'What are you talking about?' demanded Fuller. His frayed temper was beginning to snap.

'Really,' added Hales, 'this is too bad.'

'Come, come, gentlemen.' Mitchell was the urbane CO, it was a role he seemed happy in. 'We posted Mr . . . Mr . . .'

'Mr Enever.'

'And now he's seen something. That is what a good sentry is put there for.'

'You don't need to patronise him,' said Lee.

'I wouldn't dream of doing such a thing. I suggest we go down and have a look-see.'

It was the easiest way out of the problem. They rose to their feet, and made for the door. I even caught a glimpse of Mrs Avis's ankles. It wasn't a night she wanted to be alone. It was a night that I would have been only too happy to have been alone. I shifted out, edging my way along the sofa. The room was empty, the table was strewn with glasses, and there was a smouldering cigar butt. It looked like Hales's style, part of his Churchill routine.

I thought about it. I even allowed myself the luxury of standing up, but kept by the sofa. I could make my way out of the room, try the next landing, hope they came back after inspecting any passing car headlamps and the Welsh wildlife. Then I could dodge downstairs and take my chances with Anorak, whose drink problem – or solution – was unlikely to lessen as the night wore on. Or I could stay and find out what they were all up to, apart from leaping at one another's throats. I knew what the courageous policy was, stick it out.

I made for the door and eased it open. There was plenty of noise out in the drive. Mainly Enever shouting. I had a fair chance, I guessed, and made it through the door and into the hall. Then I paused.

They were coming back in. I froze. Then I decided to make for the next landing. As I did so, I heard a sound, so slight that I couldn't make it out, a fragment of white noise. The downstairs door slammed.

'If you are going to be a look-out, Mr Enever,' I heard Mitchell saying downstairs, 'then I suggest you learn to distinguish between a back light of a car on the main road and a posse of Red Indians. And between owls and war cries.'

Just after that, and before Anorak weighed in, I heard the sound again, like the fluttering of a moth. A moth in someone's throat.

It was from upstairs. I dodged back into the room, and flung myself back behind the sofa, burying my face in the material. I nearly threw up. I was about five seconds ahead of them.

Some act of folly, or desire to end the tension, led me to incline my head so that I could see them as they came in. Fuller was first, and he looked furious. Then came Mitchell,

I guessed, laughing, and Hales. Mrs Avis and sullen-looking Lee brought up the rear.

They fell silent and resumed their seats. I heard the clink of a bottle being passed round. Fuller cleared his throat. 'Well, if we can resume, after that *ludicrous* interruption.'

'Nothing ludicrous about it.' Yet Lee didn't sound so sure, more embarrassed. 'Johnny can be bloody useful . . .'

'As I'm sure Cox found out,' observed Mitchell.

'Yeah! Just like Cox found out.'

I didn't want to find out. They were all out of vision. There was a fire in the grate. Its flames sent the shadows leaping up the wall.

'Right,' said Fuller. 'It is quite simple. As some of you know, Mr Appleton is a very rich man, and despite living in Texas – or maybe because of it – he has remained rigid in his support for the Anglo-Saxon and nationalist cause.'

'So was that man of yours in Chile.' Lee was attempting to make up lost prestige by resuming the attack.

'So was that man of mine in Chile. It just so happened that he died at the wrong time, and the Jews and the banks moved rather faster than we had expected. There are no such risks with Mr Appleton. He has already spent money, generously, very generously, in the cause of a free Cuba, Argentina, Brazil, even Italy, and other projects, which I can't tell you about but which were truly spectacular and highly successful. You may have heard of some of them, you may not, but I can assure you . . .'

There was the sound of papers being shuffled. 'There's a lot of bumf here,' said Lee, 'but just how much is this Appleton putting in?'

'If you read it properly you could see.' Fuller was exasperated. 'But it's enough, and I'll come back to that in a minute. Now, we're already beginning to show what we can do, and that helped persuade him – not that he needed much persuasion – that the time has come to funnel some of his not inconsiderable resources into the heartland, into the homeland.'

'That's all very well, Mr Fuller,' said Mitchell, 'but I am not certain what you have shown him, or what you are planning to show him.'

Mitchell wasn't cheering Fuller too much either. 'Will you let me finish? Read the file. You might glean some idea of the scope of our operation.'

Lee's Birmingham accent became slower, and more nasal. 'Are we supposed to be listening to you, or thumbing through your press kit?'

'Both, Mr Lee. Both. Our movement has been riddled with crooks, adventurers, perverts, defectives, defectors, but there remains a core, a loyal core, starved of resources, starved of encouragement, denied any clear perspective. Now I think we can, with the help of Appleton's money, and with a clear vision, begin to move ahead.'

Mitchell sighed. 'What are you going to do?'

'Document two, the offensive, para two, I quote: "Parliamentary tactics, then, not only have failed, but were bound to fail, and, given the unimpeded persistence both of the conspiratorial bureacracy and a system built on head counting, will continue to fail. The solution is the application of force to pressure points within the system that will both drive the healthy parts of the organism to regroup and expel the anti-bodies and shatter the framework which encourages the growth of these anti-bodies.'

I shifted my leg. I wasn't too taken with Fuller's grasp of biology. Nor was Mitchell. He sighed and asked Fuller what he was going to do, again.

'I'm coming to that. A series of attacks on right – and fake right – targets will traumatise the body politic, provide a base from which patriots like Harry here can work effectively in countering the reds within the poorer sections of the patriotic community, while, further up the pyramid, the internationalists and phony patriots will be forced to succumb, surrender, side with us, or, and it is most unlikely, fight against us. Now the . . . the uh . . . attack on Raphael's house was a beginning, a small, but not insignificant beginning.'

The penny seemed to be dropping with Mitchell. 'Just what do you mean by that, Fuller?'

Hales cleared his throat. 'I don't think I've really had the chance to explain, Charles.' He paused, embarrassed. 'Mind you, this isn't quite how I see things.' He trailed off.

'What haven't you explained?' rapped Mitchell. 'And just how do you see things?'

Lee laughed. 'He usually sees things through the bottom end of a brandy glass.'

'Well, you know that Raphael's house was bombed,' Fuller began.

Mitchell tried to finish. 'Yes, and we picked up a little red Jew. And a few IRA murderers have probably planted a few more bombs.' Perhaps he was being deliberately obtuse, or trying to tease something out of Hales. 'Just what has that bombing got to do with you, these . . . *papers* here, and indeed your . . . offensive?'

'Look, I think we do need to inject a bit of pep into things.' Hales made the country sound like a party that was going badly. Perhaps that's what it was.

'Now I don't go along with all of what Fuller here is saying, but I do think we need a bit of a shake-out . . .'

'We'll have a shake-out all right, and we'll have a shake-out when people like me decide we need a shake-out. And not, Raphael, when people like you start setting up little games with people like . . . like Mr Lee, and Mr Fuller here.' Mitchell wasn't just angry because of what they were doing, he was angry he didn't know. I was gratified behind my sofa. If Mitchell was cooking things up, there was hope for me . . .

But it cheered up Lee as well. 'Look here, Mitchell, we don't wait around for you. I don't wait around for you. We planted that little surprise. Bastards like you don't call the tune anymore . . .'

Fuller spoke over the squabble. 'If you'd just let me finish! It's all in the papers here.'

'Damn your papers!' Mitchell shouted. 'Damn your daft ideas! How much longer do you think this charade has to last? A bunch of half-baked politicos playing around in Parliament, splashing around in a few gallons of oil, prating on about market forces, and free enterprise. And then what? You people? Time is running out all right, and I'm not consigning my wellbeing to a bunch of yobs, an old fool like you, Hales, and an overgrown boy scout like you, Fuller. There is a system all right. And it doesn't stop at the end of the slummy road you come out of, Lee, or in your club, Hales, or from wherever you, Fuller, dredge your quack ideas. We can squash you people like swatting a gnat! D'you hear?'

Fuller didn't. He continued as if lecturing an unruly class of five year olds. 'We are initiating the process. The reds will be on the streets fast enough, but we move first, we take the hour . . .'

'You take the hour – you?' shouted Lee. 'I take the hour, it's our lads who are out on the streets doing the donkey work. And as for you, Mitchell, Christ knows what you are doing here! You're one of the bastards we're fighting against. You're part of the bloody conspiracy that controls this world, part of Wall Street Money Power . . .'

'What *are* you going on about?' I was with Mitchell that time. 'I want change,' said the corporation man crushing the chargehand. 'I want ordered, planned, measured, authoritarian change. In my time. Power is not going to be stolen like fish fingers being sneaked out of a supermarket by a bunch of guttersnipes . . .'

'Don't you call us guttersnipes,' said Lee. 'We showed you, you came crawling to us in 1934. We were the masters then, and we'll be the masters again.'

'As I recall, the only person I was crawling to in 1934 was my dear mother,' observed Mitchell. 'And as for "people like you", well, "people like you" got squashed in 1934 by your glorious leader and people like me did rather well, for a while. And we're still not doing too badly now.'

Hales cleared his throat again. I think he had decided to announce that the plan, the bomb, had all been rather bad ideas. But before he could give his views, Mrs Avis came in as matron. 'I think we are getting just a teeny bit heated, gentlemen. And didn't you say that about now, Michael . . .?' She let her voice trail away.

Fuller sounded as if he were sobbing. 'They don't understand. They just don't understand. It's always the same, cant, squabbles, division.' He paused, made an effort to control himself. He even succeeded, but in an unfortunate way.

'They move so slowly here in the northlands. The Celtic

fire burns deeper in the hard rocks. The people take so long to awaken, but once stirred the fire will be all the brighter, all the hotter! Unquenchable! It is breaking through the frost, through the lies, the filth now! You must understand this, all of you! Your race is on the move!'

He paused, and coughed. 'It's time,' he sounded exhausted. He believed his script, there just wasn't all that much of it, and he didn't have the delivery. 'It's time,' he repeated. 'Maud?'

'Yes,' said Mitchell. 'It is. I think I'll turn in, or maybe just go.'

'Oh, not yet please,' implored Mrs Avis. She went to the door. It closed quietly behind her. I heard her footsteps going up the stairs. Papers were shuffled. Mitchell told Hales that he was a fool, and Hales said he had the best of intentions. Lee told Mitchell that people like him should end up on piano wire. Mitchell laughed, stood up, and I froze, but he only went over to the window between the table and my hiding place. I curled up and into the sofa. I thought he looked out, but I couldn't be sure. I heard him stretching his fingers.

From outside the room there was a murmur, a shuffling of feet, Mrs Avis opened the door. Mitchell returned to the table. I slid forward. I could just catch them as they came in, keeping my head buried in the darkness. The group's eyes were elsewhere. Behind the woman was a man, a very old man, still quite erect, with fine white hair just fringing his forehead. There was a small scar on his right cheek.

19.

The face had emerged from my mind. It was as if its exposure to the light had aged it instantly from the sepia photographs of the white hunter, yet it retained that curious deadly youthfulness. It flitted across my retina and my brain and then disappeared from view behind the table. There was a shuffling of chairs, the sound of clearing throats.

Paradise's voice was old, quiet, contained, and slightly asthmatic. 'I am pleased you are here, gentlemen. It's been a long time, such a long time . . .' His voice trailed off, then he resumed. 'Have you explained, Michael?'

'I have been trying to, father. There have been some . . . some disagreements.'

'There's no need for that. No need for that now.' Paradise was detached, dream-like. 'We should all be united now. No time to lose.'

'Good God,' said Hales.

'This is my father, gentlemen, Alexander Paradise. He has been involved in the . . . our . . . struggle longer than any of us, purified our movement . . .'
the movement, fighting before I was born, before any of us were born.' Fuller seemed to be fighting for breath. 'What I, and he, he and I, hope to see is the process coming to a successful conclusion in the period ahead.'

'Good God,' Hales repeated. 'You were supposed to be dead, man. You died – what was it – thirty years ago, forty years ago?'

'You? You're Paradise? I know about *you*,' Lee was equally incredulous. 'You were killed in 1948, South Africa, killed by black communists, that's what your son said.'

There was a pause. 'They were closing in,' said the old man. 'I had to . . . I had to appear to die . . . I went away.'

'Where? Where did you go?' asked Lee.

'I went away. Now the synthesis is approaching. We will be one. One force.'

I shifted an inch. I saw nothing more, just a fraction of space between the door and the table. I assumed that Paradise's arrival was to have been the grand finale, a stirring speech to climax the meeting of minds. But the minds weren't meeting. Not that Paradise appeared to realise this, he just went right ahead.

'The ideal will approach, because we pursued it. We have striven, fought towards the light, spilt blood, it was from the dirt of the world, but it was cleansing, once spilt it purified us, purified our movement . . .'

'There was order, you understand?'

There was silence. Perhaps he was waiting for thunderous applause, the hero welcoming the new born, the old warrior united with the new spears of youth.

'There was order. It died before I was born, a hundred years before. In 1789 the evil was let into the world, the French Revolution. The masons, the Jews, the petty tradesmen rubbed the vial and brought out anarchy, liberalism, chaos, democracy, evil! It sped across the globe.'

'I'm not *certain* about that,' Lee's interruption was almost chatty. 'In the movement now we put the failing earlier, we look back to the end of the Elizabethan era. Now there was a time! And to the arrival of William, William of Orange, I mean . . .'

'Don't interrupt!' shouted Fuller. Lee didn't reply. I just guessed at the looks being exchanged across the table. Paradise continued.

'Absolutism began to perish, the bond snapped. I was born into a bastard world. There was good in it, good in the blood, in the genius that fought against it despite the odds. I fought the cancer, all my life! The stock was good and pure, but there was no order, no leadership. The folk spread across the globe and all the evil in the world could not destroy it, but it could be tainted. We, the British, spread out across continents, *made* those countries far away, but even as we did so the evil unleashed went with us. Liberalism, democracy, corrupted the beauty of it even as it came into being, so that it could not be pure . . .'

'Now this is very interesting.' Mitchell sounded as if it was not at all interesting. If Paradise's words dripped blood, he made do with acid. 'I fail to see what this has to do with any plans . . .'

'Don't interrupt!' Fuller shouted.

'. . . that there may be to bring about some, some *changes*.'

'My father roamed the world for that empire,' Paradise continued. 'He built on the backs of the natives, in the forests, jungles, deserts, that glorious white system! That marble palace, with its pillars, across the world . . .

'He came back to Britain, went into Parliament. He was a famous man, everyone knew him, but they laughed when he warned them. He had seen it, he was in India, he knew what could happen, look at Khartoum, Amritsar! How we had to fight, have strength! That evil which eroded the palace oozed from the money-changers of Europe and New York, the financiers. At the centre was wickedness, evil. You take Russia, Holy Russia! There was order, absolutism, the orthodox church, the estates, the Tsar of All the Russias. That was how it should have been. How we should have been. Instead we brought it down!

'Our yeomen were driven from the land; their serfs poured into the cities; the slums, the ghettoes and our system created it. The money flooded in from London, Paris, New York, and the dirty liberal ideas glistened in it like oil! That land rose against it, back in 1905, the people were one with the autocracy, they poured into the Union of Russian People, the Union of the Russian Land – the reds called them the Black Hundreds – they were scared, at last they were scared, because someone had risen against the reds and Jews and moneylenders. Just when we were fighting them in the East End, that same stinking system, we were all fighting the same monster, many-tentacled, but its nerve centre, its foul being was here and in New York!'

There were rhythmic bangings on the table; Paradise was providing his own accompaniment. Mitchell and Lee had given up the points of information. The old-time religion was rarely preached with such fervour, distilled through the shattered crystals of a mind set off on some doomed and crazy orbit long ago. There were no more shuffled papers or coughs, the shadows were only shifted on the wall by the flicker of the firelight.

Yet from below I fancied I heard a sound, a muffled crash. If I did, I was alone. The old man went on.

'They came here, the reds and the Jews. As the century ended, as I was born, they poured into the city. Finance money bred in the city and the poison bred in the east. We held down India with the bayonet and the redcoats, but who held down the East End? It was gangrenous. My father fought, organised, using the same weapons as the revolutionary scum. If the mob on the street had been conjured up to smash purity and order, then we could use it, too. My father had a Russian friend, a fine man who fought with the Yellow Shirts in 1905, a great thinker, Boris Nikol'ski. My father would quote him . . . you should remember this, Hales . . .'

'What?' The MP spoke as if stirred from sleep.

' "To be a conservative at this time means to be at least a radical. Or rather a revolutionary." He was right! We had the Brothers. Have you heard of the British Brothers League?'

Hales had not.

'We were first!' shouted Paradise. 'We were fighting on the streets of East London back in 1900, and we had the people with us when I was young down in the East End, those who kept the memory, the dockers, artisans. Only the anarchist red Jew scum opposed us! The organ grinders would hand out our leaflets, collect for us. They learned down back alleys with bricks and boots and good old British fists. They learned when they saw the glass break in those rotten little shop windows, in the sweat shops, when the bones broke, when the blood got spilled! They were cleansed! And I learned! I killed for that, do you understand? I KILLED FOR THAT! It was in 1908 that I first spilt blood. It was clean! We could have gone on through the decadence of the city, into the land, in the green grass and mountains and cleansed it all of that money! But we didn't. We were betrayed, but I went on!

'They took away my father's seat in Parliament. I went into the trenches in 1916 where the stock was bled for money, the wrong cause, I killed my blood-kin in the trenches. I came back, my father was gone, the world was gone. There were so few of us. In Germany there were more. I met them when they were nothing but a tiny band of prating intellectuals, but the soldiers! The ones who had survived, they cleansed that country! But what was there here? They were no good, they stank of the factory chimneys and the dirty backyards, they were infiltrated by the reds out of that hell that Holy Russia had been turned into.

'I stayed fighting. I killed the Bolshevik pigs, but they

wouldn't listen, all those so-called fascists, retired majors and vicars' daughters in black uniforms. I ran this paper for a while, with a chap from out East, camel surgeon, fine chap. I attacked this Jew financier, and you know what? He sued me! Made me penniless . . . I had to leave the country, because I spilled reds' blood. British fascists? They're nothing!'

'I'm not too sure about you, Mr Paradise.' Any fleeting reverence from Lee had faded fast. 'We're the ones doing the bloody donkey work now, and that's why we're here now – why *I'm* here, and I want to know . . .'

'Don't interrupt my . . .'

'Your fucking father!' shouted Lee at Fuller. 'I haven't heard too much about what your fucking father is going to do in the here and now.'

There was a shocked pause. Then Paradise asked who Lee was, as if he had crawled out of the carpet. His son explained: 'He's a whiner, that's who he is, leading a gang of cheap thugs round the streets, picking up a few miserable votes from illiterates and kicking over Pakistanis in back alleys.'

'Don't you patronise me, you ponce!' shouted Lee. 'You aren't even as good as your old man. All you can do is push old age pensioners off cliff tops.'

'Astin won't be the only one,' muttered Fuller.

'Christ, you've got around to admitting it, have you, Fuller? You make me sick. That was about all you could do. Why? And why have my men running round London looking for some cheap little degenerate?'

I wondered when I was going to slip into the conversation. I decided against putting in a word for myself. It was a noisy way to run a counter-revolution, Ferret would have been unimpressed.

'I'll tell you why,' replied Fuller. He was making efforts to stay calm. 'Because he was a nothing, like you. All we have to do is snap our fingers and your miserable little movement could be mine.'

Mitchell was still trashing around, and he wanted to know who Astin was.

'A nothing,' repeated Fuller.

Paradise spoke, but his voice sounded as if he was drifting

away. 'He was my cur. He belonged to me. We went round the world. Australia, South Africa, wherever I was and my wife and my kin, he and his wife trailed behind us yapping. They could fetch and carry and do nothing else. He had to do two simple things in the end and he couldn't. His weak little spirit finally gave out. We just ensured – my son just ensured – that his body went with him.'

'What wouldn't he do?' asked Mitchell.

Fuller replied. 'We asked him to keep the explosives, for Hales's – for Raphael's place –'

'God, Raphael,' breathed Mitchell.

'He said he wouldn't, that it was too dangerous. We told him that we were going to use the bookshop as a base and he said he was too old. And those pictures, those priceless pictures, he sold them to some fool off the streets. I told him he would obey. My father summoned him, told him he had to make the sacrifice for the movement. He refused, started babbling about the police. So we put him out of his misery.'

'So that was your *big* plan, was it, Fuller?' Lee from the shadow was on his feet. 'That was the back-up? That was why we were humping plastic around the streets? Because you couldn't get one of your Chelsea Pensioners on the job? Really big international operation this is. Jesus, what am I doing here?'

Fuller stood as well. 'I'll tell you why you're here! Because we've got five million pounds guaranteed through – through Appleton, *Mr* Appleton. Just like I said . . .'

'Just like you said about your London network. I don't even believe this codger exists.' Lee's manner was turning to derision, and that seemed to restimulate Paradise.

'Appleton exists. The money exists.' It was straight and factual, but then the clouds returned to the old man's brain. 'I was in Germany during the war. I went to the Eastern Front . . . only just got out. Went back to the Cape. My wife had a house, money, she was buried there. Died in 1957. Even in the Union, cleanest country in the world, they were after me. It was hot in the South. The blacks were all around. I shot the animals in the heat, on the veldt. I shot the bearers.' He giggled, it turned into a long cough.

It was an odd sound. The boy down in the East End on a visit back in 1908; from old pictures to senility. Yet he was chilling, unlike his son, unlike Lee.

'I'm not sure about this.' Hales was making another reappraisal.

'No, Raphael, I'm sure you aren't,' said Mitchell emphatically.

'Haven't you listened to anything?' Fuller had sunk back, he was almost whining. 'Aren't you inspired? Don't you see what we can build?'

Lee couldn't. 'You won't build anything on me.'

Mitchell was straight back in. 'Raphael, you persuaded me to come up here, I thought possibly – I admit, I must have been mad – that we might have been able to use these people . . .'

'You don't use me, Mitchell,' shouted Lee.

'Yes we do, Lee, yes we do. You do what you are told to do in the end. Your kind made this shambles, you come out of the same mould as the Kinnocks and Thatchers and Heaths and Carters. Cheap grocers! Or in your case, delivery boy. You paint a little swastika on yourself, little Mosleyite . . .'

'I'm no Mosleyite, I'm no Kosher fascist!' Lee betrayed a sectarian's concern with his label.

'I'm not interested in what you are, or in decrepit Tsar lovers.'

Mitchell stopped. They all stopped. A fight was going on outside.

It had started from where I had heard the crash. They all heard it this time. It was the sound of a fight, and it came closer. I could hear just one voice, and it was Anorak's. It started deep and scared and climbed the scale as he approached and his fear grew. By the time he crashed through the door, it had given way to a gurgle. I guessed correctly that Anorak wouldn't be looking out for me, not just then. He balanced his swaying body on the doorposts. It didn't to him any good. Apart from the dark stain on his shirt, he was spewing blood. He said, 'You bastard,' the same words of abuse used by the other people in the room, but spoken with more feeling, more effort and less audibility.

Then he crashed down at the foot of the table. All I could see were his feet. He was wearing sneakers. Funny, I thought. I didn't think Anorak would be the man for sneakers, a bit lefty for him. Anorak would never give his views on this subject, or any other subject.

No one else followed him. I wondered who the 'bastard' was.

Lee was across the room, sobbing. I didn't know whether it was fear or love or fury. He stood in the doorway and looked out. When he turned back I caught his face in the subdued light. He was manic. 'Fuller, you murdering bastard.' The face was crazed, the voice quiet.

Mrs Avis was screaming, and didn't stop.

'You must be out of your mind if you think . . .' I guessed that it was Fuller who was on his feet, pushing the table aside. I was wrong; it was the old man.

His son's protests died. The old man was bellowing like some castrated bull. Then it was transformed into a howl. It silenced everyone, even his daughter. A shadow swept across the wall, there was a clatter on the table. 'They don't let *me* down, or my father, or Mr Appleton!' He was laughing. 'Michael, your time is now. You do it!'

A chair toppled. It made little sound on the padded carpet, padded carpets in a padded cell. Fuller rushed at Lee, still standing in the doorway. 'You think I'm a killer do you?' Fuller screamed. 'Then I'll show you a killer!' Metal gleamed and thrust upwards. Lee said nothing, no screams or means, he just echoed Anorak's gurgle. Perhaps Paradise had given his son lessons; it was a single upward sweep, but he couldn't extract the knife, it remained embedded in Lee's neck as he fell. Fuller pulled himself clear. He was breathing heavily. He crawled on hands and knees across the carpet. He was inching his way across the carpet, towards the sofa.

Towards me. I was in view. The message tapped slowly across my brain. I slid back into the darkness. The sofa yielded as he slumped into it.

He laughed. 'Now you see, don't you? We don't mess around.' He giggled, just like his father.

There was silence. I heard the clock ticking, loud and slow. Fuller giggled again, while his father cackled. 'Well done, Michael! Well done! You are learning. We don't take it, eh? Not us.'

Father and son roared with laughter.

Hales was on his feet. 'My God, you've done it now.' He was reverting too, it was back to school after a jape that went wrong. 'I came here . . . listened to all this talk . . . I had no *idea*.'

I felt Fuller bouncing on the sofa, like some gleeful nine year old. 'You want out, do you, Raphael? Well I can tell you that it's a bit late.'

'You're mad,' said Mitchell. 'You and your father should be locked up. You will be.'

'We'll be all right,' trilled Mrs Avis. 'We'll be fine!'

'I don't know you,' Paradise was talking to Mitchell. 'But I know your kind. You people drink your pink gins and sit around, you're the ones who blocked all change to the way things *should* be.'

Mitchell cut across. 'Raphael, get his legs, drag him out.' Hales and Mitchell dragged Lee's body out of the door. I noticed that Hales's immaculate black shoe sank into Anorak's chest as he did so. Anorak was raw meat, the blood was oozing now, he had lost his shape in death. Hales was out first. Mitchell pushed the other body aside, dragged the corpse out. They must have thrown it down the stair-well, for they were back in the doorway in seconds. Hales had blood on his hands. I didn't think that Mitchell did.

'Done it before and do it again,' said Paradise dreamily.

'It is very late,' said Mrs Avis. 'I think you should think about bed, father.'

'What the hell are you going to do, Fuller?' Physical work hadn't calmed Hales's nerves. 'What are you going to do?'

The sofa shifted slightly towards me. Fuller had stood up. He had regained the confidence of the man at the beginning of his speech, when all the party were alive, and living in a world connected to the real one. He walked towards the door, rubbing his hands. 'Better get this cleared up.' He knelt down, and picked something up. It glinted dully. 'Good of you to take it out, Mitchell, wouldn't like to lose an heirloom.'

It was the knife. Mitchell was standing by him. He took the knife from Fuller's hand. I could just see him by inching forward. He fingered it, then threw it at the sofa. I believed for one second he was throwing it at me. It hit the sofa, glanced off the arm and landed a few inches from me.

'We've played enough of these games,' he said, after a pause. 'Let's get *your* friend out of here.'

'Yes . . . We should do that.'

'There's going to be hell to pay,' said Hales.

'I think . . . I think I'll make some tea.' Mrs Avis was at some garden party in the Surrey suburbs. She bustled out of the room ahead of the three men, who dragged the body out into the hall and down the stairs.

I was alone with the old man. Lee was dead because an old trigger was pulled in Fuller's brain. Why was Enever dead? Had Fuller had him killed? Who had killed him? What was I going to do to get out?

Down in the hall I heard a crash. 'Get up, Michael!' Mrs Avis's voice was chiding.

The old man stood up, I heard his chair slip back. He walked across the room, towards where the knife had landed. He was singing to himself. His shadow spread across the sofa. An old hand reached down, strayed across the carpet. The singing stopped, and I could hear his heavy breathing. I inched back into the darkness but it was too late. His hand brushed my forehead. It was dry, dry and cold.

20.

His face was in semi-darkness, but I could still see his eyes, bright blue, the blue of youth, or madness. Eyes transmitting signals from a mind on a cold star far away.

He smiled vaguely, trying to place me. I stood up. He was tall, only slightly stooped. I was in a dream. I have only a limited capacity to absorb new shocks, and it had been overstretched during the previous twelve hours.

'I'm with Michael. Just keeping a check.' It didn't sound fatuous in that land of the deranged.

I didn't know if he believed me. Belief didn't come into it. He nodded vague assent.

If I ran, my feet would not carry me, I thought. I would crawl across the room in the nightmare, my feet dragging, my breath pumping out in short slow gasps. It would take me an hour to get to the door. As a child, I dreamt that the greengrocer came round one day. I was looking out of the window and I knew I shouldn't let him in. He was with someone else whom I had never seen before. But I let them in. The greengrocer was a friendly man in the waking world, and he was friendly in the dream. He carried a hacksaw. 'I am sorry to bother you,' he had said, 'but I have to cut your arms off, and your legs.'

'I don't want you to,' I had replied.

'I know,' he smiled pleasantly, 'but I must.'

Paradise smiled pleasantly, carried no hacksaw, and had no friend. I could feel the edge of the knife at my foot. Under the sofa, I rested my hand on its arm.

I spoke. 'Piotr Abramovitch, he was the first, wasn't he?'

His smile broadened. 'You remember. Very good, yes, that was the first, the first proper one. Do you remember the man from the Okhrana? A fine man, wasn't he? I often remember him. Do you still see him?'

'Oh, yes, all the time, he is a good friend of mine, speaks well of you. Says what a wonderful job you did that day, what a lovely picture it was of the death, with the head held up like that. Just like all those other pictures downstairs.'

'Downstairs?'

'In the room downstairs, not the ones of the dead animals, the dead men. The corpses lined up between your legs, the later ones with Michael there.'

'Yes . . . Very nice, aren't they? I took some of them myself. I've got a device, you know, for taking those kind of pictures. Always took one when I could, got the idea from my father. There are those two little British bolshies, one was in the East End in the late 1920s, the other was earlier. Then there's the one I took on the Eastern front – I was with some Dutch brigade, SS they were – they posted me with them. The difficulty there was time. The reds were on you, there is a bit of blurring on that one, shell dropped just as I pressed the catch. It's difficult during a war. The African pictures were easy, blacks in the bush, peaceful out there, as you probably know. Been out that way?'

'Haven't had the chance.' From below I heard shouts.

It was Mrs Avis. 'You rotten traitors. You can't do this. You can't betray us!'

Paradise stepped back, looked at me, and blinked. 'I don't think I've had the pleasure . . .'

'No, you haven't. I'm a friend of Michael's.'

'A friend of Michael's, eh?'

I kicked the knife out, stopped and picked it up. The blade and handle were sticky with blood. It was an old knife, with an ivory grip and a long curving blade. 'This was the one, wasn't it? The one in all the pictures?'

'Oh yes, in all the pictures.'

'The picture of Abramovitch. You killed him with this, did you?'

'Of course.'

The clamour below was increasing, there were more crashes, it sounded as if they were clearing out the garage. Funny time to be tidying the garage, I thought. Funny time to be standing here talking to a senile homicidal maniac. Reality was returning. No one knew I was there, apart from him. I could get away, he was old, his days were past . . . He was puzzled, the clouds might drift from his brain and reveal the glacier below with its jagged cutting edges. He stared at me. I held the knife across my body, motionless.

'I must go for my walk,' he said briskly.

'What?' I stared foolishly at him.

'My walk. Always take a turn in the grounds at this hour. Clears the brain. Michael and I often take a stroll together. You can come along.' He smiled again, but averted his eyes; he was unsure of me. Then he turned on his heel and made for the door. He moved fast to the landing.

'No!' I shouted. 'Not now, it isn't a good idea now. Michael's busy.'

He was on the stairs and didn't look back. 'Can't be up all night,' he said.

We had been talking loudly, but they hadn't heard us. They were in the garage. I followed him down the stairs. He stopped in the hall, looking at the light from below. He made as if to go down.

'We should go out the front way,' I suggested. 'Michael is busy.'

'Busy?' He looked at me and then strolled leisurely out. I followed him to the steps and glanced back. The hall was deserted, the light was off in the pantry. From the garage there was the sound of cans being moved. They were talking down there, male voices, no more from Mrs Avis. Any time they could come up, I thought, but Paradise was indifferent to what was going on, working on what must have been a nightly ritual. I looked at him. He was standing in the drive. The hall stank of petrol.

I had to get away. I would be clear if I made for the entrance and over the gate, away down into Rhydd-ddu. I could leave the old lunatic to stumble around in the undergrowth. He looked up at me. 'Come on!' he shouted. His voice was appallingly loud. They would all hear, I thought, Mitchell, Hales, Fuller, Mrs Avis . . . all with at least a common interest in eliminating me.

I rushed down the front steps, slipped, and crashed into the gravel. I felt pain in my ankle. I had twisted it as I fell. The gravel was embedded in my cheek, I could feel blood oozing from it, my small contribution to the total for the night. Pain throbbed through me, I swore and looked at Paradise. He was walking away, oblivious, along a cart track which led behind the house, up the hill, towards the trees. The moon was out, his silhouette was outlined against the white streak of the track. I crawled to my knees. The knife was in front of me. I looked at my hands, Lee's caked blood encrusted my palms. I didn't want to leave the knife, or they would know someone else had been there.

Light cascaded across the drive; the garage doors had been

opened. I heard a scream. It was Mrs Avis. She was stumbling out of the garage, and her brother was just behind her. There were more lights, the sound of an engine being revved. The vehicle's headlamps sent twin beams into the trees. On the edge of the forest was another car, a Rover. I was trapped on the edge of the beams, and they cut me off from the path to the gate. *They will come out, they will see me.*

They came out, but there were other thoughts on their minds. The brother and sister were together, like some parody of the babes in the wood. Mrs Avis's screams were regular, but her brother was sobbing, I wasn't sure from fury of fear, presumably both. 'So why did you do it?' He repeated it continuously.

'You're so crazed you can't even tell the difference, can you, Fuller?' Mitchell was standing in the garage entrance, his hand propped against the door. Hales was behind him, but there was another man, between them, his face shrouded in some mask. He was carrying a rifle, or a machine gun. 'You pick up dross from the streets and when it was wiped away you think it's just some little show put on for you by your father, don't you? You didn't even stop to think, did you? Anything to keep little Lee in his place, eh? You thought Lee had his little man downstairs, didn't you? You should have been pleased he's out of the way. You *were*, weren't you? People like Enever aren't fit to walk the earth, are they?'

'You're the one that's mad!' screamed Fuller between sobs. 'We had plans, we had the money, don't think you'll get anything now!'

Mitchell was amused. 'We don't need your money, Fuller. Not now, not these days. We don't need people like you or your father, or your sister, or your little friends from Aston or Hoxton or wherever. Now come back here or you'll get yourself into a lot of trouble.'

The other two didn't want to go back. But they went. The third man swung his rifle in a slow loop. He was used to it, like Paradise had been used to his knife, back in the old days. They walked towards the garage, slowly, dragging their feet.

'Get the car out, Raphael.' Mitchell gestured behind him.

Hales vanished. Then the vehicle began to edge out, the beams widening, moving towards my darkness.

I wasn't sure that my ankle would hold, but I stumbled to my feet. Pain pumped through me. It was badly twisted. I hobbled and the pain took my breath away.

Hales engaged the gears, and the Toyota came out fast. Fuller and Mrs Avis stopped and then tried to break away. Mitchell shouted at Hales, the lights swung as Hales turned the pick-up, away from me. I made for the side of the house, and towards the path, away from the danger, like an animal.

The brother and sister were less fortunate. They had only made a half hearted attempt. They shuffled towards the garage, Mitchell and the third man came out to meet them. The four went back to the entrance. I had frozen by the wall. The man with the rifle raised it and brought it down on Fuller's head. He crashed across the garage floor. Mrs Avis was down with him, clutching at his body. Mitchell gestured, and the man brought the rifle down across Mrs Avis's shoulders. The brother and sister made an untidy heap, still illuminated in the garage light. Hales opened the Toyota's door and he ran towards them. Mitchell pushed him back, and said something to the other man.

Mrs Avis had come to, she was on her knees. She really kept trying, that woman, but it was her last attempt. The man rolled something towards her, an underarm action. It wasn't cricket, but it worked. Even before it got there, I saw that flames were licking the garage walls. When it arrived, the explosion seemed to follow the sheet of flame that consumed the area. The whole world should have heard that noise and seen the glare. Momentarily it was as bright as day. There were no more screams or moans or sobs then, just the roar of the fire.

I moved out from the house, on to the path, but at its side, where the undergrowth offered cover. I ran upwards, away from the light. Above the steady roar, I heard car doors slamming. Time had lost meaning. As I reached a flatter part of the path, I glanced back. I had put some distance between myself and the remains of the party. I shouldn't have done it. One of them was turning the Rover. Its lights cut across the dark past the glare of the fire, and caught me, a fly on the window pane . . .

They had seen me. One of them was shouting. Then the car accelerated across the gravel.

I stayed on the path. I needed distance. But they could catch me in the car if I remained there too long. My ankle throbbed but I ran fast and gave myself the luxury of hoping that they thought I was Paradise. I was cheered by their clumsiness; they should have checked that he was still in the house. But then, he seemed to have been dead for so long . . .

Fuller and his sister have gone. Now make a clean sweep of the whole bloody family.

Only I wasn't family.

The car was closing in. The track narrowed, it was becoming a leaf-strewn footpath. I ran on. There was a ditch with running water, beautiful, fast, clean. I crossed it. The grass on the other side was short, easy to run on, no boulders, no stones. I heard a crash from behind. Someone had loused up the driving. I glanced back. I caught the outline of the car against the glow, and three silhouettes. The memory remains cut into my brain. The house blazed with smoke pouring from the upper storeys, one of the beams collapsed in a shower of sparks, the side of the house crumbled, like Hales's house long ago. The three spread out; one of them remaining on the path. They didn't know where I was, or who I was. It was the masked man on the path; he ran with his arms stabbing out, fast. He would catch me if any of them did, I thought. I had to go deeper in but avoid being outflanked. I plunged into the forest. It was uphill, I struggled on, away from the road, away from searching car headlamps, away from those strange murderous people.

The forest was almost impenetrable. Blood dribbled into my mouth. It was from the fall on the steps, from the bracken in the forest, from the forest floor into which I repeatedly fell. I plunged into a gulley. It was full of rain water and I went in head first. There was a roaring in my ears. I surfaced lying in about two feet of water, just enough to drown in if I put my mind to it. Just enough to drown in, if one of them found me and put his mind to it. Death by fire, or death by water . . .

I lay and listened. My fingers scooped up the oozing mud. It was deliciously cold, and thick. Then my fingers found the blade of the knife. I cut myself and swore. There was noise in the forest, not from night creatures but from the man from Whitehall, the masked man and the MP running amok in a Welsh forest.

They weren't close. The noise was receding. Then there was another sound, far away, but getting closer as the crashes receded. It was the sound of sirens, the fire brigade?

'Get back to the house!' I could only just hear Mitchell, but his voice was becoming familiar, a crisp military tone. 'Do you hear me? Get back to the cars!'

'It wasn't Paradise. D'you hear? Not Paradise!' shouted Hales.

The crashing in the undergrowth died away. The siren was still far away, echoing down the valley. I waited in the water below the forest floor. The noise of the sirens ended, then I heard engines. They were pulling out; I was safe.

I crawled out of the slime, up the bank and into the trees. I continued up the hill. My sole aim was to escape from the fire, and the sepia photographs and the crazed ideas exchanged across fine wooden tables. The trees were more spread out, the undergrowth less dense. Ahead of me the mountain loomed. Outcrops of rock were bathed in the moonlight. It was a full moon. I hit the fence, the knife still clenched in my hand. I attempted to climb across it, but it was barbed wire, and my sodden, exhausted body couldn't surmount it. I sunk back on my knees and wriggled through, tearing my clothes as I did so. The grass on the other side was short, cropped by sheep. I had escaped, I was clear at last. I knelt down and felt my ankle. It was swollen but did not hurt badly. The mud had probably helped.

I stood and walked towards the ridge. I would be able to see.

There was a sound. A rustling noise, then a thud as something heavy moved. A rock had fallen. I was nearly on the ridge. I dropped into the grass. The bleat was very near, the sheep was nearly on top of me. I laughed, a throaty wheezing noise filtered through phlegm and mud and ditchwater.

I made the ridge. My ankle began to throb again, pain ticking like the clock in the house. The moon was drifting behind the clouds. Below me the mountains fell away sharply. I was further up than I had thought. There was a covering of scree and boulders, then almost a sheer drop. On hot sunny days peaks like this were for slow climbs with friends and sandwiches, and clothes untidily tied around one's waist as the day passed and the ascent became more arduous. Time to think and lie back in the heat . . .

I had not watched the outcrops pass below me that night. I looked back. The forest was dark, silent, but through it there was a glint of fire. The house blazed on, columns of smoke, outlined at source by sparks drifting into the night sky towards Beddgelert. I scanned the darkness for a road, where a Rover and a Toyota and a fire engine might be making their way, but saw nothing.

I decided to walk along the ridge and head back to the road from Rhydd-ddu to Nantlle. I had no plans, just a walk across the countryside. The wind was cold, but refreshing. I was free, safe, out of the world of sofas and curtains. The ridge dipped and then rose to a higher peak. I moved upwards, laughing, swinging the evil old knife from side to side.

I noticed the rock when it was too late. At least it was the same ankle, I staggered, crashed down, screaming obscenities into the wind. The knife clattered across the rocks. I sobbed with pain.

'You came did you? You're here now, aren't you? I saw you down there you know, I watched you; reds, Jews, blacks, pigs! You traitors! You thought you would drag me down to your own filthy sties did you? That's what you thought was it? Well you can't. I have learned over very many years, very many years.'

Paradise stretched out the vowels. Each word was extracted with great effort, great precision. The moon moved out of the clouds and the light spread across his face; a death mask. The blue eyes were buried in black valleys, the cheeks white and the skin tight across his high cheek bones. His scar was long, deep and dark.

'I got rid of you all. All of you years ago. You want to come back? Again? I remember you all, I took your pictures, snaps of rats . . .' He stooped down and picked up the knife, his knife.

'I remember all your names. I made notes. They are back at the house in my files, Leary, Cropley, Mpambe, the black in Rhodesia that very hot day, that man in Stettin . . . You were all irrelevant, you know, even your deaths, your miserable deaths, you were just a pastime, an amusement. What about my movement? I've been building all these years . . . The time is coming . . .'

His voice rose and fell; sometimes he was silent, sometimes the wind snatched the words.

'It's no good you coming back now to complain . . . demand your rights. You have no rights . . . You can't frighten me, I don't frighten easily, you curs. You talk of liberty? Cheap words for cheap little plebs scuffling in the dust. Do you know that, Cropley? Remember how you begged me on your knees? You weren't the bloody Bolshevik then, were you? Not then . . .'

The knife dangled in his hand.

'What about Abramovitch, Paradise? What about him? Where's his picture?'

He stared at me. 'Michael's friend.' He spoke as if reciting a guest list.

'Your son is dead. Your daughter is dead. Your house is a ruin and you are the last of your line, stuck up a mountain.'

'Who are you?'

'I'm the one with the picture for your collection. Abramovitch, remember him?'

'Frying Pan Alley, 1908.' Paradise made it sound like the beginning of a lecture. 'Nasty little red Jew all the way from Russia. One of the rats that crawled out after they failed to drag it down . . . Failed that time . . . Slithered over here. The Okhrana were after him. They contacted us. We had links. Couldn't get a thing out of the authorities, they knew they could rely on us. "Blood my cub", that's what my father said, and he did too, like Michael tonight, but I shouldn't have waited so long . . . We watched him. Saw him in Aldgate that day; piece of luck really . . . Followed him through those stinking streets. Watched him land like a fly on all that rubbish . . . We would have got the man in the shop, too, the one selling those pamphlets, but we never had the chance. They didn't usually go in for that sort of thing, the Okhrana, they liked to keep them under surveillance . . . they made an exception . . . I slit him from ear to ear . . .'

He was in a trance. I could imagine little Maud and little Michael falling asleep at night with tales of their father's adventures in the butchery trade.

'Then we took the picture. Difficult with the light, the Russian had a place nearby.'

'And now you have lost the picture.'

He glared at me, swinging the knife and slicing at the air. 'You have the picture.'

I felt inside the remains of my jacket. There was a sodden mass of paper next to my wallet. The photograph was there. I pulled it out. 'Abramovitch's picture, Paradise.'

He could move fast. His knife caught the tips of my fingers, cut the middle one, I dropped the photograph. He picked it up, kneeling to do so with the long, stained blade still pointing at me.

'You are the one.' He stared at the long-dead Russian. I was uncertain whether he was talking about me or Abramovitch. 'You aren't coming for me!' he howled. He looked around.

I could hear sheep chewing the grass.

He swung the knife and sprang towards me. The blade came down in an arc. Experience, ritual and madness transcended old age. I slipped under him, he landed on me, the knife slipped from his hand. I grabbed it, the cutting edge upright. He was on his knees. I kicked him, and he half fell on the blade and screamed, sliding forward. The photograph dropped from his hand and blew away in the wind. He was on the very edge of the ridge. I still had the knife. He fell into the scree. I dropped the knife and it clattered on the stones. His body rolled down the slope and, as it became steeper, towards the sheer face. I watched him trying to grip the rocks. A rotten branch from a long-dead tree splintered in his hands. The knife followed him down. He cried out. Then his body fell into the void. I wondered if Astin had gone in the same place. His cry was carried on the wind. His body thudded on the rocks, and then there was silence again. The moon was going, I was cold.

21.

I lay for a long time and shivered; maybe three hours, an hour, ten minutes. I ached. The ankle became part of a great pain, deeper than the cut hand and the face and the leg and exhausted lungs. Deaths, faces, Astin, the shop, the Russian. Mrs Avis was talking to a policeman but there was fire all around now. She was laughing, flying into the air, very strange. Her brother was looking out of Hales's window, there were big crowds, flags of all nations, sheep and goats and wildebeest and lions, tigers, kangaroos, all coming across the grass to meet me, such lovely cropped grass. Behind it was a white palace that stretched across half the horizon, with long white pillars set deep in the grass. But from out of the foundations seeped that awful dark red, soaking the green grass . . .

The white tent was up again. The children played in the grass, kicked the ball that wasn't a ball.

I awoke. It was cold. Rain was falling lightly. I crawled along the ridge, talking to myself, singing songs. I descended where it was less sheer, half crazy, soaked, slowly down to the road. On the last of the inclines, I saw the road from Rhydd-ddu to Nantlle. At the end of the valley was the lake, glinting faintly, and beyond that the coast and Caernarfon. Below me was a hamlet, the hamlet I had passed through on my way up that morning ten centuries ago.

I reached the road and lay on the soaking verge. There were some ruined cottages, quarry workers' cottages. I had to sleep. I stumbled towards them. There was another building which looked as if it was inhabited. I didn't care if I woke them. Good Samaritan time . . .

I banged on the door. No one came. I smashed a window and crawled inside it. It was deserted, a place for far-away weekenders tucked up in suburban villas in Cardiff or Birmingham or Barnet. There was a camp-bed and I collapsed on it.

When I woke, it was still raining. My clothes were strewn across the floor. Everything in the cottage was damp, but there was a cooker, and tins, and a calor gas light. I found a towel, grey with coal dust, hanging over the sink. Wrapping it around myself, I opened the door and stared out. The rain, in long columns, skimmed down the valley, obscuring the cliff face opposite and leaving Snowdon buried in watery mist. There was no sun. I had no idea of time, just black, grey, heat, cold. I went back inside. It took a long time to find a tin opener, a long time to find some matches and they were damp. I lit the gas. There was a kettle. The water was stale but I didn't care. I made some tea, ate some corned beef and beans, swallowing the food like an animal, taking perverse pride in my grossness, my voraciousness. It was dark in the cottage. There were just two rooms. The place was littered with malt whisky bottles stuffed with candles. I lit some of them. There was a framed picture on the wall. The owners, I guessed. Father, mother, small kid in shorts, standing outside the cottage on a sunny day. I shivered. I couldn't light a fire. My clothes were too wet to move in. I lit the oven of the cooker and baked my clothes with the door open. Then I returned to bed and a damp sleeping bag. I was woken at night by the smell of scorched clothes. I took my jacket out, my jeans. My underpants were baked solid with mud, ditchwater, the piss of fear . . .

There was enough light to reach the cupboard. I found some aspirins, swallowed them with cold tea, and squatted in front of the oven. The heat was lessening. I would be out of gas if I left it on. I extinguished it and returned to the sleeping bag.

I dreamed strange dreams. The palace returned, and the occupants. There were photographs everywhere, sepia figures from murders unsolved for seventy years, from long-gone wars. Paradise was a frequent visitor, usually in the moonlight, with his scar livid, silver. I awoke sweating and terrified. Grabbing the last candle, I made for the picture on the wall. It was going to be Paradise, I knew, there was no safety anymore. The man had fairish hair and a neat walrus moustache, no scar, or murder in his eyes, no dead animals or children born into death. The wife had the smile of peaceful, smug middle-class England. There should be an Austin Cambridge parked somewhere behind the cottage, I thought.

The following morning I decided to leave. What day was it? I wondered. I guessed it was Tuesday. I dressed, ate some remaining cold beans, cleared up. I believe in domestic order. The rain had gone, there was watery sunlight, and flecks of golden light coming off Snowdon.

I made my way down the road. I was sorry about the weekenders' window, and my small thefts. I didn't know what to do. Where were my unknowing companions of that night? I wanted to see the Cutlers, meet normality again. It was cold, but not an unpleasant winter day. There was no traffic, so the walk was long. More than an hour passed before I reached the village. A bus full of children on their way to school was parked on the edge of it. Their noses pressed against the windows, their breath misted the glass.

Birds sang. Behind the village were great heaps of slate, grey and gloomy. But I was happier. I would go into Caernarfon, tell the police . . . Tell them what? That I had murdered one of the older local residents? Tell them of grenades and fascists and plots?

The Cutler house was unchanged. The curtains were pulled back. They must be up, I thought. I banged on the door, pressed the bell, waited.

No one came. At the next door a small child stared at me, a teddy bear clenched in his hands, as if I would attempt to wrest it from him. He had fine fair hair. I smiled at him. He started wailing and ran, his small body bouncing across the tiny front garden. I banged on the door again. It was simple enough. Caradoc had gone to work, Jean had gone out, gone for a walk, gone shopping . . . I didn't believe it. The child stood in the corner of his domain, underneath the window, staring suspiciously at me.

I must have looked very dirty. I was panicking. Why weren't they there? A man strolled by, an old man with a cloth cap and a neckerchief, a relic of the 1930s. He nodded at me, and I at him. But it wasn't a friendly gesture on his part and just an attempt by me to regain entry into commonplace humanity. I walked down the path, I had to get out of the village. I broke into a run, until my ankle sent urgent messages up my leg. The bus was already moving. I waved and it slowed before the scarecrow figure and then halted. Momentarily the shouts of the children died as I paid my fare. I was relieved that my wallet was still there. I had nothing smaller than a five pound note. The driver glared at me, with an expression mingling annoyance and suspicion.

I smiled fatuously at him. 'Caernarfon.'

'Caernarfon? Nothing smaller?' He reached into the cash tray.

'No, sorry.' My voice trailed away. I was bedraggled, a big spender, and English. The children looked at me as if I was one of them caught in the act.

I found an empty seat and watched the valleys give way to the flat coastlands.

A small girl was playing with her watches. She had two, both quartz, strapped tightly side by side on her thin white wrist. She was in the next seat. She pressed the buttons on the side of the dials; it was only eight o'clock. I must have been up since dawn.

The coach pulled into the square of Caernarfon. I stepped out, and checked the timetable for London. There was a coach leaving in twenty minutes. It was already waiting. I went into a cafe and drank three cups of tea and ate a ham roll, tearing at the bread. The fear from Nantlle was still with me. I didn't know why but I felt I was being watched. I wouldn't go to the police, perhaps it was they who were watching me. I was an atom, far from my universe, needing the anonymity of the city. I bought a ticket at the coach office, strolled down the parade opposite the castle and bought the papers; the local, and the *Guardian*. I stuffed them under my arm. I felt the damp inside my socks curdling my toes. I saw I had ten minutes to wait and the coach was still locked, with the driver leaning against a tree, smoking. Shoppers crossed the square. A woman with a red hat was picking up the debris of a collapsed carrier bag. The driver tossed his dog-end away and climbed into the coach. I made towards it. Passing the woman I paused and helped her pick up her groceries. She smiled, but her expression changed to curiosity as she saw my dishevelled appearance. Muttering her thanks in Welsh, she stuffed her belongings into an overflowing basket. I was still half on my knees, my line of vision obscured by a tree. I saw a cop surveying the scene. A man content, in his territory, all was well . . .

I could go up to him, tell him, he would escort me to the station, just for a statement of course.

He wasn't just standing there, he was watching for something. Waiting for someone, I thought. *You fool*, I told myself. *Perfectly harmless.*

No, he's looking for me. He doesn't know me, he doesn't know what he is looking for.

The policeman was bored, as if he had been waiting too long for someone who would never arrive. Or waiting for too much of his life for something to happen in that square other than an occasional Saturday night brawl.

I waited. He was looking towards the castle. I walked swiftly to the coach and I didn't look back. The driver lit another cigarette as I climbed the steps. He didn't give me a glance. I made my way to the back of the coach, sank into the seat, swung my knees up and peered out of the window.

The policeman was still looking at the castle, his hands on his hips. More people boarded the bus. Most of them looked like locals, travelling a few stops down the coast. There were few of them, there was plenty of room.

The driver started the engine. It vibrated through the coach. I reached for my papers, and glanced again out of the window. A Rover was parking, the first I had seen since that night. *The* Rover? I felt sick, and then relieved. It wasn't the same one. A fat woman in tweeds got out, knocking her hat askew in the process.

The coach inched forward. There was another car, another Rover, and it had stopped. A man swung the door open. I had hardly seen him that night, but I was almost sure that it was Mitchell. He walked briskly across to the cop, tapping him on the shoulder. The policeman turned, smiled. They laughed and looked around them. The coach accelerated down the narrow streets, and they were lost from view.

I had sunk into the seat, attempting to bury myself in it. I hardly moved until the coach was clear of Caernarfon and up on to the Bangor road. The world was plotting against me, the world of the police and Mitchell.

I read the papers. There was nothing in the *Guardian*. My eyes searched restlessly through the pages, looking for bad news, *the* bad news, a picture of me running from the fire, waving a knife . . .

Then I looked at the local. It was on the front page. 'TRAGIC FIRE AT RHYDD-DDU' it said.

'At least two people are believed to have died in an inferno which completely gutted the 200 year old Sirius House in the early hours of Sunday morning. The fire, which is believed to have started when a gas explosion ignited oil storage tanks, could be seen as far away as Beddgelert.

'By the time the fire service arrived the blaze had already consumed the property, which had been owned by a retired London businessman, Mr Noel Fuller. It has not yet been ascertained whether Mr Fuller is one of the victims, due to the condition of the corpses.

' "He was a real gentleman," said a neighbour, Mr Tony Rees, a farmer, "one of the old school."

'One of the bodies is believed to be that of a woman, and there are fears that if Mr Fuller survived the blaze he may have panicked and come to injury on the mountains.

'This is the second time in recent weeks that tragedy has struck the area. Two weeks ago a London bookseller, Mr Selwyn Astin, was killed when he fell from a nearby crag.

'The house has been a landmark . . .'

I folded the paper. There had been no murders, just a gas explosion, and Mitchell on holiday in Caernarfon out of season. They would find the body soon. Someone would be strolling across the mountains, looking for his sheep and he would see the corpse.

What had Mitchell done? Bribed the entire fire brigade? Waved a little card and made a few discreet phone calls? Put out a word to the police and told them to watch out for . . . whom? They didn't know who I was. I was anonymous, a figure on a fiery landscape running into the night.

Crazy old Paradise, or someone else?

When a telex machine blows a fuse it races. The key hits the same letter, the same white space, until the paper dissolves and it hammers the surface underneath. My brain was a blank surface, and the key hammered the darkness.

The coach took a long time to make Birmingham. It was dark before London loomed. They might be waiting for me at Victoria.

I dropped off the coach in Baker Street. I don't like the pub on the corner opposite the tube. It tries to be traditional but satisfies itself with the unfortunate stranded in the limbo between Central London and Regents Park. I entered and bought a drink. They nearly refused to serve me, the stubble was growing. The beer was foul, it assumed the tastes already in my mouth. It was only a half pint, but I left most of it and stumbled back into the night. I was used to the night now. It was usually night in my new world. I caught a bus for Highbury and walked across the fields. The house was, as usual, in darkness. My door was still swinging, with its lock ripped off, and the smell of stale urine was stronger. It reminded me of the smell of wolves, or what wolves ought to smell like. The rubbish was a few days older.

I made an effort to clear things up. There was little I could do about the mattress, so I dragged it down into the basement. I knew there was another one down there, a leftover from some long-gone resident, better than the one I had.

You have to try and keep some order, don't you? You can't just let things fall apart.

I didn't have any food. I thought I should go out and get some. The shops stay open late at Highbury Grange. I was in a little Indian supermarket; my wallet was empty, all I had was sixty pence. I bought a pie, and some beans, a little tin so small that it was almost all tin and no beans, and some long-life milk. I can't stand the stuff. I like proper cow's milk, but they didn't have any.

I went a long way back to the house. You can't be too careful.

They are pretty clever, these people. They've got eyes all over the place, they can see what you are doing from a satellite, parking your car – not that I have a car – picking your nose, pushing old men off cliff tops . . .

It wasn't my fault! He came at me, it was him or me.

I looked very carefully before I went up the hill. God, I was half way to Finsbury Park. But the house was still quiet.

I put the pie in the oven, and found a couple of green sprouty potatoes to have with it and the beans. They were all right when trimmed and boiled. It was quite tasty. I was very hungry.

I went to bed.

22.

I woke up and read the paper. There was a stack of them in the hall, a history of my missing days, but without my history. Nothing.

I was uncertain, I was tired, still tired. I looked out of the window. There was no one there, no one out of the ordinary, no Anorak; a woman in a red hat with a bag; not a broken carrier or anything like that, just a bag.

I kept falling asleep. I thought that maybe I was sickening for something, after all that time on the hillside . . .

I decided to go out, take a walk. It was early afternoon. I had to find a way of filling the day. I wondered what I would do. I had lost interest in the book. The appeal of the 1930s was fading.

I remembered I had no money so I went to the bank, which was near Highbury and Islington tube station. As I passed the newspaper stall outside, I saw a headline and bought the *Standard*.

'MP DIES' it said. 'Raphael Hales, the 55 year old Conservative MP, died early today. Mr Hales suffered a heart attack at his home in South London late last night and was rushed to Kings College Hospital but was found to be dead on arrival.'

That was all. I checked the stop press. He had been found by his servant, it said; nothing more.

Astin, Fuller, Paradise, Avis, Lee, Enever, now Hales. They were all gone. There were just two of them left now, and me. I was cold, the sun was shining.

I had to make contact; but with whom? I decided to find Ferret. He wouldn't be at home, I thought; I would try his site, it was off the Caledonian Road, he had told me. By the time I found it, darkness was falling again. He was outside.

'Well, well Raven, back again, have a good holiday?' He was with a couple of other guys.

'Yeah,' I said.

'You don't look too good.' He laughed, 'Well, it all happens while you're away, eh?'

'Hales you mean?'

'Yeah, well Gold anyway.'

'What about Gold?'

'He's out, isn't he?'

I stared at him foolishly. 'Out?'

'Look, man, I could keep this up for hours but we're supposed to be on strike, and I've got a meeting in ten minutes.' He looked at his watch.

'This is important, Ferret.'

He tapped one of his companions on the shoulder. 'See you in a minute, pal.' Then he turned to me. 'So is this, Raven. If we don't hold this thing together today, then we all go down the spout.'

'What do you mean, Gold is out?'

'I mean that you should read the papers. Gold was released on Monday. The police said that it had all been a fucking mistake. It was a gas explosion after all. Now if you don't mind . . .'

The tide was coming in all around me. 'I don't believe . . .'

'Yeah, well you better. And what with old Hales kicking it today, it just shows that God is on the side of the righteous after all. Now, it's been wonderful to speak to you, I'd just love to know what happened on your winter vacation, but right now . . .'

'For Christ's sake, I've been up all bloody hours . . .'

He glared at me. '*You've* been up all bloody hours! Do you know I was up at six this morning outside this bloody place? Being told by surly bastards in nice warm lorries to go and get a job while I was standing here handing out leaflets with my thumbs droppin' off in the cold? In the pitch dark? And it's been the same every fucking day, including Sunday! Give us a break, man!'

'Oh shit . . .' I spun on my heels.

'Look, man, I'll see you down the Compasses, about eight, all right?'

I did. By then I had been drinking for two hours, the night was continuing, I felt I was delirious. The first twenty minutes or so I could hardly move past the strike. Then he listened; he was incredulous.

'Are you sure you're all right, Raven?' he asked when I finished.

'What d'you mean?'

'Are you sure you're all right in the head?'

'No, I'm not even sure of that.'

He sighed. 'Well let's just suppose that this Mitchell guy was a plant . . .'

'He wasn't, or not the way you're implying. He was deadly serious . . .'

'If he was a plant, then he could probably have folded the entire operation. The strain should have been enough to put Hales under the turf. A neat little security number.'

'It wasn't that. Mitchell was serious enough. He was – is – organising something, and now he's made sure that everybody who knew about it has been knocked off.'

'Apart from you.' He laughed. 'I wouldna' like to be in your shoes.'

'They don't know who I am.'

'What about the picture?'

'It went west on the hillside.'

'Are you sure they don't know?'

'No, but Hales was the only one who caught a glimpse, the only one who would have known me.'

He scratched his chin. 'Wonder what'll happen to you. What are you going to do?'

'I haven't a clue.'

'You're gonna have to write it down. We'll do a report. I mean this stuff could be incredible, if we can get the back-up stuff.'

I looked at him. 'What do you mean back-up stuff?'

'Supporting evidence and that.'

'Do you believe me?'

He ran his finger around his glass. It was twenty seconds before he answered. 'You've always been a liberal, John, always run around with some weird ideas . . .'

'Jesus!' I shouted, I was angry, but scared.

'Hold on, I didn't say I didn't believe you. It's just that – well – it's pretty odd.'

'You're fucking right it's odd.'

'Can you check on this Mitchell fella?'

I did, the following day. I looked through the Ministry of Defence lists, went through all the right routines. His name wasn't there. I rang Moira. Someone else answered, said she had gone back to the States.

I haven't seen anyone much these last few days. I've been thinking. Then in the paper I saw the other day that some guy called Enever had been killed in a car crash in Shoreditch. It had happened in the early hours of the morning. He had a passenger with him, also killed, name of Lee. Friends said they had been coming back from the North. It didn't mention their politics. Apparently the car had exploded, but foul play hadn't been suspected, just something wrong with the fuel tank. Apparently they had only been identified from their dental records. It was a terrible sight, one of the few passers-by had told the *Hackney Gazette*.

I wondered why Mitchell had bothered. Perhaps he wanted to make sure that everything was returned to the right place in the file. And, after all, you don't want mangy, possibly rabid dogs from Hoxton littering up the Welsh countryside, do you? It would look out of place.

I have some friends in the country, in Suffolk. I decided to go and stay with them. I was very careful, I rang from a call box. I went down there.

I can't get Abramovitch out of my mind.